THE DARK HEART
OF
ROGER LOMAX

Sandra Savage

CONTENTS

ACKNOWLEDGMENTS

In memory of Auntie Nan – *My* Auntie Hazel.

Chapter 1

The match, scraping against the sandpaper edge of its box filled the room with sound and the smell of sulphur. There were four candles arranged on the low table, three small, white tea lights, encircling a thick, blue wax pillar. Roger lit them, methodically, ending with the blue pillar and blew out the flame now burning halfway down the matchstick.

A long, brown stem of Nag Champa Incense was placed, carefully, in its soapstone holder alongside the candles and ignited, using one of the tea lights, before being extinguished immediately, allowing the curl of scented smoke to begin to drift into the air. Roger straightened and took a deep, satisfying breath into his lungs, his ritual lighting of the candles and incense accomplished once again. How he loved ritual.

He looked around the room and counted the chairs, twelve in all, not including his, which stood apart from the rest and checked his watch. Nearly seven o'clock. They'd be here soon and he mustn't be caught unprepared.

There was a gentle tap at the door. "Damn," Roger muttered under his breath as he switched off the overhead strip lights. "Too keen, too keen, why is there always someone too keen."

"Can I ask you to wait a few moments, please?" he called to the closed door, "if you don't mind?" There was a muffled cough and then silence.

He flipped open the flat, plastic box and removed the silvered CD from its resting place. With the expertise of countless repetitions, he inserted it into the player and pressed the button. The muted sound of panpipes began to resonate through the incense and candlelight as he lowered himself into his chair and inhaled the energy around him. "There," Roger sighed, now he was ready, now he would open the door and let them in.

He watched the second hand of his watch tick-tock its way to exactly seven o'clock before calling out to the waiting women on the other side of the door. "You can come in now."

After a few seconds hesitation, the handle of the door turned and a grey haired head peered into the dimness of the room. Roger smiled, his face rosy and smooth in the candlelight, his pure, white hair silhouetted against the darkness behind him. "It's alright," he assured the owner of the grey hair benignly, "come along in." He indicated the circle of chairs, "Sit anywhere you like."

The elderly woman, did as she was told and sat down, her eyes seeming to stare at Roger as they tried to focus in the candlelight. She was followed by a succession of eleven other women, some like herself, but others more middle-aged, some younger, each with differing levels of confidence, as they nodded and smiled to one another. No one spoke, except Roger, giving a word of welcome here, a comment on the weather there, allowing them all to take in the ambience he had created for them and become aware of his presence.

Roger closed his eyes and placed each foot flat on the floor, grounding his energy and raising his consciousness, aware that every eye was on him, wondering, apprehensive and expectant. He pictured the women in his mind's eye, the usual mix he'd seen many times before, all looking for something to fill their empty lives, failed wives, sexually dried-up prunes and nervous plums, he'd met them all, wanting to feel alive, to be touched by a man's hands again, or maybe touched for the first time. Whatever their needs, Roger knew how to satisfy them all, bringing them back for more each week and feeding his power within. For he knew how to heal them, he was Roger Lomax, the greatest healer of them all.

The sound of the panpipes faded and stopped. Roger let the silence build to a peak of anticipation before opening his eyes and establishing contact, individually, with every female in the room. "Thank you for coming," he said graciously, "and welcome to you all." He noted the nods of those who accepted his thanks. "Tonight," he began, "I want to take you to a place of deep relaxation, where anything you wish can be yours, a special place, where you can go at any time, when you feel alone or unhappy, or in need of love, a place where you can be at peace with yourself."

He waited for the appropriate response of anticipation before continuing. "Is everybody ready?"

There was a shifting of position in the chairs as shoulders were shrugged and then relaxed and legs were uncrossed, at Roger's request. "Feet flat on the floor please," he instructed, "bare feet preferably." Shoes were obediently slipped off around the room and pushed under chairs as the energy began to rise.

"Now, I want you all to close your eyes and come with me on a journey." With practised ease, Roger fast-tracked the CD, till the sound of waves, washing gently against some distant shore was picked up by every ear in the room. His powerful voice, took on a deep, mellow tone as he began the guided meditation.

"Imagine, if you will, that you are standing on the most beautiful beach, the sand golden and warm beneath your feet and the blue sea foaming its white-edged waves around your toes. Feel the heat of the sun and the coolness of the sea. Hear the seagulls calling to one another as they swoop over the waves.

Over the next half hour Roger's voice took them, through the power of their imaginations to a place of relaxation and peace, each one focussing more and more on their personal journey into their sub-conscious. He could feel the air vibrate around him with the energy he was creating, a powerful energy, filling his chakras with light.

Roger pressed a button on the CD player and the sound of a flute soft and soulful, filled the room. "Be at one with your spirit," he said, "ask your guardian angel for anything you wish and it will be given unto you."

He glanced down at his watch, luminous in the dimness. 'Perfectly on time, as usual,' he smiled to himself, before closing his eyes and breathing, once more, into the energy.

After ten minutes exactly, the flute music ended and Roger began again. "It's time to return now," he intoned, "you can go back to your secret place as often as you wish, but now, it's time to leave and come back into the room, back to reality." His face took on its closing smile. "Welcome back," he nodded, "welcome back."

Twelve pairs of eyes gradually opened into the candlelit room and blinked into awareness again. Involuntarily, arms and legs stretched out and smiles crossed faces as each woman nodded to the other, their approval of Roger. "He was so spiritual," they said of him, "so warm and loving. Not like the men they knew, cold and unfeeling. No wonder they were so full of aches and pains. No wonder they needed Roger's healing touch as often as they did."

Roger smiled his benign smile, knowing their thoughts about him and drinking in their adoration. "If anyone wishes healing, then please, speak with Vanessa as you go out and she'll arrange a time for me to see you." He stood up now, his tall, heavy frame towering over them and clasped his hands in prayer-mode in front of his barrel chest. "Till we meet again," he bowed, before descending once more into his chair, closing his eyes and grounding his energy. He listened till the murmur of female voices faded and the reception door closed behind them, before opening his eyes and switching on the strip light. "Women are so wonderfully gullible," he smiled, extinguishing all but the blue pillar candle, "don't you agree?" He looked up at the black spider which had appeared on the wall above him, its spindly legs gripping the smooth white surface.

Laughing softly to himself, he blew out the final candle flame and gathered up the soapstone incense holder. "Goodnight Spider Black," he said, "happy hunting."

Chapter 2

Vanessa was bent over the table in the small reception room, her frizzy red hair held away from her eyes by her left hand as her right hand totalled up the takings for the evening on her calculator. "Two hundred and forty pounds," she murmured, before entering the amount carefully in the ledger. She was glad she'd learned book-keeping, instead of going to art school as she'd wished, because now she was so useful to Roger, helping him with all the mundane things that needed doing, so he could concentrate on his great gift.

Mrs Rawlings put her head around the door without bothering to knock. Nobody knocked for Vanessa. "Can we come in now Vanessa?" she cooed.

"Of course, please come in, I won't be a moment." She closed the ledger and replaced it with Roger's appointment book. Mrs Rawlings was followed by five other women, who had remained in the waiting room after the others had left.

"We all need to see Roger, my dear," she began, crossing the room and taking on the role of self-appointed spokesman as she went, "don't we ladies?" She turned and smiled at the queue of women behind her, before returning her gaze to Vanessa. Where on earth had Roger found this mousy woman, she wondered, not for the first time, with her bulging watery-blue eyes and colourless complexion and not to mention those drab clothes she always wore.

"What evening would suit you best?" Vanessa asked meeting the pitying eyes of Mrs Rawlings. "Roger will be healing tomorrow, Wednesday or Friday." She knew what Enid Rawlings thought of her, not because she was psychic, but because Roger had told her often enough what a dreary little thing she was.

"Oh, tomorrow, please."

Vanessa wrote her name down in the appointment book and filled in the date and time on a small card. "I've put you down for your usual time," she said handing over the card, "that'll be sixty pounds please."

Mrs Rawlings rummaged around in the bottom of her handbag for her purse and produced three £20 notes. "There," she said, "freshly minted." Vanessa took the money with a smile. She may be dowdy, but she didn't have to pay for Roger's attention, she had one over on all of them, she was Roger's wife.

Appointments were made for the remaining women, each willingly paying over her money. Vanessa recorded the time in the appointment book and placed the notes carefully in her tin box, till all the women had been issued with their appointment cards and left.

£240 from the Circle and £360 for the treatments she calculated. £600 in total, Roger would be pleased with her.

She gathered up the books and moneybox and placed them in the small, brown attaché case, given to her last Christmas by their daughter Sophie, to make it easier for her to carry the takings home on her bicycle. Giving the room a last look round, she left for home, closing the door quietly behind her. She didn't drive, Roger didn't think it suited a woman to drive a car, although in the winter-time, she wished she could go in the car with him, instead of on her bicycle, but it was one of Roger's rules that they would always arrive at and leave his Circle separately, so as not to interfere with his meditation preparation beforehand and his 'grounding time' at the end. But, usually she enjoyed the cycle ride home with the attaché case strapped onto the little pannier on the back and the breeze blowing through her springy hair, as her legs pushed the pedals round and round. Sometimes, one of the town's residents would nod to her as she passed, but mostly nobody noticed her, except the dogs' at their owner's gates or the cats' out on their nightly prowls. They noticed her. Wherever she went, doggy tails would wag and furry cat bodies would slide softly past her legs and be rewarded with a gentle stroke along their length or a scratch under the chin. Vanessa loved animals, but there weren't any in the house, another of Roger's rules. "No pets" he'd told her, "particularly cats, never cats."

He hadn't even relented when Sophie had said a kitten would be fun to play with. Normally, Sophie could twist her father round her little finger, but not this time, the answer had still been no!

Vanessa leant the bicycle against the wall at the back of the house and carried her case into the kitchen. Sophie was sitting at the oak table drinking coke with one of her school friends and barely glanced up as Vanessa entered.

"Hello darling," she smiled, kissing Sophie on the back of the head, "everything OK?" No answer. "And Jane," she added, "how are you, Jane?"

With twelve years of good manners behind her, Jane replied, "Very well, Mrs Lomax, thank you for asking."

Sophie's straw had reached the bottom of the glass and she was making sucking noises with the last few drops of liquid. "Sophie," admonished Vanessa, "don't do that." Sophie pushed her fingers through her strawberry-blonde hair and stood up.

"We're going upstairs," she said coolly, ignoring Vanessa's words, "Jane's mum's coming for her at nine." Vanessa felt a faint stab of hurt at her daughter's indifference. She should have been used to it by now, but it still hurt, especially as she loved her so much. Roger had secretly wanted a girl child, right from the moment Vanessa discovered she was pregnant so despite the hastily arranged marriage, he had been ecstatic when his daughter had been born. He was forty-two to Vanessa's seventeen when the marriage took place and now, Sophie was twelve, thirteen on her next birthday in November and growing more and more beautiful with each day.

It had been wonderful when Sophie was first born, breast feeding her and singing her to sleep when she cried. Vanessa had never known such closeness with another human being and craved the company of her child almost like drug addicts craved their fix.

"Did daddy ring?" Vanessa called after the disappearing backs.

"No!" came the singular response.

Vanessa sighed and began to make herself some tea. Roger was always late, or out somewhere and on the odd occasion he was home, he spent all of his spare time with Sophie, or locked in his study and not to be disturbed, especially not by her.

The 'phone in the hall began ringing and Vanessa ran to answer it. "Hello," she said, "is that you Roger?"

The soft voice of Kim Mason replied. "Hi, 'Nessa, no it's not Roger it's Kim, but he's asked me to call you." Vanessa felt herself wince, "he's going to be a bit late home tonight, I'm afraid, so not to wait up 'Nessa dear. I've persuaded him to give my little group a demonstration of his gift and well, you know how it is, people just can't let him go once they've got his attention." Her voice held a note of finality about it that brooked no further discussion, "Anyway," she hurried on, "I'd love to chat for a while, but I must go, they're waiting to start. Goodnight 'Nessa." The phone clicked and purred.

"There," Roger said, "that was easy enough now, wasn't it?" Kim took a cigarette from the packet on the floor and lit it, inhaling the tobacco deep into her lungs. "Now, now," murmured Roger, letting his hand glide over her nakedness, before removing the cigarette from her fingers. "You know you're not allowed to smoke till afterwards."

Kim flipped over onto her stomach, allowing her breasts to swell onto the fur throw. "Have I been a bad girl again?" she whispered, teasing him with her eyes from behind the fall of her hair.

Roger's hands pushed her legs apart. "You have," he said, feeling her surrender, "and you know what happens to naughty little girls, don't you?"

Kim opened her legs further. "No," she breathed, arching her back till her breasts were fully exposed and her nipples peaked. Roger pulled her across his legs, squeezing her breasts with one hand while the long fingers of the other, stroked her with practiced ease.

"They get spanked," he hissed, "they get spanked very, very hard."

Kim squealed and began to squirm in mock fear. "Now, let's see you raise that round bum of yours a bit higher for Roger." He was sweating now, as he began throbbing with pleasure.

"No," Kim gurgled, "I won't." Roger pushed her head down onto his hardness.

"No answering back," he chided, as his hand smacked her quivering softness. He could feel her tugging and sucking him with her mouth as his hand found her raised buttocks again and again.

"Roger's ready," he breathed, his urgency increasing with the redness of her skin. He pulled her on top of him and sat her astride his belly. She was the most beautiful woman he had every penetrated, her breasts firm and proud and her flat stomach sucked in, in anticipation of his entry.

Roughly, he pulled her hair with both hands and brought her mouth down on his, kissing her with increased urgency as he felt himself plunging into her depth. He pushed and withdrew, slowly and deliberately, whispering obscenities in her ear, then biting her neck and breasts till he heard her scream with ecstasy as the rush of orgasmic pleasure imploded inside her. Almost simultaneously, Roger felt a surge of power and release. The candles blurred into the darkness of the room as the heat in his groins coursed through him. This was what he lived for, this was what drove him, the ultimate experience of sex with a young, submissive woman, who understood his needs and met them full on. She'd been an easy conquest, he mused, his mind drifting in and out of awareness, but then what woman wasn't, for him.

In the aftermath of their lust, none of them moved till Kim rolled onto the floor and lay on her back, her eyes closed and her breathing easing.

"More," she murmured, sensually, opening her legs again in anticipation. She stroked the hair around Roger's neck as she pulled his head towards her, "Now, punish me again," she whispered, "please."

Chapter 3

It was past midnight before Vanessa heard the scrape of Roger's key in the lock. She felt herself tense, her eyes staring into the darkness around her. Straining her ears, she listened for every sound, which would track her husband's movements through the house as he made his way upstairs.

'Please, please let him come to bed with me?' she prayed silently.

His footsteps sounded nearer and louder in the silence of the slumbering house, as they approached their bedroom door. Vanessa held her breath.

Should she call out his name, maybe cough to let him know she was awake?

But before she could do anything, his footsteps moved away.

She could hear the gentle knocking on Sophie's bedroom door and the click of the lock as it closed behind him and her hands gripped the pillow, pulling it over her ears. Vanessa felt the choking sensation tighten in her throat as tears forced themselves from her eyes. 'What had she done to displease him?' she wondered frantically, 'why did he choose to spend the night in his daughter's room again, instead of with her, his wife?'

The questions chased around her head as her misery deepened. Hadn't she given him everything he'd ever asked for, including a beautiful daughter? She knew he loved Sophie, just as she did, but couldn't he spare just a little of that love for her?

Pulling the duvet over her head, Vanessa shivering with unhappiness, tried to sleep, but sleep eluded her and as the sky began to lighten, she pushed back the duvet and swung her legs over the edge of the bed. She gazed at the long, white limbs stretched out before her, Roger used to love her legs and their paleness, wrapping them around him and stroking them from knee to thigh as he lay between them, his head resting on her breasts.

She had been sixteen when she had caught his eye. A young, naïve student at a further education college learning book-keeping and computers so that she could try to earn a living working in an office. She had wanted to go to Art School but hadn't been bright enough or talented enough, but she was good at math and hadn't put up any objection when her father had pointed her in the direction of the local college. Roger had been a lecturer in Marketing at the same establishment and was known by the rest of the male staff as always being on the look-out for a 'pretty young thing' to conquer. With two failed marriages behind him, his views on women were restricted to two things. They had to be young and they had to do as they were told, especially when it came to sex. And the younger and more biddable, the better he liked it. Vanessa had presented the perfect opportunity, and he had lost no time in seducing her.

What he hadn't counted on was getting her pregnant, but the thrill of the conquest had made him careless. His first reaction was to get out of the mess and quickly, insist Vanessa had the child aborted, but before he could put any plan of escape into operation he was summoned to the Principal's office and instantly dismissed for gross misconduct. Some bastard had reported him.

Vanessa's distress was palpable as she pleaded with Roger to forgive her. After all, she had been the one who had tempted him beyond endurance and allowed herself to become pregnant and now, she had cost him his job. "Father will help," she had insisted to a stony-faced Roger, "he's got pots of money and would help us till you get another job. Please let me speak to him, tell him how much we love each other?" The thought of some easy money appealed to Roger's empty pockets and he wondered how much he would need to get as far away from Vanessa and this silly pregnancy business as he could.

"And what college would hire me now!" he stated savagely, "your stupidity has cost me everything," he rounded. "How much money has your father got Vanessa, enough for me to leave the country and never come back?"

Vanessa had flinched, her head and shoulders drooping in despair. She loved Roger and couldn't live without him. "I don't know," she stammered, "let me speak to him, please." Her blue eyes, red-rimmed with tears stared at his chest, afraid to look into the anger in his face.

The meeting with Vanessa's father did not go well for Roger. Unlike his daughter, John Anderson was made of much sterner stuff and pinned him down to an agreement to marry his pregnant daughter in return for a house in Vanessa's name and £2,000 a month till Roger found work. Vanessa's obvious devotion to him, coupled with her father's offer of financial gain persuaded him to do 'the honourable thing', so on a bright spring day in May, he and Vanessa were married. Sophie was born the following November and Vanessa's happiness seemed to be complete.

She padded towards the bedroom door, her bare feet sinking into the soft carpeting and headed across the landing to the stairs leading down to the kitchen. The door to Sophie's bedroom was firmly closed. Vanessa felt isolated and alone, as she stared at the white barrier. Shut out not just by the door, but also by the invisible wall around Roger and their daughter, who seemed to be so in tune with each other and so out of tune with her.

Chapter 4

The kitchen was cold in the early morning as Vanessa boiled the kettle. Roger wouldn't be awake for hours yet, not with such a late night and Sophie could sleep the clock round. She looked out of the kitchen window at the stillness and peace of the little back garden. The sky was just starting to lighten as the low whistle of the kettle began to permeate the silence. Hurriedly, she turned off the gas and poured the water over her Lady Grey teabag before taking the steaming brew to the back door. If she was very quiet she could watch the early morning birds begin to arrive in the garden looking for breakfast. It was her favourite time of day, often indulged.

Suddenly, a flash of white caught her eye, dipping behind the shrubs, along the wooden fence, before emerging almost at her feet. Vanessa stared. There before her was a beautiful, white cat.

She leant forward, hand outstretched in greeting. "Hello," she whispered, "aren't you the pretty one." The cat came nearer and confidently brushed against her leg, allowing her to stroke his snowy head. Then she noticed his eyes. There was one blue eye and the other was golden. "Goodness," she breathed in astonishment "and where have you come from?"

The cat purred loudly, then before Vanessa could do anything else, he turned around and walked off, back the way he'd come.

Vanessa stood transfixed. There were a few cats in the neighbourhood but not one like that. Not one so beautiful and those eyes, different coloured eyes. She smiled, without even realising it, and sipped her tea. The meeting with the cat felt somehow comforting, but would go no further she knew, not with Roger's abhorrence of all animals, especially felines. She shivered and returned to the kitchen and her wifely duties.

By the time Roger stirred, the sun was moving away from the kitchen, round the side of the house and into Sophie's bedroom window. How he hated this house, Roger thought, so provincial, so ordinary, just like Vanessa. Then he glanced over at Sophie, lying asleep next to him, her blonde hair framing her young, young face. He pushed a lock of hair gently from her cheek. "One day," he whispered, "one day you'll want me as much as I want you." He felt himself harden, "But not yet my temptation, not till you're ready."

He rolled easily off the bed, holding his breath till he was sure Sophie slept on before making for the door. She already knew daddy loved her more than anything else in the world, even mummy... especially mummy.

He always made sure he came into his daughter's room after she was asleep and left before she awoke. He had patience, didn't he and anyway, she secretly wanted him in bed with her, he told himself. Yes, one day, one day.

Vanessa heard his footsteps on the stairs and the kitchen door opening.

"Roger," she turned brightly, "good morning darling, did you sleep well. I didn't hear you come in. Did the evening go well? Kim phone..." Vanessa felt her voice falter under his stare. She was asking too many questions again, speaking too much.

"Breakfast?" she finished anxiously.

Roger picked up the morning paper from the sideboard. "If I must," he replied sourly, pulling out a chair and rustling open the paper, bringing any further interchange to a halt.

It's always like this, Vanessa stressed to herself, no matter what she did, it was always the wrong thing, the wrong words, the wrong way she looked. She moved around the kitchen on automatic pilot, as quietly as possible, as she sought to prepare a meal for Roger that he would at least eat, never mind appreciate.

Wordlessly, she placed a plateful of scrambled eggs in front of him and began filling his cup with fresh coffee. His hand reached out and grabbed her wrist. "Not coffee, I want TEA!"

Vanessa felt herself begin to shake. "Sorry, Roger," she murmured, "my mistake."

He pushed her away. "Call yourself a WIFE."

Vanessa felt fear form in her stomach as she watched his wrath building. But, it wasn't her he vented his anger on this time, it was the eggs. Very slowly, he tipped the plateful of food onto the table. "Give it to one of your animal friends," he sneered, "it's all it's fit for."

Vanessa stood frozen with fear, as Roger threw the newspaper at her and stood up. "I'll eat elsewhere," he growled, "somewhere civilised."

She stood immobilised till she heard the front door slam and Roger's car rev up and drive off. Tears began to wet her cheeks as she stared at the eggy mess. Not for the first time, she tried to understand how she always managed to upset her husband, no matter how hard she tried to be the wife he wanted. She went to the kitchen sink and splashed the cool water onto her face.

"What's the matter now?" a voice asked wearily. Vanessa quickly mopped her face with a tea towel as Sophie came into the room, still bleary-eyed from sleep. "Why did daddy slam the door?" Vanessa took a deep breath and turned to face her daughter.

"And, what's all this mess on the table?" Sophie's eyes widened as she surveyed the scattering of cooked eggs.

Vanessa used the towel to scoop up the eggs and deposit them in the bin.

"There was a little accident," she replied, fixing on her 'mummy' smile. "Clumsy me," she shrugged.

Sophie sighed. 'Why couldn't her mother be like Jane's mum, perfect, simply perfect?' Vanessa could feel the disdain coming at her in waves and her smile crumbled. Even her daughter thought she was useless.

"I'm going into town this morning, banking and shopping, you know," Vanessa said quickly, trying to ease the tension in her shoulders, "we could go together," she continued, "maybe buy you something pretty, have some ice-cream..."

Sophie eyed her with mild pity. A look she'd perfected from watching her father. She screwed up her nose. "Can't, going to Jane's house, her mum's taking us to the cinema." Vanessa took a deep breath as she felt the tears of hurt rising again.

"That'll be nice," she smiled, "maybe another Saturday then. Breakfast?"

Sophie shrugged. "Suppose so."

Vanessa dutifully fed her daughter and phoned Mrs Munro to thank her in advance for taking Sophie with her and Jane to the cinema. Mrs Munro's warm, confident voice replied. "My pleasure Mrs Lomax, I should have mentioned it at the Circle last night, but it completely slipped my mind. I was just soooo relaxed. Roger is wonderful, isn't he?"

"Yes," Vanessa agreed tightly, "yes he is."

"Bye, bye." The line went dead and Vanessa hung up.

She waited until she heard Sophie calling out her goodbye as she left the house and listened to the silence. She liked silence, it felt safe. She looked at the clock. She'd better hurry if she was to get to the bank before it closed and deposit last night's takings. Roger would never forgive her if she mucked up that job as well.

Picking up her cashbox and pay-in book, she hurried to the garage and wheeled her bicycle out onto the road. The day was fresh and bright, warm enough not to bother with her thick anorak. She slung her handbag over her shoulder and set off. She loved the freedom of cycling, smiling to a few people as she passed them and feeling the gloom and anxiety of breakfast time, lift.

Parking her bike by the tree outside the bank she hurried in and made the cash deposit. Mr Parker, the teller, watched her with interest. She could easily become a teller, like him, but seldom looked up from her task and never spent any time on small talk.

Once outside, she sighed with relief, job done. She was lifting her bike clear of the tree when a flash of white caught her eye again. There on the trunk was a notice about a missing cat. She looked closer. It was him! The beautiful white cat with the strange eyes was staring out at her.

"Oh no," she thought, "missing!" She looked for a contact number. She would have to get in touch and tell the owners she'd seen their cat, just that morning in her garden. Give them hope that their cat was at least alive.

But there wasn't a phone number, just an address. Laburnum Cottage, 4 Willow Walk, West Hampton. Vanessa took a note of the address and forgetting all about any shopping she had intended doing, headed off to find Willow Walk. Down by the river, she seemed to remember, not that far from home. Vanessa followed the path beside the stream. It had been a long time since she'd been down this way, remembering, as she pedalled, childhood walks with Sophie and paddling with her, the cool water gurgling around the stones and their ankles.

She found herself singing silly nursery rhymes and giggling at her naivety.

The path turned off to the left and joined a proper tarmac road. There were a group of cottages in front of her, three to the left and three to the right and one at the very top of the cul-de-sac. Vanessa counted, 1, 2, 3 then 4, the one at the top and dismounting, pushed her bike towards the cottage.

No one seemed to be around, but the peace and gentleness of the little hamlet began to pervade her very being. Trees whispered in the breeze and the scent of roses from the nearby garden filled her nostrils. "Beautiful," she breathed, as she approached Laburnum Cottage.

Leaving her bike leaning against the garden wall, Vanessa pushed open the small wooden gate. The path was uneven and showed signs of years of use.

She leaned forward at the blue door, to see if there was a nameplate, but there wasn't, just the number 4. Her ears strained for sounds of life but found none. Tentatively, she knocked on the door. No answer. She wished she'd brought something to write on, leave a note, but there was just the pay-in book in her attaché case on her pannier.

Before turning to go, Vanessa was taking a last look round when she saw it again, the white flash of fur. It was the cat, surely. She moved towards the shrubs at the side of the garden. "Here Kitty," she called. "It's alright, I won't hurt you."

"I'm sure you won't." Vanessa swung around to be met with the bluest eyes she'd ever seen, framed with grey hair, held in a topknot.

"I'm sorry," she blurted, "I knocked and no one answered and then I saw the cat and..." she trailed off. The blue eyes seemed to look right through her.

"I know," Mrs Hazelwood said kindly. "I've been expecting you."

Vanessa giggled nervously. "Expecting me?"

"Certainly," smiled Mrs Hazelwood, "Noble told me you were coming."

"Noble?" Vanessa queried.

Mrs Hazelwood nodded towards the feline, "Yes, Noble, he's my cat."

"Your cat, you mean the missing white cat with the coloured eyes is yours?"

Mrs Hazelwood nodded. "I thought I'd lost him this time, might have known he was on one of his missions."

Vanessa wasn't quite sure what to say. "He was in my garden this morning," she explained, "and then I saw the notice on the tree saying he was lost and I came to tell you he was alright... but, he's here!"

"Would you like some tea, my dear?" Mrs Hazelwood said patiently, "it's Lady Grey, your favourite."

Vanessa was becoming more confused by the minute. 'How did she know I liked Lady Grey tea,' she asked herself, 'and the cat, Noble, HE told her I was coming?'

"This way," ordered Mrs Hazelwood. Her small figure disappeared round the side of the cottage and into the back garden. Vanessa followed. There on a white wrought-iron table was a tray holding a teapot, cups and saucers, sugar and milk, a plate of biscuits and a dish with lemon slices neatly cut.

"Please," said Mrs Hazelwood, "sit down."

Vanessa sat and watched as her hostess poured out their tea. "Milk or lemon?" she asked.

"Milk please."

"Noble likes milk," she continued. The white cat slipped out from behind a blaze of Delphiniums and glided towards his mistress. She poured a little milk into a saucer and placed it on the grass, smiling as Noble lapped it up.

"Please, drink your tea before it becomes cold," Mrs Hazelwood said matter-of-factly. Vanessa did as she was told.

"Do we know one another?" she queried hesitantly, returning the cup to the tray.

Mrs Hazelwood looked surprised. "No."

Vanessa was more confused than ever. "It's just that you seem to know things about me that…"

Mrs Hazelwood held up her hand. "I've already said, Noble told me about you."

Vanessa sat back uneasily. 'I seem to have wandered into another world,' she thought, deciding to leave as soon as possible and to forget the strange woman and her cat.

She smiled as she stood up. "Well, I'm glad you've got your cat back," Vanessa said, keeping her voice calm and soft, "I'm sure he's also glad to be home."

Mrs Hazelwood nodded in acknowledgement. "Come again Vanessa, whenever you like, I'm always here and so's Noble."

Vanessa started. "You know my name!" she exclaimed, "but how do you know my name?"

Mrs Hazelwood tutted, "I keep telling you, Noble told me."

Vanessa took several steps backwards before turning and hurrying down the path to where her bike awaited her.

She pedalled faster than she had ever done before and got back to her house in a state of fluster and heat. Pushing the bike into the garage, she almost ran into the kitchen. And into the wide back of Roger.

"What the hell?" Roger swung around. "You!" he glared.

The sight of her husband brought her back to reality. "I'm sorry," she stuttered, "I've been rushing around all day, you know, getting things done… I'm sorry."

Vanessa moved towards the door. "You're healing tonight Roger, so I'd better get the appointment book and then there's the paperwork from the bank to file away…" She felt his strong hand grip her upper arm.

"STOP," he shouted. "Where have you been?"

Vanessa squirmed to free herself. "Nowhere," she murmured. She couldn't tell him about the strange lady and her cat… no, especially not her cat.

Roger pushed her away. "Get on with it then. Mrs Rawlings's appointment is at seven o'clock and I don't want her to be kept waiting because of YOU."

Vanessa nodded and ran from the room trying desperately to calm her breathing.

By six-thirty she was at her desk at Roger's consulting room, as was Mrs Rawlings. "I'm a little early," said Enid Rawlings, patting her blotchy red neck.

"It's been a frightful day and I need Roger's healing more than ever this week." She dabbed her eyes with the edge of a white handkerchief.

Vanessa nodded empathically. "He won't be long," she said.

"Tea while you wait?"

Roger's client smiled weakly. "No, thank you. My bladder you know."

The pair lapsed into silence. At six-fifty-five Roger arrived.

Chapter 5

As usual, the air changed when Roger entered a room. His presence seemed to push through the invisible. Enid Rawlings also changed, her shoulders lifted and her neck stretched up, tightening the loose skin under her jaw line.

He glanced at Vanessa before turning his full attention to Enid.

"In a moment," he smiled, "you're just that little bit early," he chided.

Enid Rawlings's face coloured slightly as she tipped her head down, suitably chastised.

"I'll buzz you when I'm ready," he muttered to Vanessa as he passed her desk and went into his consulting room, closing the door behind him.

Roger's room was his private domain. Only those he allowed in ever saw behind the door and were cautioned to keep his privacy protected at the end of their therapy session with him.

On the walls were his many framed certificates in Hypnotherapy, Massage, Reiki and NLP. After losing his lecturing job at the college he had been searching around for something suitable to his abilities and had come across an advertisement in the local paper offering hypnotherapy training.

Everything about the subject appealed to him. Hypnosis, controlling minds, vulnerable women and making money, all had formed in his psyche.

He had taken to the therapy like a duck to water and Vanessa's father was only too glad to fund his training. The quicker he got Roger off his financial hands the better.

Roger excelled in his new chosen profession. Given his deep voice and commanding presence, he very soon built a reputation for himself as a wonderful healer, especially amongst the women he treated. Then there were his hands. Healer's hands they all said. So warm, so soothing, so powerful.

What wasn't certificated on the walls was his misguided expertise as a sex therapist. This 'skill', as he preferred to call it, had been picked up from books and the internet, as well as his many sexual experiences.

When Kim had come to him for hypnotherapy to stop smoking, he had used his hypnotherapy skills to control her mind and his sexual expertise to push her to more and more base levels. She took to spanking like a duck to water, he remembered, and in one so young! But he'd wanted to try more and more. Do more and more. Expertly, he manipulated her mind, till she would do anything for him. He never advertised the fact, but he used some of the techniques he'd practiced first-hand on her, in one or two of his healing sessions, when required, or rather when the mood took him.

Ah, Kim. Their now shared lust for sexual pleasure and new sensations kept them together, despite Kim's occasional unease at Roger's preference for younger and younger flesh.

Roger switched on two Tiffany lamps and the green lawyer's lamp on his mahogany desk. The heavy curtains draped across the bay window were pulled shut and the sound of soft music drifted into the space. He pressed the buzzer under the rim of his desk and waited.

Almost instantly the door was pushed open just enough to let the figure of Enid Rawlings enter.

"Ah, Enid," Roger smiled, "come in, come in." His eyes followed her as intently as a spider watches a fly enter its web. 'Was he in the mood?' he wondered.

Without speaking, Enid took up her usual position on the padded treatment table and closed her eyes. Lying semi-prone, she strained to hear Roger move towards her. But, he kept her waiting.

Just as she was beginning to get anxious she felt his hands rest on the top of her head. He was behind her and, yes, he decided, he was in the mood.

Enid's hand fluttered to her neck and chest. "Is that where the tension is, Enid?" Roger's voice sounded like melting honey in her ear.

"Yes, Roger," she rasped, "and my bladder, you know the problems I have with my bladder."

She was so obvious, he told himself. So sexually frustrated, she was ready to explode.

"And do you want Roger to fix things?" he continued, moving around the table till he could see her face. She nodded silently, nervously unbuttoning her cardigan for him. He pressed a lever on the side of the table which lowered the upper half down to the fully prone position. Enid wriggled and gripped the sides in anticipation of Roger's touch. She knew it was wrong, but what could she do, she was in his hands, powerless and… the thought brought an involuntary gasp from her lips.

"Hush now," whispered Roger, "we don't want the world to know our little secret."

Agonisingly slowly, his hands pushed the cardigan aside and lifted Enid's bra upwards revealing her bare breasts. The heat from his hands massaging them to attention brought a flush of blood to her neck. "Nice?" he asked quietly. Enid gulped and nodded.

"More?" Again she gasped in anticipation.

"Yes, yes." She felt her skirt being lifted as Roger's hand moved smoothly up over her knee, then thigh, then under the edge of her white pants. Frilly, like he preferred.

"Is this where you hurt?" he asked, pushing the frill aside and down to where she was wet. His practiced hand knew exactly where to rub her to build the sexual excitement she craved. "Now, open your legs for me Enid, and no noise, remember, or I'll stop."

Her back arched and her legs opened. Roger was in. His fingers worked deeper and the strokes became longer until Enid could feel herself going beyond any point of return.

"Now," she screamed, "now," as she gripped the table tighter and tighter.

Roger clamped his free hand over her mouth. "Ssshhhh", he commanded, "no noise, I told you, you're not doing what I say again." He held her there, on the tip of his finger till, finally and moving almost imperceptibly, he brought her to orgasm.

A surge of power swept over Roger. How sweet total control felt how all-consuming.

Enid slumped back onto the table, tears flowing from her eyes and a smile spread widely across her face. "Thank you," she said softly, "thank you."

Roger washed his hands at the tiny sink in the corner and thought of Kim. He'd be with her that night and then he'd show her how much he could do to her and what he expected her to do to him.

Slowly, Enid Rawlings adjusted her clothing and put on her outdoor coat.

No words were spoken as she left. Roger's rules.

Fifteen minutes later Roger buzzed Vanessa again, time for the next one.

His need for control now abated, the following two clients were treated using Hypnotherapy and Reiki, both of them blissfully unaware of what had happened there earlier to Enid Rawlings.

This was the part of his practice which frequently bored him, but the money he was making more than compensated for the inconvenience. And, anyway, there was still Kim to see and their trip to London to arrange at the end of the session.

By the time his last client had gone and he'd treated himself to a whisky from the bottle he kept in the bottom drawer of his desk, Vanessa had left for home. Just to make sure, he buzzed her in the reception room. No response. "Good" he breathed, refreshing his glass and picking up the phone.

It rang twice. "Kim Mason," said the voice.

"It's me."

There was a murmur of soft laughter. "If it's the 'me' I've been expecting you're late."

Roger immediately felt aroused. She wanted to be chastised again. God she was a glutton for punishment.

"Don't be cheeky, darling," he laughed, "and slip into something uncomfortable, I'll be with you in twenty minutes."

It was Kim's turn to tease him back. "That long," she said, "by the time you get here I'll be off the whole idea."

"See you in ten." Roger hung up and drunk the last of the whisky.

He looked around his domain proudly. How strong he felt, in control of himself and his life. Perfect.

He picked up the phone again. Vanessa answered.

"Is Sophie in bed?" he asked.

"Roger!" she felt herself alert and tense at the same time. "Yes, yes she is. Why?"

"Don't ask questions all the time. You know it annoys me."

"Sorry Roger." Vanessa's shoulders began to droop. "I suppose you're going to be late again," she asked, "didn't the clinic go well?"

"Oh, shut up Vanessa," he replied, "and don't wait up."

The drive to Kim's flat took longer than twenty minutes. No woman would tell him when to arrive and she'd better be glad to see him when he did get there, or she'd be in trouble. He felt himself harden at the thought.

He could picture Kim, naked and agitated, longing for him to knock on her door and take her where she stood.

His pace quickened as he pushed open the front door. No need to knock, she was waiting, ready and waiting. No time to waste knocking on doors.

His eyes adjusted to the candlelight as the scent of Frankincense assaulted his nostrils. The shape of Kim spread, face down, on the fur throw came into his view. Her hair tumbled down her back and her red nails pinched and bunched the soft fur, on which lay a small whip. Black and woven with nine tails.

"Forgive me," she breathed. "I didn't mean to hurry you."

"But you did hurry me, Kim, and now…" Roger stripped slowly, removing his garments and dropping them all around her. Kim could feel her body pulsing with desire and lust. He picked up the whip, drawing it across her hips and between her legs. "Turn over," he commanded, "now." First her head turned then her shoulders and breasts and finally her hips and legs. She gazed at Roger, fully erect and put her hands together in prayer.

"Please, please," she begged, "punish me for being so bad, so wicked. I deserve to be whipped." The words were coming in hoarse whispers as she rubbed her hands over her breasts and down onto her hips. The first sting of the whip landed across her breasts. The second sting was on her thighs. She rolled over and raised her buttocks high into the air. "Again," she cried, "again."

Roger felt his breath quicken and come in harsh gasps. The lash stung again and again till it drew blood. "Now," she groaned, "NOW." Roger threw the whip aside and knelt behind her.

"Like this," he roared, thrusting into her with the strength and power of a wild stallion. The heat seared through them both, their screams of lust matching one another's, till the force of his erection was spent and Kim's orgasms had ebbed.

They lay, exhausted. The candles spluttered and went out. Just the moonlight through the window lit the room.

Roger pulled her towards him.

"Now," he murmured into her hair. "It's my turn."

Chapter 6

Vanessa spent another restless night alone in their bed. As usual, Roger had gone straight to Sophie's room to sleep. She understood his reasons. Ever since Sophie had suffered an asthma attack during the night when she was about eight years old, Roger had preferred to spend as many nights as possible in her room. "Just in case," he'd told her, his fatherly concern brooking no objections from Vanessa.

It had upset her at the time, and still did. "If anyone should sleep in their daughter's room, surely it should be her."

She turned and pulled the duvet over her shoulders, trying to push the thought from her mind that Roger may have used Sophie's asthma attack as an excuse to stop sharing his bed with her. She hated herself for thinking this way, for goodness sake, Sophie couldn't help having asthma and Roger was her father.

She looked at the clock, almost five-forty and she was wide awake. Slipping out from under the bedclothes she pushed her feet into her furry slippers, pulled on her dressing gown and, with her usual stealth at that time of day, she crept past her daughter's room and downstairs to the kitchen.

She glanced at the calendar pinned to the corkboard. In another two weeks she'd be thirty years old. She winced as she looked at her reflection in the darkness of the window. Her hair hung in messy tangles around her face. She took out a hand mirror from a drawer to look closer. Staring back at her were washed-out blue eyes and thin lips. "Thirty!" she exclaimed to herself sadly. She touched her skin. It felt dry and tight. No wonder Roger ignored her.

She brushed away two tiny tears that had crept into the corner of her eyes and boiled the kettle. Thirty years old and the highlight of her day was her early-morning cup of Lady Grey Tea.

She wrapped her dressing gown tightly around her, tying it with its terry-towelling ties and took her mug of tea to the backdoor.

The silence of the morning and the arrival of the birds always calmed her soul and she determined she would try harder than ever to make Roger love her again, the way he used to when they'd first met. It used to be that he couldn't wait to be with her. He once loved her red hair with its corkscrew curls and when Sophie had been born, Vanessa felt that she'd been doubly blessed. To have a wonderful husband and beautiful baby daughter was more than she had ever dreamed of.

Her thoughts were interrupted by a rustling noise near the fence running down the side of the garden. Her eyes adjusted to the early morning light and met those of the white cat. The old lady's cat! It must have wandered off again.

She put down her mug and bent over towards the cat. Noble, yes, that was his name, she remembered. Silently, the cat moved nearer, his eyes focussed totally on hers. This time, he let her stroke his beautiful head for a few seconds and even sat down at her feet, letting her get to know him.

Vanessa somehow felt very privileged at his attention but then, as before, he turned tail and left the way he had come.

Vanessa smiled. She knew he'd get home himself this time, but felt strangely comforted, as before, by his appearance.

Roger was his usual grumpy self when he came down for breakfast, but Vanessa was determined he wouldn't destroy her good mood this time.

After all, she would soon be thirty years of age, a fully grown woman. She was sure he'd think of something special to mark the occasion, but Roger had other ideas.

Sophie trooped into the kitchen, eyes half-shut and kissed her father on the top of his head. Roger's eyes immediately lit up as he turned to look at her, pointing to his cheek indicating he wanted another kiss. But Sophie didn't notice and scuffled across to the cooker where Vanessa was making a batch of pancakes. She didn't see Roger's face darken, but her mother did.

She tousled her daughter's hair. "Still sleepy," she cooed. Sophie nodded.

"Can I have jam on my pancakes?" she asked, reminding Vanessa how young she still was. "And daddy, can he have some too?"

Vanessa glanced at Roger, who had returned to burying himself in his newspaper.

"Of course," she said, with just a hint of mockery, "daddy can have anything he wants, can't you daddy?"

Sophie plopped down beside her father. "Can I have anything I want too?" she said coyly.

Never one to miss a chance to draw his daughter nearer to him, Roger pulled her onto his knee. "Of course, sweetheart, what can daddy do for you?"

"Weeeeelll," began his daughter, "Jane's mum and dad are buying her a pony," her eyes were wide open now, "and I want one too."

Roger cringed. "Now, now, Sophie, you know daddy doesn't like animals."

"But it's a pony daddy, not a hairy dog or furry cat and it won't live here," she whined.

Not wanting to disappoint his daughter, but with no intention of buying her a stupid pony, he stood her in front of him. "In a couple of weeks," he said, "daddy is going up to London and when I'm there I'll see if there are any ponies for sale and if there is, I'll bring one back with me."

Sophie eyed him suspiciously. "Really?"

"Really." What Roger failed to mention was that it would be a toy pony and not a living one. But his lie would have to do for now, till he could think of something else to tell her. Sophie sat down at the table and began to eat her pancakes, occasionally glancing at her mother for reassurance. Her father had agreed too easily.

But Vanessa's mind was racing. 'London, in a couple of weeks' time,' she thought. 'Was that her birthday surprise? Roger was taking her for a weekend in London!'

As soon as Sophie left the table, Vanessa began to smile to herself at the thought of a whole weekend, just her and Roger. It would be like old times.

She would buy something new, something sexy and her hair, she would have her hair done the day before and Sophie could stay with her grandfather or maybe Jane Munro's mum would have her for the weekend.

"Have I said something to amuse you?" Roger asked sarcastically.

Vanessa returned abruptly from her daydream. "Oh!" she stammered, "I was just thinking about... London."

"What about it?"

"Well, it's the weekend of my birthday, and I thought, maybe…"

Slowly, Roger placed his newspaper on the table. "And you thought that WE, YOU AND ME, would go to London TO CELEBRATE!"

Vanessa backed off. "Well," she fought back weakly, "aren't we?"

Her husband stood up and pushed his chair back making a loud grating noise on the quarry tiles.

"If you must know, I'm going to London for a conference that weekend and if you'd been doing your job properly, you'd have noticed I've written it in the appointments book. So check it out and don't make yourself any more stupid by booking in clients on those dates."

"Oh," he finished sourly, "and happy birthday when it comes. Sorry I'll miss it," but under his breath he added, "not."

Vanessa felt her world crumble. Her thirtieth birthday and Roger had to go to a conference, so no surprise, no celebration, just her and her alone, singing, *"Happy Birthday to You, Happy Birthday to You, Happy Birthday dear Vanessa, Happy Birthday to you."* This time, she couldn't stop the tears from forming and wept till there were no more tears to cry.

In his car, Roger dialled Kim's number on his mobile. Her answerphone cut in. "Just a reminder, darling, about our weekend in London. I've booked the usual hotel and let Darko know we'll be at his club on the Saturday." His stomach tightened at the thought. "Wear something, well, hedonistic," he urged, you know what Darko likes. Speak soon." He flicked the phone shut. "Two weeks to go," he muttered. He couldn't wait.

Chapter 7

The two weeks leading up to Vanessa's birthday, found her more and more isolated. Sophie never missed an opportunity to be near Roger, stroking his hair as she passed him at the kitchen table, snuggling down on the floor between his legs when he sat in his chair in the evening. Not that he spent that much time at home, Vanessa mused sadly. She knew what her daughter was up to, dreams of her very own pony never far from her thoughts, but Roger seemed to soak up her attention like a sponge.

On the Saturday he was leaving for London, Sophie was up and about at an unearthly hour for her, running excitedly around her father, picking imaginary flecks of fluff off his coat and handing him his briefcase and car keys.

She never once mentioned the promise of a pony. She didn't need to. Roger was well aware of the manipulation that was going on. He beamed at his daughter. "Now be a good girl while daddy's gone and, well, who knows..." he teased. His daughter may be a tiny manipulator, but Roger was the master and no female, not even Sophie would ever be able to outwit him.

Vanessa stood quietly in the background till Sophie, flushed and smiling, ran from the bedroom.

"I hope the conference goes well, Roger," she ventured. "When will you be back?"

The earlier euphoria dropped from Roger's shoulders like a stone.

"I'll be back when I'm back," he retorted.

Vanessa felt herself wince. "It's just that I need to know... for your appointments," she added quickly. Roger sucked in air loudly.

"If I need to let you know exactly when I'll be back, I'll phone." He waved his mobile in front of her. "See," he said through gritted teeth, adding sarcastically, "don't phone me, I'll phone you." And with that, he picked up his suitcase and was gone.

Vanessa stood still, listening to the noises around her, her daughter singing in the shower, her husband slamming the front door and opening his car door, the engine being started, then the sound of the car driving off into the distance.

The next day was her birthday and there wasn't even a single card for her, never mind a present. Was she so invisible, she wondered?

Sophie padded into the bedroom, her hair in a towel and another draped around her shoulders. "Will you dry my hair for me?" she asked. "I'm meeting Jane later and we're going to the stables to see her pony." Her young eyes sparkled with anticipation. "And," she added, "when daddy comes back, I'll have my very own pony too."

Vanessa followed her daughter through to her bedroom. She knew Roger wasn't going to bring back a pony for Sophie and dreaded the disappointment she was going to watch her experience.

"Sophie," she said gently, "it might be that daddy won't manage to get you a pony in London, they mostly live in the country." Her daughter's eyes were reflected in the dressing table mirror where she sat. She pondered this information for a few moments before slowly turning to face her mother.

"Why do you have to ruin everything," she said her voice calm and confident. "Just because daddy isn't going to bring you anything back from London, don't try to spoil things for me."

Vanessa stepped back, stung by her daughter's haughty tone. The one person in the world she loved, even more than Roger, had finally turned against her. Roger had done his job well she thought. She understood him wanting his daughter to be his 'best girl' but did he really have to take Sophie away from her altogether?

The knowledge that she meant no more to her husband and now her daughter, than a biddable servant, instantly seemed to drain her love for them from her heart and replace it with a cold emptiness.

"Sorry," Vanessa said meekly, "of course, you're right. Daddy WILL bring home a pony for you. Silly mummy."

Reassured, Sophie shrugged. "Now, dry my hair," she demanded smugly.

And Vanessa did.

After her daughter had left, the emptiness of the house matched the emptiness she felt in her heart. The sun shone through the window and the garden blazed with summer flowers. 'Go outside,' she decided, 'go anywhere away from this house.' Her need to breathe fresh air was almost overwhelming. Quickly, she pulled on her cardigan and picking up her bag, went out to the garage and got on her bicycle.

At first, she just cycled aimlessly, going as fast as she could, letting the wind blow away the hurt till finally, breathlessly, she found herself down by the river. She sat down by the cool water, slipping off her shoes and letting her feet dangle in the ceaseless flow running over them. She felt the warm sun penetrating her skin and closed her eyes, listening to the rustle of the leaves on the trees and the occasional birds twittering somewhere in the shrubs.

A sense of peace returned to her soul and her breathing slowed back to normal. She re-ran the morning encounter with Sophie and Roger's hostility towards her before he left for London and felt again, the ebbing of love from her heart.

She knew she had always been a good wife to Roger and did everything he'd wanted, no matter how much it had sometimes upset her. She remembered his touch, getting rougher as the years had gone by, the loving seeming to turn into something else. But she never complained. It was just Roger, having his needs met, he'd said, they were just different from hers that was all.

And, when Sophie had been born, Vanessa's needs had truly been met.

The love she had felt for her daughter had almost consumed her. There was nothing she wouldn't do to make her happy and, everyone, except Roger, had said what a wonderful mother she was. That she had produced such a beautiful child always brought tears to her eyes when she thought of Sophie, but, not this time. This time, there were no tears of love for Sophie, Roger had seen to that, turning their daughter away from her and towards him at every opportunity.

She felt the isolation begin to descend on her again when, coming through the grass towards her, tail held high and feet elegantly stepping, came the cat.

Vanessa blinked in disbelief. Noble seemed to have developed the knack of turning up just when she felt at her loneliest. He came closer, but this time, sat down a few feet away and meowed. At first, Vanessa wasn't sure it was the cat that had made the noise as she'd never heard him make any sound before. Then, he did it again. Vanessa stood up and as she did so, Noble moved off. Instinctively, she picked up her things and her bicycle and followed him. Almost immediately, she realised where he was heading. Back home, home to Laburnum Cottage and his mistress.

As they neared Willow Walk, Noble quickened his pace and ran ahead of Vanessa. It was almost as if he was heralding her arrival.

Mrs Hazelwood nodded to him on his entrance to the cottage and rose to put on the kettle. "She's here again, is she Noble?" Noble meowed.

Vanessa parked her bike at the gate as before and stepped up the path. Although the front door stood open, she knocked tentatively. "Come in," the voice called to her, "tea's nearly ready."

Vanessa did as she was told and looked around the front room for its owner. The room was crammed with strange ornaments and symbols. Crystals sat on the window sill, plants grew in pots to the height of the ceiling and herbs hung on strings from a rope strung above the fireplace. The whole place smelled of cinnamon and lavender. Probably from the candles dotted around the room, Vanessa thought. What a peaceful place.

Movement behind the door leading to another room caught her eye.

She coughed and a head appeared around the door. "Ah, Vanessa," said Mrs Hazelwood. "I see Noble's found you again." Vanessa nodded, amazed that she accepted the fact as normal.

"I'll bring the tea in here, if that's alright," Mrs Hazelwood said, "please, sit down."

Vanessa sat down on the edge of a deep purple velvet sofa. "Thank you."

She was handed a cup of Lady Grey tea, as before.

"Thanks," Vanessa said, taking the tea. "You're very kind," she continued, "but I don't even know your name, never mind how you know mine, and, as for Noble!"

Mrs Hazelwood took up a position directly opposite where Vanessa sat and placed her cup on the small table beside her armchair.

"My name is Mrs Hazelwood," she said patiently, "Hazel Hazelwood and you can call me either one you wish, though I would hope you'd call me Hazel."

Vanessa nodded.

"I'm what some people call a Medium. I have second-sight you understand, always have had since I was a child. I knew things were going to happen before they happened and I sometimes get 'messages' you know," Hazel looked upwards, "from the spirit world."

Vanessa's eyes widened, "And Noble?"

"Ah, Noble," smiled Hazel. "He's a very special cat. Found me about ten years ago. Just walked in and never left." On hearing his name, Noble came into the room and jumped onto Hazel's lap, purring.

"Is he a Medium as well?" Vanessa asked incredulously.

Hazel pondered the question. "I don't rightly know," she said, "but he does seem to know things, things invisible I mean. He knew you were lost," she nodded sagely, "and that's why he's brought you here to me."

Rather than panicking when she heard this, Vanessa felt totally at peace. 'This place did feel like home. It was like coming safely into harbour after a storm at sea.'

"But I'm not lost," Vanessa replied, "I know exactly where I am."

"You may know where you are physically, my dear, but in your heart, I feel you're just a little bit lost," Hazel said kindly. Vanessa blinked and bent to sip her tea.

"It's just temporary," she whispered, "everything will be alright, I'm sure. I just have to keep on loving them, that's all, but sometimes it gets really hard."

Hazel rose from her chair and crossed to the sofa, sitting beside Vanessa and taking her hand in hers. "I know," she said softly, "I know." And somehow, Vanessa knew Hazel Hazelwood did know.

A knock at the door interrupted the moment and a very tall, lanky young man came into the room. "Auntie Hazel," he called and then, noticing Vanessa made to back out again. "Sorry," he said, his face reddening, "I just dropped in, didn't know you'd have company."

"Oh Donald," smiled Hazel, "come in, come in, Vanessa's a friend," and turning to Vanessa added, "you don't mind if Donald joins us, do you?"

Vanessa shrugged and muttered, "Not really I suppose, no, of course not." After all, it was she who was the unexpected visitor more than Donald. The room suddenly seemed overfull with the arrival of Hazel's nephew, who was exceptionally tall and seemed all legs and arms. He had to almost bend double to kiss his Aunt on the cheek.

Hazel bustled out of the room to fetch another cup and Donald extended his hand to Vanessa. "I'm Donald Martin," he proffered, "nephew to Auntie Hazel and computer nut," he added shyly.

"Vanessa," she responded, "Vanessa Lomax, Mrs and total technophobe."

Donald grinned. "Hurrah, someone who knows less than me about the machines." He took off his thick spectacles to polish them, revealing dark brown eyes and huge eyelashes. Vanessa thought he looked more like a giraffe than a human. She had never met such a physically awkward man in her life, but at the same time she sensed he didn't have an unkind bone in his body.

Hazel came through with a new cup and poured Donald his tea.

"He's the one who printed the poster for me when Noble went missing," she advised proudly, "the one you saw outside the bank."

Vanessa smiled. "Mmmm very eye-catching too."

"And it worked," Hazel added. "It was Vanessa who came to tell me about Noble. He'd turned up in her garden that very morning, before finding his own way back."

"Clever Noble," Donald smoothed, as the cat brushed past his legs, "we were getting worried about you," he added. "Missing for three days, he was."

Vanessa coughed. "Well, I see you both have a lot to talk about, so I'd better get back. Sophie, my daughter, will be home soon and I don't want to..."

Two pairs of eyes watched her rise from the sofa and make for the door.

"Before you go my dear," Hazel said, "I've got something for you."

"For me," Vanessa turned startled, but Hazel had disappeared into the kitchen. She returned with a small glass pot and handed it to Vanessa.

"What is it?" she asked.

"It's skin cream," Hazel said. "I make it myself from lanolin and Attar of Roses, among other things and I want you to have it."

Vanessa took the jar and unscrewed the lid. The smell of roses hit her nostrils. "Why it's beautiful," she said, "but I must pay you..."

Mrs Hazelwood held up her hand. "No payment necessary, Vanessa," she whispered. "It's a present from me and Noble, for your birthday."

But before Vanessa could ask anything more, Hazel guided her to the front door.

"Goodbye my dear," she said, "and Happy Birthday for tomorrow."

The door closed slowly but firmly.

'How did she know...?' thought Vanessa, but then realised that Hazel Hazelwood seemed to know lots of things about her, to which there was no logical explanation.

Vanessa took a deep breath and clutching her present tightly in her hand, walked down the path and headed for home.

Chapter 8

Roger completed the drive to Kim's flat smoothly and, for once, on time. Kim was waiting.

"Ready darling?" he asked, his eyes travelling from her cleavage to her eyes.

"Ready," she breathed into his ear, "and willing." She slipped her arm through his, her high-heeled shoes making a delightfully sensual smack on the pavement with each step.

Once in the car, Roger's hands gripped the steering wheel. Already he was anticipating the night ahead. "Is Darko expecting us?" Kim asked.

"Of course," Roger answered. "And when I spoke to him, it sounded like he couldn't wait either."

Darko was the owner of the private 'Swingers Club' in Soho, where Roger took Kim as often as possible. Darko had known Roger before he had met Kim and his first impression of Roger was as dark as his complexion. His opinion of him hadn't altered much over the following months, as he watched him gravitate towards the younger and younger girls, brought in from Thailand. Darko expertly arranged the hedonistic evenings, providing not only 'recreational drugs' and alcohol, but sex partners to meet all his clients' needs. His philosophy being that if he didn't meet their needs, someone else would. And he liked the money.

The drive to London was taken in silence, Roger and Kim both lost in their own fantasies about what was to come and it was late in the afternoon before they arrived at their hotel.

Roger had booked separate rooms, which served to heighten the anticipation of seeing Kim in all her 'finery' when they got to the club. He also wanted privacy to prepare himself for the night ahead, no food, it only made him sleepy, one shot of whisky, didn't want to be too drunk to perform and Frankincense for his body. He just loved the smell of the oil on his skin. He lit the candles he had brought with him and lay naked on the hotel bed. He breathed in the scent as he massaged the oil over his chest and abdomen, his thoughts drifting in and out of his mind, awaking and then calming his sexual arousal. "Not yet," he chided himself, "later, much later."

There was a tap at the door. Startled, Roger called out, "Go away."

"It's me," Kim's voice came through the door. "I want to go NOW."

Roger cursed, annoyed at having his ritual disturbed and frustrated at Kim's inability to control herself.

"Go back to your room," he commanded, "I'll come and get you when I'M ready."

The mood now vanishing fast, Roger got up, extinguished the candles and popped two Viagra into his mouth, washing them down with the last of the whisky.

"She had better be worth this aggravation," he muttered to himself. She would pay, they both knew, for disrupting his preparations.

When he finally knocked on Kim's door, she was pouting with frustration. She stabbed out a cigarette and stood up. She was wearing a full length black leather coat, buttoned high enough to conceal her cleavage and belted at the waist. The only things visible were her black patent leather high heeled shoes.

Roger's eyebrows arched. "Well," he murmured, "what have we here?"

Kim sniffed as Roger drew her closer to him. "Feeling dominant tonight are we?" he asked urgently.

"Maybe."

His grip tightened on her arms. "Just as long as you don't try to dominate me, Kim dearest," Roger spat, "you know that's a game you'll never win."

Her eyes tried to outstare his, but couldn't. "I wouldn't dare," Kim smiled, her body bending submissively as he pulled her hair back.

"Good. Now, do as you're told and get moving." He smacked her buttocks through the leather. "And there'll be more of that, if you're a good girl, later tonight."

After checking the peephole in the door, Darko opened it. "Welcome," he bowed to Roger, "and Kim," he cooed, "leather, mmmmm, nice."

The heat and dimness of the inner room washed over them as they made their way to the bar. Glistening bodies brushed up against them as they were looked over by the others and Kim could already feel hands trying to find their way through her coat.

"Aren't you hot Kim?" Darko had come up behind her. "In that coat, I mean."

Kim turned to face him. "I'm very hot," she breathed, "but I need help to unbutton it." Darko started to sweat as his hands began their job. He could never stay cool around Kim and she knew it.

"There," he whispered, as her coat fell open, revealing black lace hold-up stockings, a tiny satin thong and black silk tassels dangling from her nipples.

"Now, isn't that better?" he sleazed.

Before she could say anything, she felt Roger twisting her arms behind her.

If there was one thing that aroused him more than anything, it was sexual competition, especially competition from Darko. He pulled her coat from her shoulders and dropped it to the floor. Kim shivered as he moved in closer behind her. She'd been waiting for Roger all day to take her and to do it in front of Darko was just too delicious.

But suddenly, Roger pushed her towards Darko. "You want her," he sneered, "take her. She's all yours Darko my man, I've got sweeter meat waiting for me." Without saying another word Roger stripped naked and dropped his clothes where he stood. "Watch and learn," he gloated, moving unerringly through the naked bodies towards a tiny Thai girl, sitting, waiting, in a school uniform, just for him.

Darko turned Kim's face away from Roger and his lust and towards him. "He's pathetic," he said, his voice husky with desire, "let a real man show you what you need," pushing his erection into Kim's hand. "And, if you object... then I'll have to punish you."

Kim felt hot and wet. "Then I object," she murmured, placing his manhood expertly between her legs and immediately forgetting her hurt at Roger's rejection.

Darko led her to another room where cocaine was waiting for them. "Just to get things warmed up," he whispered, "ladies first." Kim snorted the white powder just as Darko began her punishment. She gasped as his hands squeezed her nipples and his teeth bit into her neck. She felt herself go out of control as the cocaine took hold and Darko got more aroused and brutal. She heard herself scream in ecstasy as he drove into her. This was what she loved, what she lived for.

"Again," she gasped, "harder."

His thrusting was fast and furious till, finally spent, Darko lay on top of her, his breathing coming in rapid gulps. Roger couldn't compare to him, he told himself. Not now, not ever.

He pulled Kim to her feet. "You want more?" he demanded. Kim's eyes opened momentarily, before closing to oblivion as she slumped to the floor, satisfied! Darko smiled to himself, leaving her where she lay. "Now, what else have we got tonight?" he murmured, his eyes roaming over the sea of nakedness before him, finally resting upon his next conquest, a black goddess, her head rolling backwards and her hand stroking herself enticingly.

Roger, having satisfied his lust for young flesh, was also looking for more action. When he saw Darko move in for the kill with his next victim, but before he could go looking for Kim, two small hands reached around him and he felt hard little nipples rub against his legs. Turning, he found another Thai girl on her knees, her head upturned towards him, pleading to be taken. How could he resist, he shrugged. Kim was forgotten.

The night ebbed and flowed as sexual appetites were satiated and refuelled again and again, but for Kim the night was over and she was unaware of what had happened to Roger till early morning. As she tried to come to her senses, she struggled into a sitting position. Her stockings were ripped and she'd lost one of her shoes. The thong and tassles had gone and her breasts and neck were bruised and inflamed. She staggered through to the party room, blinking her vision blurry and still unfocused. Bodies were everywhere, some sleeping, some still entwined in sexual positions awaiting another arousal.

There was no sign of Darko, but there, lying spread-eagle on a low bed in the corner of the room was Roger, his arms around two Thai girls, all of them naked and asleep. Kim felt sick. She knew Roger liked them young and biddable, but these girls were... no more than children. She gulped, as another wave of nausea and self-loathing engulfed her. She had to get out of here she told herself, searching around for the coat she had on when she'd arrived.

It was lying on the floor by the bar, where Roger had dropped it. She picked it up and put it on, glad to be covered up. She found her other shoe and put them both on as she weaved through the bodies, to the door. She was twenty years of age, but suddenly felt very old indeed. "What am I doing?" she asked herself, her feelings for Roger and her own feelings about her sexual needs, getting increasingly repulsive to her.

She ran out of the door into the early morning and breathed the air deeply to try to clear her head. This isn't love, she told herself, tears beginning to run down her cheeks, Roger didn't love her at all. She brushed away the tears.

It was all just sex, that was all he ever wanted, she now knew for certain. How could she have been so obsessed? Her head began to clear. She had to get back to the hotel, gather her things and get home from London before Roger realised she was gone.

A black cab, trawling for early morning trade crawled into view. Kim waved him down. "Waverley Hotel," she said, slumping down into the cavernous back of the taxi. If the driver was surprised at her appearance, he didn't show it. He'd seen it all in his time, hadn't he? Just another silly girl, thinking she was going to be swept off her feet by Prince Charming, only to find it was all about being used by men for sex.

Kim told the driver to wait, hurried into the hotel and found her handbag and suitcase. Quickly, she threw on a dress, to cover her nakedness and pulled the leather coat tightly around her.

"Paddington Station," she told the driver, "and hurry."

The driver nodded and within twenty minutes, he deposited Kim at the echoing railway station. She searched the boards for the next train to West Hampton. Luck was with her, there was a milk train running through to Reading in fifteen minutes.

Her feet sounded loudly on the station walkway as she made her way to Platform 4. The nausea hit again, but this time, not so badly. She just wanted to be home, and as far away from London and Darko and his Swingers Club, but especially from Roger, as fast as she possibly could.

The train pulled in and Kim and a few other people boarded. She found a seat at the back of a carriage and curled up in the corner. The train doors locked automatically and it began to pull out of the station. From the corner of her eye she saw movement on the platform and the figure of Roger running alongside the train. She squirmed down further into the seat. Had he seen her she wondered feverishly? He'd make her pay for running out on him that was for sure. But instead of feeling aroused by this, for the first time, Kim felt empty. She was out of his grasp she now felt for certain and that was the way it was going to stay. For the first time since falling under Roger's spell, Kim felt herself back in control of her life and she was going to live it her way from now on.

Roger cursed to himself as he watched the train roll into the distance. He was sure he saw Kim on it and felt his fists clench, but there was nothing else for it but to go back to the hotel, collect his things and make the long drive back to West Hampton alone.

Chapter 9

The house was still empty when Vanessa returned from Willow Cottage. What a strange day it had been. She had gone from misery to elation, thanks to Hazel Hazelwood and her kindness. She fingered the jar of cream.

'Roses,' she smiled. 'How did Hazel know they were her favourite flower,' she wondered, 'and how did she know it was her birthday tomorrow?'

She opened the jar and scooped out a small amount, rubbed it between her palms and smoothed it onto her face. It felt wonderful, cool and soothing and she could almost feel the tension of the last two weeks releasing with the scent of the flowers. She looked at herself in the mirror on the living room wall. She seemed different, somehow. She looked closer. The eyes that looked back at her had lost their redness and the lips that had felt thin and dry, now looked soft and fuller. Startled, she ran her hand through her springy red hair. Even that seemed to have lost a bit of its dryness.

Gently, she replaced the lid on the jar. Tomorrow was her birthday, she reminded herself and she was going to enjoy it, no matter what.

And the woman that looked back at her from the mirror agreed.

She heard the door open and close as her daughter returned. She didn't want the sourness of their earlier encounter to continue any longer and determined that she would try to build a bridge back to her. After all, she was a child and although, at times, she seemed quite grown up, Vanessa knew instinctively that love was what her daughter needed, regardless of how it sometimes appeared.

"Hey," she began brightly, "how was the pony?" Sophie's eyes were shining, the earlier encounter also seeming to have been forgotten by her.

"Oh, mum," she sighed. "He is the most beautiful thing you've ever seen. He's chestnut with a white blaze on his face and I fed him an apple and polo mints." She clasped her hands together and danced around the room. "I can't wait till daddy comes home with mine."

Vanessa flinched. She didn't want to say again that there wouldn't be a pony from Roger, but couldn't help but feel a sensation of dread creeping into her heart. How would her daughter react when she eventually found out the truth?

"Well, let's just be patient," Vanessa soothed, "now I have another surprise for you?"

"You do?"

"Yes," Vanessa continued, "tomorrow is mummy's birthday and I thought it would be a good idea to go out somewhere nice for Sunday lunch, just you and me."

"What about daddy, isn't he coming?" asked Sophie.

"Well no, darling, he's still in London, remember, at the conference. I don't expect he'll be home till much later."

Sophie frowned. "Does that mean we'll be going to some crummy little tearoom?"

Vanessa held onto to her smile. "Of course not, I was thinking more of the new place in High Street, you know the one, The Green Room it's called, used to be Mr and Mrs Howards' hotel."

Sophie brightened. "Yes," she agreed, "Jane's mum took her there last week and she says it's gorgeous."

Vanessa breathed a sigh of relief. "And, I'll get up early and make us a carrot cake for when we get back. You know it's your favourite."

"OK," she trilled as she skipped from the room. "Can I watch tele in my room," she called out, almost as an afterthought, rather than asking her mother's permission.

"Fine," Vanessa called back. Well, so much for building bridges, Vanessa thought, ten minutes in her company and her daughter couldn't wait to disappear into her bedroom. Not much of a bridge, she told herself with a sigh, but tomorrow, she reasserted, will be just great.

Sunday morning dawned to find Vanessa still sound asleep. When she eventually did surface, it was gone nine o'clock. She could hardly believe it. She had never slept past six o'clock since Sophie had been born. Still, the feeling was lovely, as she stretched and took in the warmth and quietness of the day. Then she remembered. "Of course," she whispered to herself, "today is my birthday and my body is obviously giving itself a gift too."

Sophie was still asleep, as usual, so instead of her usual quick shower,

Vanessa decided she would have the luxury of a bubble bath. Quickly, she ran the taps and poured in some shower gel, hoping it would have the desired effect. It did. She slipped out of her nightdress and submerged herself in the foamy water. "Luxury," she murmured, "I must do this more often."

Dreamily she sponged herself with the warm, soapy water and felt almost heavy, she was so relaxed. When the water began to cool, she slowly pushed herself up and out of the bath. She caught sight of herself in the bathroom mirror as she wrapped a towel around herself. Again, startled, she realised somehow she was different. Dropping the towel, she took a closer look. She pulled her hair up in a bunch on top of her head and took in her trim waist, long legs and small, round breasts. Nothing drooped, she noticed. In fact, it was almost like she was seeing herself as she used to be and not the dowdy wife and mother Roger so despised. She dried herself and brushed her hair. There it was again, the feeling that she was somehow beautiful again.

She picked up Hazel's jar of cream and, just as before, she scooped a little onto her hands and applied it to her face. Almost afraid to look, she glanced sideways into the mirror. Once again, she seemed transformed. Her skin seemed to glow, her eyes had a sparkle and her lips were pink and plump.

She studied the cream again. "Surely not!" she exclaimed. But the cream had been made by Hazel Hazelwood and who knew...

Instead of her usual trousers and top she selected a dress from her wardrobe she hadn't worn for years. It still fitted perfectly, and along with a pair of summer sandals, her look was complete. Well almost. Vanessa searched in her dressing table drawer, unearthing a seldom-used lipstick and some mascara. She was truly very pretty, she thought, but how this change had happened so suddenly and completely was beyond her. The smiling face of Hazel came into her head. She would be pleased, Vanessa felt sure. "Thank you," she said to no one in particular, before leaving the bedroom and going down into the kitchen to make the carrot cake.

Donning an apron to protect her dress, Vanessa set about mixing and stirring and grating the carrots. She found herself singing softly as she worked and within the hour, the carrot cake was made and in the oven. She was sitting at the table sipping her Lady Grey tea, when Sophie shuffled in, her nightie hanging off one shoulder and her face contorted in a huge yawn.

"Sleep well?" Vanessa asked. Sophie nodded, still yawning.

"How about some orange juice and a bit of cereal for breakfast?" Vanessa asked, "don't want to spoil your appetite for lunch."

Sophie's eyes began to blink open and for the first time took in her mother's new appearance. Her eyes widened.

"You look... wonderful," she gaped, "you look just like Jane's mum!"

Sophie couldn't have given Vanessa a bigger compliment if she'd tried.

"Well, thank you darling," she smiled warmly, "it's not every day I have a birthday, so I thought I'd dress up a bit."

Vanessa busied herself getting Sophie her breakfast, grinning to herself when her daughter couldn't see her face. The smell of the cake cooking began to fill the kitchen and, at the same time, fill Vanessa with a new found confidence.

Sophie watched her mother closely as she drank her juice and ate her cereal, having difficulty in believing what she was seeing. She seemed to have changed overnight.

"Now, if you're finished," Vanessa continued briskly, "hop into the shower and put on something nice for going to the Green Room."

Sophie nodded and then, for the first time in a very long time, ran over to her mother and gave her a big hug. "Happy Birthday mummy," she whispered, her small hands reaching round Vanessa's waist.

Vanessa was almost speechless with surprise. "Well, thank you Sophie... now hurry along and get ready, I've booked the table for half past twelve."

Vanessa almost exploded with happiness. Suddenly, everything was right in her world. The sun was shining, the cake was ready to come out of the oven, she had found a way back to her daughter and, more wonderful than that, she felt she had found a way back to herself.

She lifted the carrot cake out of the oven and placed it on the cooling rack. She'd top it with the sweet creamy frosting when they came back from lunch.

She glanced at the clock, almost noon. Even time was working in her favour.

Sophie came bouncing into the kitchen. She had on her white jeans and trainers and a bright pink t-shirt with a picture of a horse on the front.

"Ready," she said, for once looking forward to going out with her mother, who was so pretty. She hoped Jane and her mother would be at the Green Room so that she could show off. She'd been getting fed up of her mother always being the boring one, but not today she wasn't, her mum was the best.

The Green Room lived up to its name. There were potted plants positioned to give privacy and add softness to the room and the walls were covered in wallpaper showing leafy branches with little pink rosebuds all over them. The tables were draped with white linen and the cutlery gleamed in the sunlight. Small bowls of fresh flowers were on each table and the waiters all wore white shirts and black waistcoats with GR embroidered on them in green.

In one corner was a small bar, where three or four people were sitting, chatting, enjoying a pre-lunch drink and the tables were filling up fast.

The waiter guided Vanessa and Sophie to a table for two at a window and offered them menus and, with a bow, left them to make up their minds about what to order. Vanessa watched Sophie studying the long list of dishes. She really is a beautiful little girl, she thought, trying to be so grown-up and failing miserably, as she leaned over to her mother and whispered, "What should I have? There's so much to choose from."

Vanessa suggested the roast chicken, or perhaps a salad, knowing her daughter's taste for simple foods. "I'd really like a burger," Sophie whispered, "and chips."

Vanessa looked down the menu for the Children's Choices and there it was. Beef burger, chips and salad.

"Well, just this once," she grinned, "as it's my birthday."

The waiter took their orders, nodding knowingly at Sophie's choice and smiling wisely at Vanessa's order of chicken and celery salad, ciabatta bread and a glass of chilled Chenin blanc to accompany it.

"Any dessert?" the waiter asked.

"Perhaps later," said Vanessa returning the menus. As the waiter left the table, Vanessa became aware of someone at the bar, staring at her. She frowned and turned away.

But when she looked again, the man was still looking at her. And now, he was getting up and coming towards them.

For a second Vanessa couldn't believe her eyes. Coming over to her table was the lanky figure of Donald Martin. Seeing her mother's stunned look, Sophie turned just as Donald reached them.

"Vanessa?" he queried, "it is you?" Vanessa felt her face colour as she forced herself to smile.

"Mr Martin," she said formally, "how nice to see you... again."

Thankfully, there was nowhere for him to sit, so he squatted down beside Sophie. "And is this your daughter?" he enquired, "the one you mentioned..."

"Yes," Vanessa quickly interrupted, "this is Sophie."

Sophie extended her hand and said, "How do you do," very politely.

Vanessa began to feel more and more uncomfortable. She didn't want to have to explain to her daughter who Donald was and, especially, didn't want to have to tell Roger about how they'd met.

Donald became aware of Vanessa's discomfort and stood up. "Well," he said, "nice to see you again, and you Sophie. Enjoy your lunch."

With that, he returned to the bar and joined the others but for Vanessa, the encounter had left her shaken.

She hadn't really taken in Donald's appearance at Hazel's, except for the fact that he looked, to her, like a giraffe, but she found it hard to believe that he was the same person. At Hazel's he had seemed like an overgrown schoolboy, but in the restaurant, he took on an air of authority and composure and, yes, he was actually quite handsome in an academic sort of way.

The sports jacket and chinos, the loafers and denim shirt, open at the neck, revealing his chest hair.

"Who was that?" Sophie asked, inquisitive and intrigued. She had seldom seen her mother speak to a man before and never when daddy wasn't around. Vanessa shook out her napkin and sipped some of her wine.

"Oh, that's... er... Mr Martin from the bank. He works there and when I do daddy's banking, Mr Martin takes in the money." Vanessa was aware she was rambling and prayed that the meal would arrive quickly, so that she could divert Sophie's attention on to that and away from Donald Martin.

"Mmmhhh," said Sophie, in her best bored voice, "is that all."

Vanessa's breathing returned to normal. "Look," she said, "here comes your beef burger."

The waiter served the food and Sophie tucked in, seeming not to give Donald Martin another thought.

But for Vanessa, the encounter gave her much to think about. Not least, her guilt at having lied about him to her daughter.

Chapter 10

The drive back to West Hampton was a nightmare. Roger hated driving on a Sunday, especially on the motorway, all those bloody caravans and day trippers clogging up the lanes. His tension was made worse by thoughts of Kim. "Nobody runs out on me," he muttered to himself, "she'll pay and pay dearly for her disobedience."

And then he remembered, the pony. He smacked his hand on his forehead. He'd meant to buy Sophie a toy horse before leaving London to pacify her, but now, it was too late. Even shops in Reading that open on Sunday would be closed by now. A sign for motorway services came into view. They always sell lots of soft toys and stuff, he remembered, surely, they'll have a toy horse.

The services was chock-a-block with people and Roger had to push his way through the crowd to get to the shop. There were teddy bears and dolls, games and puzzles, toy cars and model aeroplanes and... yes... he spotted it on a shelf, a toy pony, aptly entitled My Little Pony. He lifted it down and flinched at the price, before joining the queue at the cash desk to pay for it. He looked at the plastic horse, with its synthetic mane and tail and his heart sank.

This stupid, plastic oddity wasn't going to placate Sophie in a million years. Angry at himself for getting into the situation, he turned on his heel and replaced the toy back on the shelf. He had spent years making sure Sophie loved and trusted him and now... I'll make it up to her, he told himself, win her back. He was so close to totally controlling his daughter that he couldn't give up now. Not over a silly pony.

It was late evening when he finally pulled into the driveway, fatigue from the night before and the slow drive washing over him. He couldn't face Sophie's disappointment at him tonight, letting her down, losing her trust. That could wait till morning. Right now, he just wanted to sleep. He buzzed open the garage door and drove in, closing it behind him. Once inside the silence, he flipped the back of the seat flat and stretched out. Within minutes, he was asleep.

He woke with a start, his whole body was cold and his feet were freezing. He checked his watch, two-thirty, "Sod this," he murmured, "time for bed."

He knew Sophie would be sound asleep, so there would be no confrontations at this hour. Letting himself in through the back door into the kitchen, he switched on the spotlight under the overhead cupboard. Something smelt good and he realised he was very hungry.

Then he saw it. Sitting on a plate on the counter was a cake, and around the cake a scattering of little candles. Roger sniggered. Of course, Vanessa's birthday cake. He cut himself a chunk of the cake and then another, washing it down with a glass of milk. At least she was good for something, he snorted.

Now that he had satiated one appetite, he decided he would satiate another.

Vanessa. It had been a while, but he shrugged, 'conjugal rights and all that.'

He made his way upstairs, but this time, opened the door of his own bedroom. He peered into the gloom, dropping his clothes where he stood.

"Vanessa," he hissed theatrically, "it's your birthday surprise." He tiptoed nearer to the bed and pulled back the duvet. But Vanessa wasn't there, no one was there.

He snapped on the bedside lamp and pulled the duvet completely off the bed. He felt his anger swelling inside him. Where the Hell... and where was Sophie? The thought of his daughter missing and out of his control shook him to the core. Calm down, he told himself, check her room. Thoughts of Sophie lying in a hospital bed or, worse, lost forever, flooded his mind as he made his way quietly to the door of his daughter's bedroom.

He listened. Silence. Hardly daring to breath, he inched the door open, his breathing eased, he could make out a shape on Sophie's bed, she was alright. He went in, closing the door behind him and crept closer, he'd sleep in his daughter's bed as usual, start manipulating her mind again. Better than bedding his wife, he smirked, who he would make pay for leaving his daughter alone in the house.

He stopped, inches from the side of the bed, shock reverberating through his system. There, lying next to Sophie, her red hair spread over the pillow, one arm round his daughter's shoulders, was Vanessa.

Shaking with rage, he backed out of the room. He got back to his bedroom and pulled on his dressing gown. There would be no more sleep for him tonight and tomorrow, there would be Hell to pay.

Vanessa was up early the next day as usual, and he heard her move past the bedroom and down the stairs. The kitchen was still cool this early in the day and she pulled her dressing gown around her before filling the kettle. She breathed in the stillness. Yesterday had been wonderful, she smiled to herself, reliving the previous day. It had been a shame that Sophie had had such a bad dream that night, but comforting her till she fell asleep had reawakened all the motherly love she thought she had lost. She hadn't meant to fall asleep beside her, but she was so relaxed it had just happened.

She made her usual cup of Lady Grey tea and stood sipping it as she watched the sun come up and the light begin to flood the garden.

It was a sudden awareness more than anything else, that made her turn around.

To her shock, Roger was standing in the kitchen doorway, his dressing gown flapping open and his face set with rage.

Vanessa almost dropped her cup. When had he got back, she wondered wildly, she'd heard nothing, no car, no noise at all, but there he was standing in front of her.

"Roger," she exclaimed in a high voice, watching his face for any reaction, "when did you get back from London? I didn't hear you come in, you didn't waken me..." her voice trailed off as she was aware again of rambling.

He moved closer to her, till her back was against the kitchen sink and she had to tilt her head back in order to keep looking at him.

"No, you didn't hear me come in dear wife," he rasped menacingly, "because you weren't in our bed, were you?"

Vanessa pushed her hair back and tried to inch around him, but he had placed his arms either side of her so she couldn't move.

She smiled nervously, trying to gauge his level of anger. "No," she stammered, "I was with Sophie in her room. She'd had a nightmare and couldn't get back to sleep... I'm sorry," she blurted, "I didn't know you'd be back so late. You should have let me know..."

"So, it's all my fault, is it?" Vanessa couldn't understand why Roger was so angry. Sophie was her daughter as well and she needed her mother last night. She hadn't done anything wrong.

Roger's face told her there was no point in trying to explain further and with a leer, he undid her dressing gown.

"Too busy taking care of your own needs, were you that you forgot I have needs as well?"

Vanessa felt her blood run cold. So this was the cause of his anger. She hadn't been available for sex when he wanted it. She closed her eyes as her dressing gown dropped to the floor. "Now, turn around," he ordered.

Vanessa turned away from him, her mind locked on yesterday, as she felt her arms being pushed sideways along the worktop. "Bend over," he ordered. Protest was useless, Vanessa knew. All she could pray for was that it would be over quickly.

Roger grunted like an animal forcing himself into her. Vanessa gasped, as a pain shot through her. "This is for not being in bed last night when I came in," he spat "and this is for being in bed with my daughter." Under the force of his thrusting, Vanessa's knees almost buckled. "And, you won't do it again, will you," he demanded. Vanessa could hardly breathe. "WILL YOU," he repeated roughly in her ear.

She shook her head, "No Roger," she whimpered, "I won't do it again."

He pulled her red hair back, forcing her to raise her head, as he rode her like a horse. She felt him pull her harder onto him as he came. She was sure she was bleeding. His breathing slowed and Vanessa froze, till he pushed himself away from her. "Now," he said, "get me some food and make it edible, not like that stupid cake over there."

Through the tears Vanessa became aware of two eyes watching her, one was blue and other one golden and they were framed by a white face and two pointed ears. "Noble," she muttered. He had seen everything. She watched as he made his was down from the low branch of the apple tree and disappeared into the shrubbery. A feeling of peace came over her. She had a witness to her abuse and Noble would somehow tell Hazel. Hazel, she silently decided, would know what she should do.

She picked up her dressing gown, wrapped it around herself and began frying bacon and eggs, toasting bread and boiling water. She knew she had to do as she was told for now, but her hatred for Roger was beginning to form in her soul, overcoming the fear she usually felt around him.

The kitchen door opened. "Daddy," yelled Sophie, "you're home from London." She threw her arms around his neck. "Did you get it?" she asked, trying to keep the excitement out of her voice.

Roger glanced at Vanessa. "Don't you have something to do upstairs," he said, "like now?"

Vanessa looked at Sophie, "But Sophie," she protested, "she needs her breakfast."

Roger's face darkened. "She'll share mine," he stated flatly, "now go."

Vanessa hurried from the kitchen and upstairs to the bathroom. She ran the shower and stood under its comforting deluge till her legs stopped trembling and the blood was washed away. Too hurt and confused to wonder how things had got this bad, she slowly dried herself and dressed in her usual trousers and bland top. She took a brush to her hair and looked at herself in the mirror. The happy face of yesterday was gone, replaced once more with tension and misery. She reached for Hazel's cream and smoothed some on her cheeks. Once again, her skin relaxed under the soothing balm and she felt a little of the joy of yesterday seep back into her mind. She took a deep breath. Whatever Roger had in store for her in the future, she told herself, she would survive. She opened the bathroom door and was almost knocked down by her daughter hurtling past her, eyes blinded by tears.

He's told her, she knew, and not kindly.

Sophie's bedroom door slammed. She knew better than to try to comfort her daughter right now, but later, when Roger left, she would make it alright again.

Vanessa slipped back into the bathroom and locked the door.

She knew she couldn't stand up to Roger's physical power, but that didn't mean he was stronger. And as she counted the long minutes till she heard him leave the house, she knew she had to get strong and she knew she had to go to Laburnum Cottage and Hazel.

Cautiously, she opened Sophie's bedroom door. Her daughter was in bed, the duvet pulled up to her chin and fast asleep. The tears had been replaced by exhaustion and Vanessa quietly closed the door again.

Downstairs, she telephoned Sophie's school to explain her daughter's absence then called Jane's mum. "Mrs Munro," she called brightly, "is it alright for Sophie to come over later," she asked, "Roger has a Circle this evening and I have to be there to arrange the appointments.

"Of course," came the soft reply, "I can't go to the Circle myself this evening, Mr Munro's at a meeting at his Lodge and nothing is more important than that," she added resignation in her voice, "so we'll expect Sophie around six."

"Great," Vanessa said, "and thanks again, I really appreciate this."

She would let her daughter sleep as long as possible, hoping she would feel better when she woke up. She knew she couldn't miss the Circle. That would make Roger even angrier and she didn't want that again, both for her sake and Sophie's.

Chapter 11

Roger had calmed down, but it was an unnatural calm. Telling Sophie had been hard, but more for her than him, after all, he was the one in control and what he said was what happened. When she had begun to cry with disappointment, he had felt himself begin to be aroused, but now wasn't the time. That would come when she had been brought under his control again.

That unfortunate episode when she'd turned to Vanessa for love would have to be redressed and soon, but right now, he had bigger fish to fry, Kim and her disobedience.

He checked his watch. The Circle wasn't till seven o'clock, plenty of time to deal with Kim. Silently, he climbed the stairs to her flat and looked through the letter box. There was no sound, but he knew she was there. Waiting, hardly daring to breathe, waiting to be punished by him.

And Kim was waiting, but not with bated breath. She had spent the night going over and over in her head how she had managed to sink so low as to find herself, naked and abused in a sex club and by the time day was breaking, she knew. Roger had messed with her mind, manipulated her thoughts during the hypnotherapy sessions she had had with him when she'd first gone for help to stop smoking. It was the only explanation that made sense. In that moment when she had looked at him, naked and asleep with two Thai girls beside him in Darko's Club, she had felt such revulsion, it had swept aside any desire she had ever felt for him, or had been manipulated into feeling for him. Now, all she saw was an overweight, middle-aged lecher and it was his turn to pay.

She unlocked the door and stepped back into the centre of the room.

Her grip on the iron poker tightened. She knew she had to face him eventually, but this was one encounter she had to win.

She watched and door handle turn and the door swing open.

Fear spread through her body as he came into the room, closing the door quietly behind him, a warped smile never leaving his face.

"Well, well," he laughed, "what have we here?" Kim backed further into the room. She had to keep calm, keep him away from her, not get sucked into his grasp again.

"Get out of here," she told him, trying to keep her voice steady. "I never want to see you again. And, if you touch me or come near me again, I'll…"

Roger moved toward her, almost daintily for a man of his bulk, and grabbed her arm. "You'll what," he sneered, removing the poker from her grip, "tell Vanessa, get the police?" He twisted her arm around and forced it up her back. The pain shot through her shoulder but she didn't scream.

"You see," he mouthed, "you'll do as I say, till I say it's time to stop and not before." Kim felt herself fold to the floor. She should never have let him in, she now knew, she'd thought she could handle him, but she couldn't. He'd won again.

As she lay there, the picture that had filled her head during the night returned. Roger and those two Thai children. Disgust filled her again and alongside it came anger.

"So, what would Kim like Roger to do to her to punish her this time," he sleazed, but Kim wasn't in the mood to be punished. Pushing into him with all her strength, he toppled backwards and fell over the coffee table before crashing down onto the floor. Kim saw her chance and ran from the room and into the street. She had to get away from him as fast and as far as she could, she now knew how dangerously out of control he was.

Like a fugitive she circled round the block of flats and sneaked into the park across the road. She could see Roger's car from there and she waited. Eventually, he would have to leave, only then could she go back in and get her things. She had to get as far away from him as possible. There would be no going back to her old life, she knew, but right now she just had to stay safe.

It was late in the afternoon before he came into sight. He had stayed in her flat for three hours waiting for her to return. How sure he must have been of her, that she wouldn't call the police. She could see he was hurt, as he limped to his car, which gave her a blip of satisfaction. He drove off, but Kim waited for another hour before she felt able to return to her flat.

The door stood open but the walls echoed his displeasure. They were covered in black graffiti. BITCH, WHORE, SLAG, she read, there was a scrawled dagger with blood dripping from it, swearwords and obscenities covered the walls and the furniture had all been upended. Kim felt sick with fear. The hatred in the room was almost palpable and she knew that it wouldn't end there. She had to disappear and fast.

She gathered together some essentials, money, credit cards, passport, car keys and a few clothes and locking the door behind her, she ran downstairs to her car. She'd book into a hotel for the night and tomorrow decide her future.

His foot aching on the accelerator, Roger drove to his consulting rooms.

He had a Circle at seven o'clock and he couldn't afford to miss that. He needed the money. In fact, he was going to need lots of money if his plan was going to succeed.

He cursed Kim under his breath. The slut had pushed him hard and his ankle had hit something sharp as he'd fell. He could feel it throbbing. But, thoughts of revenge would have to wait, right now, he had money to make.

He hobbled into his room and headed straight for his desk drawer and the whisky. Rapidly downing a shot, he untied his shoe and examined the swollen ankle. The evening he had planned would have to be curtailed, but that was alright, none of these feeble women ever argued with him. They would come when he called and love him for it.

He lay down on his treatment table and let himself relax. It had been a bad day all round, but nothing he couldn't handle, after all, he was Roger Lomax.

He pulled on a long black robe and made his way into the large room where the Circle would be held. The chairs were set, as he'd left them and his candles and incense awaited him. His ritual could begin again. By the time his devotees arrived he was ready for them, calm and assured and ready.

At seven o'clock exactly, he called, "Enter." The door opened and in they came, twelve ladies, all coming to feed off his power, all needing him.

By the time the Circle was closing, Roger was back in full control. He nodded as each bright eye and smile thanked him and left the room. He breathed deeply till he heard the last voice leave the reception and the door close.

Still limping, he went in the small reception area. Vanessa had done her duty, as he knew she would. Flicking through the appointment book, he was pleased to see ample bookings for the coming week to bring in a lucrative amount of money. He closed the book, returned to his consulting room and reacquainted himself with the whisky bottle. Tonight he would sleep here. Tomorrow was another day.

Chapter 12

While Roger had been dealing with Kim, Sophie had slept and Vanessa had paced the floor. She heard her daughter coming down the stairs. It was mid-afternoon. She waited, hoping for the best, but fearing the worst. But Sophie seemed... well normal, when she came into the room.

"Sophie?" Vanessa said, a query in her voice, "alright?"

Cool eyes surveyed her. "Yes," she said, "but no thanks to you."

Vanessa flinched. "ME!"

"Daddy explained everything," she continued, "he'd wanted to bring me a pony from London, but YOU, told him not to." Sophie's mouth tightened. "Why did you do that?" she continued, "I was right, wasn't I, just because you didn't get a present for your silly birthday, you made sure I didn't get my pony."

"Sophie," Vanessa started, shocked at Roger's deceit. "NO, I wouldn't do that to you, NEVER."

She made a move towards her daughter, but Sophie drew back.

"We'll have a nice lunch," she said, mimicking her mother, "and carrot cake," she continued, "we'll go to the Greeeeeeen Room."

A mixture of hurt and anger glowed in her daughter's eyes. Vanessa's shoulders drooped. "Oh, Sophie," she whispered, "you're so wrong about this..."

But Sophie wasn't listening. "I suppose I'll be going to Jane's later," she stated, all emotion gone from her face, "but I think I'll just go now, no reason to hang around here." And with a last look of contempt at her mother, she left the room and the house.

Vanessa sat stunned. She couldn't believe that it was just a day ago, that she and her daughter had spent such a wonderful time together and now, it had all gone. Thanks to Roger's lies, the status quo had been resumed.

Suddenly, the memory of the cat came into her head. "Noble," she said softly.

Almost on automatic pilot, Vanessa cycled to Laburnum Cottage. She hardly saw the rest of the world as it passed by her and her journey seemed timeless. The cottage was sleeping in the sun as she dismounted and parked her bike. Hazel was in the front garden, picking herbs for her creams and potions and flowers for the front room. Without turning, she said, "Vanessa dear, go on in, I'll be with you in a minute."

Vanessa did as she was told, no longer phased by Hazel's intuition. She sat herself down on the purple velvet sofa, in the front room, her ankles and arms crossed in front of her. Her eyes were drawn to a stained glass angel hanging in the sunlight, reflecting its beauty into the room as it moved slightly in the air from the open window.

Hazel came in and took in the sadness of the young woman. "I'll just put these in water and make us some tea," she said kindly. She noticed Vanessa's eyes fixed on the angel. "Do you like her?" she asked. Vanessa nodded.

"Good." Hazel smiled. It was time for Vanessa to understand.

They drank their tea in silence as Hazel waited for Vanessa to release the tension in her face.

"Do you want to tell me about it?" she asked gently. Vanessa stared at her hands.

"Hasn't Noble told you?"

Hazel patted her hands. "No, not exactly," she replied, "he can't tell me in words, but he was very angry when he came in this morning. His tail wouldn't stop whipping from side to side and he meowed loudly every time I tried to comfort him. So, what is it, what's wrong?"

Once she started talking, Vanessa couldn't seem to stop and Hazel didn't try to stop her either. She needed this to be out in the open.

By the time she had finished telling Hazel everything that had happened since her birthday, the tears had dried and Vanessa felt completely still and empty. Hazel had held her hand all the time during the telling of her ordeal and squeezed it gently before letting it go.

"It's time for you to understand," Hazel began, determination in her voice.

Vanessa turned to face her, confusion in her eyes. "Understand?"

"Yes, Vanessa, understand. Firstly, it wasn't an accident that I knew who you were before you came here." Vanessa sat passively as Hazel continued. "I told you before that I was a Medium and, through me, someone from the spirit world has made contact. She's been very worried about you."

"She?" Vanessa whispered.

"Does the name 'Jennifer' mean anything to you?"

Vanessa's eyes widened. "Jennifer was my mother's name."

Hazel nodded, satisfied. "Then if that is true, you must know that everything else I've said is also true."

Vanessa closed her eyes. Her mother had died when she was barely six years old. Cancer, they'd said. It seemed from that day, her father had also died, shutting himself off from the world and leaving Vanessa in the care of a series of Nannies. Any closeness that may have developed with her father as she grew up never happened and even today, they barely had any contact. She knew if she needed money she could go to him, but no love was ever shown. He'd been more than happy to pay Roger to marry her and even when Sophie had been born, his attitude had never changed. Sometimes she wondered what life would have been like if her mother had lived, but she had stopped wondering that when she'd married Roger. And now, Hazel was telling her that her mother was speaking to her from where... Heaven?

Hazel's blue eyes smiled at her. "It's alright," she said, "I know it's hard for you to believe, but... well, when you've been around the spirits for as long as I have, you learn to doubt nothing."

"What else has she... I mean, my mother, told you?"

Hazel's eyes fixed on Vanessa's. "She hasn't told me the future, if that's what you're asking, but she has said that I've to tell you she is always watching over you and will be with you, no matter what happens. She's your real guardian angel."

Vanessa turned again to the angel in the window. "Do you think she's as beautiful as that one?"

Hazel followed Vanessa's eyes. "More beautiful," she said.

Noble strolled into the room, his tail held high. He came over to Vanessa and jumped up on her lap, purring happily. "He saw everything," Vanessa said, stroking his soft furry head.

"He loves you," Hazel stated in her matter-of-fact voice, "and so does your mother... and me," she added.

Vanessa could hardly keep the tears from re-starting. She nodded vigorously.

"Thank you," she said, "thank you."

"Now," Hazel continued softly, "time to go home. Just remember that you are loved and watched over." And, for the first time in a long time, Vanessa felt that she was.

Hazel took Vanessa to the door. "I wish my daughter would love me too," she whispered.

"But she does," Hazel replied, "both of your children love you."

"But, I only have one..." Vanessa corrected her. Hazel smiled and gently, but firmly, closed the door.

The journey home was much easier and, although nothing had changed when she got there, she knew that something had changed in her.

It was gone six o'clock by the time she headed off to Roger's consulting rooms and the Circle. She had missed a phone call from him while she'd been at the cottage and was left with a curt message saying he'd expect her to carry out her duties as normal and that he wouldn't be home later that night.

'Good,' she thought, it would just be her and Sophie and maybe, just maybe, she would be able to make her understand.

When she got to the consulting rooms, the lights were on and the door unlocked. Roger had got there before she arrived. She knew not to go into his domain, so began busying herself with her mundane administration tasks. The women arrived in ones and twos and at seven o'clock precisely, she heard Roger call for them to 'enter'. As soon as they had gone through, she began to balance the ledger and update the appointment book. She counted the money quickly into the moneybox and satisfied that everything was in order, she quietly crept out of the room.

She would pick Sophie up earlier than usual and hope that Roger meant what he had said on the answer machine. This was a chance for her to show her daughter that she loved her just as much as Roger and that she hadn't done what he had told her.

Mrs Munro was welcoming, as ever. "Vanessa, you're early. Sophie's just finished supper." She turned around and called into the hallway. "Sophie, it's mum, can you get your coat please." Pulling the door behind her, however, Mrs Munro adopted a concerned look. "It's none of my business, of course," she began, "but Sophie seemed quite upset when she arrived. Is she alright?"

Vanessa grimaced. "She's fine Mrs Munro, just fine," she replied not giving out any information except to say that Sophie had a bit of a cold coming on.

Not convinced, but not wanting to interfere, Mrs Munro nodded. "Well, let's hope she's better soon."

Thankfully, at that moment Sophie appeared at the door. "Bye Mrs Munro," she smiled, "and thanks for the macaroni cheese, it was delish."

With hardly a glance at Vanessa she moved past her and down the path.

Again, Mrs Munro looked concerned. "Kids," Vanessa shrugged, hoping that her daughter hadn't told her friend the lies Roger had fed her.

Before anything further could be said, Vanessa said goodbye and followed Sophie down the path. Her idea that she could win back her daughter's affections easily now became a distant wish.

Quickly, she caught up with Sophie. "Daddy won't be home till after you're in bed tonight, so is there anything you'd like to do till bedtime." There was no answer. Vanessa hated it when Sophie gave her the silent treatment. She never knew what she was thinking or how she felt and it was an art she had learned and perfected from her father.

Remember you are loved and watched over, Vanessa told herself, over and over till they reached home. By the time she had returned her bicycle to the garage, Sophie had gone straight upstairs to her room. There would be no reconciliation tonight.

Sadly, she went into the kitchen to make her Lady Grey tea, digging her hands deep into the pockets of her thick cardigan, with the sun gone, the cold of evening made her shiver. Her hand touched something hard. Her first thought was it was some forgotten object she'd popped into her pocket for safe keeping. Her hand wrapped around the flat, cool surface and brought it into the light. There in her hand was the glass angel!

Vanessa gazed at it in amazement. "How on earth?" she muttered, running her fingers over its face and shining wings? She clutched it to her.

"My guardian angel," she breathed. "I **am** loved and watched over."

A deep calm seemed to envelop her as she held the angel up to the light.

How the angel had got into her pocket, she didn't know, but for her it was a physical reminder from the ones who truly loved her and, instinctively, knew it would keep her safe, no matter what happened.

Chapter 13

The hotel room, in which Kim found herself, was small but clean and warm and, more importantly, she could afford it. She thought of her lovely flat, now wrecked and bearing the scars of Roger's evil anger. She shuddered at the thought of what he might have done to her, had she not escaped when she did.

Although she wanted to put as much distance between herself and Roger, her finances wouldn't stretch to a holiday abroad. She dug out her address book from her handbag and flicked through it. Most of the names there were also known to Roger and she didn't want to have to return to her parents' home. They had made no secret of their displeasure when she'd decided to train as a massage therapist, saying it wasn't a suitable job for a girl. At the time, Kim had thought them just old fuddy-duddies, but her experience with Roger had made her rethink everything about her life. She shut the thought from her mind as she reached the last page of the book – xyz. There on the page was the name Liz Young.

"Of course," Kim exclaimed. She had known Liz since college and they'd always kept in touch, till Kim's involvement with Roger that is. Kim reached for the phone and it was picked up on the third ring. "Liz," Kim began brightly, "it's Kim. Blast from the past."

To her relief Liz sounded pleased to hear from her. "Kim Mason," she squealed, "this is amazing, I was just thinking about you."

"Well, that's good," replied Kim. "How are things with you anyway, love-life on the up and up?" She heard Liz sigh.

"Actually, it couldn't be more down at the moment. The latest 'love of my life' upped and left a couple of months ago, so I'm back on my Jack Jones again. But, never mind about me, how are you?"

"As a matter of fact Liz, things aren't too good at the moment. I need a favour, a big favour." She hesitated before going on. "My love life has hit a brick wall too," she moaned, "but well, unlike you, I can't get my ex to move out."

Carefully, she tried to sense Liz's mood. Positive or negative?

She decided to take the bull by the horns. "So, the thing is, Liz, I need somewhere to crash for a few nights. Just till he takes the hint and moves out..."

For a moment, Kim thought Liz was going to say sorry and hang up, but instead she said, "Great. That's what friends are for and maybe we can support one another to get over the **bastards.**"

Kim breathed a sigh of relief. "So, is it alright if I come over tomorrow? You're still at the same place I take it?"

"Well, I'm doing the early morning slot tomorrow, so won't be back till around three o'clock, but anytime after that would be fine."

"That'll be perfect, Liz. And thanks, I owe you big time."

They said their goodbyes and Kim went into the bathroom, took a shower and climbed into the single bed. Liz Young was a presenter on the local radio station, 'Hampton fm' and their friendship had deepened when she had sought out Kim's professional help three years ago. The pain of her marriage breakup had tensed her up so much, she had trouble doing her job, but Kim's deep tissue massage had done the trick and she'd been able to keep working. Sinking into slumber, Kim felt safe again and once some time had passed, she felt sure she would be able to return to her flat and a new life, without Roger.

The next day, when Kim awoke, it took her a minute or two to realise where she was, then it flooded back. She pushed the duvet off and muttering to herself, headed for the bathroom. Today she told herself, would be just fine. She shook the trauma of yesterday from her mind and concentrated on getting dressed and heading down to the dining room for breakfast. She hadn't eaten since breakfast yesterday and realised she was starving. The smell of cooked bacon and fresh coffee filled her nostrils. This wasn't a day for cold cereal and fruit, Kim needed something substantial to fill up the emptiness she felt. The small dining room was also empty except for, what Kim guessed was a sales rep, tucking into a heaped plateful of food as he played with his mobile phone.

She sat at a table in the window and wondered how she would manage financially. Massage therapy work hadn't been as lucrative as she'd hoped and now that Roger's 'gifts' would be no more, she felt a knot of fear forming in her stomach. "Tea or coffee, Madam?" The arrival of the waiter interrupted her thoughts.

"Emmm, coffee please and could I have the full English please?"

The waiter nodded, poured Kim her coffee and returned ten minutes later with the hot food. The breakfast tasted wonderful and very filling, which was just as well as it was going to have to keep her going the whole day. Lunch was off the menu.

At three-fifteen she knocked on Liz Young's door.

It was thrown open by an exuberant blonde-haired woman, wearing a silk patterned blouse, harem pants and in bare feet.

"Liz?" Kim queried, beginning to think she'd come to the wrong door. The last time she'd seen her friend, she had been wearing a sober trouser suit and buttoned up blouse, her hair had been brown and her face make-up free. And now... she was well, a free spirit.

"You look great," exclaimed Kim. "What a change."

Liz ushered her in and took her small suitcase from her.

"Well, that's thanks to you and maybe a little bit to 'the bastard'," she winked. "He liked to choose my clothes for me and well," she twirled, "sometimes he was right."

Kim took in her surroundings. The flat was spacious and decorated in soft shades of pink, cream and blue. Cushions were scattered over two large sofas and the wooden floor was carpeted with thick-piled rugs. An unlit crystal chandelier gleamed overhead and side lights cast pools of light and warmth into the room. "Beautiful," Kim murmured, Liz has done very well for herself.

Liz came back into the room bearing a bottle of white wine and two glasses.

"I've put your case in the bedroom next to mine," she told Kim, "but first," she clinked the glasses, "let's celebrate."

Liz poured out the wine as Kim relaxed. "Thanks," she said, "for everything."

They raised their glasses to one another and sipped the chilled Pino Grigio. "Now," continued Liz, "tell me about him then, this mystery lover who won't take the hint and LEAVE."

Kim wasn't sure how much to tell her friend, but knowing how gossip can get around, even with the best of friends, she decided to make up a credible scenario.

"Well you know how it is," she began, "older man, younger woman. I was quite enjoying the attention actually till he decided to leave his wife. Turned up at my door late one night bearing a holdall and a carrier bag and just, moved in. To tell the truth, I thought he'd go back to her, once he realised that looking after him wasn't part of my agenda. But, no, and he's been there now for about six weeks. Finally, last night, I told him he had to go, but he flatly refused. So, I decided I'd get out, leave him to it and hope he returns to the matrimonial home some time soon." Liz had listened to everything in silence, sipping at her wine and re-filling their glasses at the end of Kim's story.

"Does he have a name," Liz asked, "this old man of yours?"

"He has," replied Kim, trying quickly to think of something suitable, "he's called George."

Liz looked at Kim askance. "George," she repeated, "just George?"

Kim felt herself begin to colour, here she was taking her friend's hospitality and lying to her.

She glanced at her hands, took a deep breath and told Liz the truth. If she couldn't trust her, then who could she trust?

"So, you see," she finished, "I'm really scared to go back to my flat until I know he's given up."

"And his wife," Liz asked, "does she know any of this?"

"NO... no... at least, I don't think so."

"God help her," Liz said, quietly.

"And there's another thing," Kim added. "I'm broke."

Liz raised her eyebrows. "What about your therapy business, isn't that going well?"

Kim grimaced. "Not really, and if I go to the therapy clinic, Roger could easily turn up there and make things very difficult for me, so..."

"Well, that's one problem that's easily solved," she said briskly. "There's always room for another 'goffer' at the radio station and I've got a bit of clout there, so if you'd like...?"

Kim hugged her friend. "Liz Young," she grinned, "how can I ever thank you?"

"Well," Liz replied, the mood lightening by the minute, "you could start by helping me cook us a celebration dinner."

Kim shook her head in amazement at her friend's hospitality and kindness. "Consider it done."

Over the weekend, Kim settled into her temporary home. She would go back to her own flat soon, to clean it up and repaint the walls, but every time she thought about it, she panicked and backed off. Liz had to work over the weekend, but when she returned on Sunday afternoon, she had good news.

"I've spoken to my boss," she told Kim, "and he's fine about you coming to work at the station. He's insisted it's on a trial basis and that you'll be working directly for me, but apart from that, you're in."

Kim couldn't thank Liz enough. "You won't regret this," she insisted, "whatever you want me to do, I'll do it, and if I don't know how, I'll learn."

The radio station was hidden up a side street on the other side of town. From the outside it didn't look very impressive, but once inside, it opened out to a beautiful reception area with two long corridors leading off it. Piped music could be heard through hidden speakers and potted plants filled the corners alongside blue covered seating.

Liz introduced her to the receptionist. "Anything you're not sure of, just ask Linda, she's been here for yonks and knows everything and everybody."

Linda smiled her best receptionist smile. "Welcome to Hampton fm," she said, "you'll love it here, won't she Liz."

Liz looked at her friend, knowing what she knew and how scared she was of Roger, she slipped an arm around her shoulder. "You betcha!"

She followed Liz down the long corridor. To the right of her were offices, where people were busying themselves on phones, computers and photocopiers. And to the left were the studios.

Turning into one, Liz held up a finger to her lips. "Sssshhhhh," she whispered, "there's a programme just finishing." Kim stared into the darkness. On the other side of the glass where the presenter was sitting, there was a man with earphones on, signalling to the presenter. He seemed to be counting down, at the end of which, he gave a thumbs up. Liz waved through the glass.

"Who's that?" Kim asked.

"That's the sound man," Liz told her. "It's him who makes sure the sound quality is right and that the programme is running to time. Would you like to meet him?" Kim nodded, not sure what to expect. "My programme starts in fifteen minutes, so he's off duty now. C'mon."

They made their way through the studio, Liz acknowledging her colleague as they went, and opened the door into the adjoining room. "Hi Donald," smiled Liz, "I'd like you to meet a new member of the team. "Donald Martin, meet Kim Mason," Donald rose from his chair to greet her and kept rising. Liz laughed, "he's a bit on the tall side," she giggled, "but he's harmless."

Kim felt at home, instantly, with the lanky sound man.

"Pleased to meet you," she said. "This is my first day, so, I'm not sure what I'll be doing."

Donald grinned at Liz. "Want me to show her the ropes?"

Liz nodded, looking at her watch. "If you would Don, I'm on in ten minutes, so maybe you could get Kim a coffee or something and explain a bit about the place?"

"Done," said Donald, removing the headphones from his head and beckoning to Kim to follow him.

Liz waved her off. "See you later," she mouthed as another sound man took over from Donald.

The small canteen was empty, but a pot of coffee was sitting on the machine and cups and saucers were lined up on a side table.

Kim watched as Donald got their coffees. "Sit anywhere," he indicated, "how do you take your coffee?"

"White please, no sugar."

They sat facing one another at a small table and Kim got a closer look at her guide. Apart from being very tall, she saw that he had amazing eyes, although hidden behind horn-rimmed specs, she could see they were dark brown with very long lashes. His smile was slightly crooked and his manner totally relaxed. For his part, Donald thought that he had never seen anyone so beautiful as the girl in front of him and he had difficulty stopping himself from staring at her.

"So, how do you know Liz," he asked, trying to sound interested but not intrusive.

"Oh, we're old friends from way back," Kim said, "I'm staying with her just now, while my flat gets... redecorated."

Donald nodded. So, she lived alone, he mused, now that was just the news he wanted to hear. "Once you've had your coffee, I'll show you around, introduce you to the others and find some jobs for you to do," he smiled, "and I'm sure Liz will have plenty to occupy you, once you find your feet."

Kim tried to repress a squeal of delight at the way things were turning out. A few days ago, she'd had to run from her flat, terrified and now, thanks to Liz, she felt she was on the threshold of the new life she craved.

Chapter 14

Since finding the angel in her pocket, Vanessa had seemed to find a new calmness and peace in her life. Sophie was still being difficult but they were, at least, back on speaking terms.

The only encounters she had with Roger were at breakfast and occasionally at his consulting rooms. He had taken to leaving cash for her every week to cover housekeeping needs and had changed the bank account so that Vanessa could pay in money only and not withdraw it. If she needed any more, he'd told her, she'd have to ask him for it.

Vanessa felt like a chattel, but if it meant only being in Roger's presence once or twice a day, she accepted it. He still came in late at night and slept in Sophie's room, but after his 'birthday present' she almost felt physically sick at the thought of him touching her again.

The arrangement could have sustained for long enough, but one day in June Vanessa had fainted. She'd been in the bank, paying in Roger's fees, when blackness enveloped her. Mr Parker, the teller, had run around the counter to help her up. "Mrs Lomax," he called his voice tinged with concern, "Mrs. Lomax." He patted her cheek and was relieved when her eyes fluttered open.

"What's happened..." Vanessa heard herself say, coming round and finding herself lying on the floor. A small crowd had gathered.

"Call an ambulance," said someone.

"No," Vanessa protested, "I'm fine. Please Mr Parker, help me up."

The teller took her through to the back office and sat her down. He got her a glass for water which she sipped gratefully.

"How foolish of me," she murmured, "I don't know what came over me."

Mr Parker smiled with relief, "Perhaps you should see a doctor," he suggested. Vanessa nodded. She felt so peculiar, she decided she would.

Worried that the stress of living with Roger's new regime was affecting her, as soon as she reached home, Vanessa phoned for an appointment with Dr Adams. But only a locum was available if she wanted to see a doctor that day…? Vanessa booked the appointment.

The locum was very young, just out of medical school Vanessa felt.

"So what's the trouble?" he asked, adjusting the stethoscope hanging around his neck and turning away from his computer screen.

"Well," Vanessa said, "this morning, in the bank, I fainted."

Pushing down the urge to make light of things with a joke about bank loans, the young doctor cleared his throat, "Well, let's start by taking your blood pressure." Vanessa sat silently, till the procedure was completed.

"Normal," he pronounced. "So, not low blood pressure then."

He smiled at Vanessa and turned his attention back to the computer.

"You're married and just turned thirty. My first question would be, is it possible that you're pregnant?"

Vanessa gasped. "Pregnant!"

"Well, it's very common for fainting to be the first sign. Are you or your husband taking 'precautions'?"

Vanessa shook her head. Sex with Roger had been so infrequent over the last couple of years, she had sometimes forgotten to take her birth pill. She felt tears forming as she remembered his 'birthday present' to her.

"Mrs Lomax," the young locum asked kindly, "would you like a pregnancy test, find out one way or another?"

Vanessa nodded.

He buzzed through for a nurse, who responded immediately.

"Mrs Lomax requires a pregnancy test nurse, could you see to it?"

The nursed smiled, "Of course, this way Mrs Lomax."

She ushered Vanessa out of the surgery and into the nurses' room.

By the time the test was done and Vanessa was waiting for the result, she knew it would be positive. She'd missed a period. Her periods had become erratic due to her forgetfulness about the pill, so she'd thought nothing of it… till now.

The nurse returned. "Good news Mrs Lomax," she beamed, "it's positive, you're four weeks pregnant."

Vanessa felt she was going to faint again.

"Are you alright?" the nurse asked, seeing the colour drain from Vanessa's face.

"Yes, yes, I'm fine."

"Do you want to see the doctor again?"

"No, it's alright, thanks. I'll just go home now."

"Tell your husband the good news," the nurse grinned, "I'm sure he'll be over the moon."

"Yeah," Vanessa agreed bleakly, "over the moon."

Vanessa made the journey home in a daze, wheeling her bicycle alongside her. Lost in thought, she didn't hear her name being called and it wasn't till she felt a tap on her shoulder that she turned. The tall, rangy figure of Donald Martin was smiling down at her.

"I thought it was you," he continued, "I was just off to lunch at the Pig and Whistle, you're quite welcome to join me if you like. Are you alright?" he asked, suddenly noticing the strain in Vanessa's face and the tears brimming her eyes.

Before she could answer he took the bike from her and linked his other arm into hers. "C'mon," he said, "you need to sit down." He guided her across the road and down the street into the pub.

"Do you want a drink?" he asked his concern deepening as he saw that her hands were trembling.

"Tea," Vanessa whispered, "please."

Donald quickly gave the order to the barmaid, "And a half pint of mild for me, he added."

The lounge bar was relatively quiet as they found a table in the corner. Donald waited till the drinks were brought to the table and the barmaid had gone. Vanessa wrapped her hands around the filled cup and gulped the hot liquid down. The heat permeated into her body and her hands warmed up.

"You needed that," Donald said, pouring her a second cup from the metal teapot.

"Is there anything I can do to help," he asked, trying to match the image of Vanessa in the Green Room to the distraught figure before him.

Vanessa raised her head and took a deep breath. "I'm pregnant," she stated almost defiantly.

Donald blinked. "Isn't that good?"

"Not really," Vanessa replied, her shoulders beginning to sag again.

"I'm sorry," Donald said, feeling useless to help. He didn't know much about women and even less about pregnant ones. His passion had always been his computers and his job at the local radio station.

"Maybe Aunt Hazel can help," he offered. "Does she know?"

Vanessa put down her cup, suddenly remembering Hazel's pronouncement that 'both her children loved her.'

"I think she knew before I did," Vanessa answered mysteriously, getting up to go.

"Thanks for the tea Donald," she said, "it was just what I needed."

She shook his hand and left. Donald slowly finished his beer and returned to the bar. 'What a strange lady,' he thought. But his thoughts were interrupted by the arrival of his lunch date.

"Donald," waved Kim. "Sorry I'm late. Have you ordered?"

Donald felt his heart leap at the sight of Kim Mason. She'd only been working at the station a short time, but already they were friends and, if he was lucky, they'd be more than that in the future.

Chapter 15

As the weeks went by, Vanessa tried to make a decision about her future. The pain she had endured at conception may have been great, but the connection she felt to her unborn child was slowly diminishing it.

She felt that her marriage to Roger was all but over and that she would try to build a new life for herself and Sophie away from this place. Roger needn't know about the pregnancy, she decided, but her own father did. She would go to see him the next day and beg his help, both financial and emotional.

Surely, he would see her need and unblock his heart.

If Vanessa felt the phone call to her father had been strained, seeing him again, after more than a year, was worse.

He had agreed to her visiting him as long as she was alone. He didn't want to see Roger and not even Sophie, his only grand-daughter, so on a hot day in August after Roger had left for his consulting rooms and Sophie had gone on a school trip, she made an extra effort and dressed up a bit, before leaving the house to visit her father. Hazel's cream helped again to make her feel special and loved and it was with a light step she boarded the cross-town bus.

She had spoken to her father now and then over the year, but it had always been much the same, a few platitudes and then an awkward silence.

The day was clear and warm and her father's house was bathed in the late morning sunshine as she arrived. The drive up to the front door was wide and paved and the lawns and flower beds either side looked carefully tended and full of colour. She could smell the scent of roses all around her and their perfume gladdened her heart. This visit was going to go well, she told herself. Surely her father would give her the help she needed, when he knew about her pregnancy and desperate circumstances.

The door was opened by Mr Dobson. He and his wife had worked as housekeeper and handyman for Vanessa's father since her mother had died and were devoted to his wellbeing.

Mr Dobson's eyes lit up at the sight of Vanessa.

"Your father is expecting you," he smiled broadly, "and lunch will be served at twelve-thirty I hope you're hungry," he winked, "Mrs Dobson has made a roast chicken salad and a tarte tatan for afters."

Vanessa smiled gratefully, "Oh, Mr Dobson, thank her for me won't you and if it's alright, I'll stop by your flat before I go."

Mr Dobson nodded in agreement. "Your father's in the library," he indicated the door at the far end of the hall, "he's been a bit more tired than usual of late, but, well you'll see for yourself."

Vanessa took a deep breath and nodded, a small knot of concern forming in her stomach.

Her father was sitting with his back to the door, looking out of the window onto the garden. He turned to greet her when he heard her come in.

Vanessa crossed the room to where he sat and almost gasped when she saw him. His once handsome face was sallow and thin, with deep lines etched into his forehead and around his eyes. Something was very wrong with him that was for sure. This wasn't just tiredness, even she could tell that.

"Don't look at me like that," he said, gripping the arms of his chair, as Vanessa dropped into the chair opposite him.

"Daddy," she whispered, trying to ignore the fear that had now grown into a tight ball in her stomach, "what is it?"

"Oh, nothing to worry about," he said trying to be bright, "just a bit liverish that's all. Part of getting older, you know. Doc says I've to take this awful medicine for a while then everything will be fine."

Vanessa sat back a little in her chair. "Why didn't you let me know you were ill?" she asked.

"No point," said her father, "Mrs Dobson does for me and Mr Dobson looks after the garden, so no need to worry you."

There it was again, he was shutting her out just like always.

She could see the droop in his shoulders and the whiteness of his knuckles, but she had to find a way to break through the barrier he had quickly and expertly erected around himself.

"I've got some news to tell you, hopefully good news."

John Anderson turned his attention back to Vanessa, expectantly.

She kept her eyes fixed on his as she pulled herself up erect and smiled her broadest smile.

"You're going to be a grandpa again," she said, "I'm going to have a little brother or sister for Sophie."

Vanessa swore she saw tears forming in the corner of her father's eyes.

"Life goes on, eh," he said softly. "And what does that husband of yours have to say about it. Is he pleased?"

Vanessa couldn't hold the eye contact a moment longer.

"Well," she whispered, "he doesn't know yet."

"Any reason why not?" her father asked.

Now it was Vanessa's turn to feel tearful.

"Oh, daddy," she murmured, "Roger doesn't love me anymore. Our marriage is a sham. Ever since Sophie was born, he changed. Oh, he has lots of time for his 'little girl' but I'm just the housekeeper and cook now. Sometimes I think he wishes I were dead."

John Anderson took in his daughter's distress. How like her mother she looked and he wished more than anything he could do something to help her. But the cancer that was growing in his liver was unstoppable and he knew he would only get weaker and weaker. No match for Roger when he would inevitably come calling.

He braced himself for her next question.

"So," she said helplessly, "if there's a way Sophie and me could perhaps come and live here for a while, just till the baby's born...?"

"Sorry," he said abruptly. "I'm too old to have children running around the house and as for Mrs Dobson, well, she couldn't cope with all the extra work. No, Vanessa, I'm sorry, but the answer is no."

Vanessa felt crushed. Never had she needed her father so much and never had she felt so rejected.

Without another word she stood up and left the room and the house. No point in hanging around any longer, she knew now that she was on her own, no one was going to come riding to her rescue. She ran down the drive and into the street, tears battling with her willpower to stop them from falling.

John Anderson rang through to Mr Dobson.

"Tell Mrs Dobson there will only be one for lunch today, my daughter had to leave sooner than expected. And Dobson," he added "she doesn't know about the cancer, nor will she. Do you understand?"

"Yes sir," he answered sadly, "I understand perfectly."

"Did he tell her?" his wife asked when he'd hung up the phone.

Mr Dobson shook his head. "This is probably the last time we'll see little Vanessa now till after he's dead."

He looked at Mrs Dobson. "C'mon old girl, let's get lunch for him, then we'll have a nice cup of tea."

Vanessa walked blindly all the way home and collapsed, exhausted onto her bed. How could her father just leave her to her fate like that? And Sophie, didn't he care anything about his grand-daughter?

The questions circled her brain till she fell asleep. Some things just didn't have any answers.

She woke to the sound of Sophie coming up the stairs. "Mum," she was calling, "where are you?"

Vanessa struggled into a sitting position. "In here, Sophie," she replied.

The door opened and her daughter looked in, a slight frown on her face.

"What are you doing in bed at this time of day?" she asked her mother.

"Oh, it's something and nothing," Vanessa replied, trying to sound more convincing than she felt.

Sophie sat on the end of the bed. "What does that mean?" she probed.

Vanessa hesitated, considering whether to tell her daughter about the pregnancy, but deciding now wasn't the right time.

"I've just had a bit of a tummy bug, that's all, but thank you for asking Sophie that was nice of you."

"Mmmmmhhhh," Sophie seemed to be mulling over the truth or otherwise of the answer. "It's just that daddy met me from the trip and told me that he's planning a surprise for me for my birthday and... well, you will be alright by then, won't you?"

"Well, I hope so," Vanessa said, swinging her legs over the side of the bed and getting up. "What's the birthday surprise anyway?" she asked, feeling a twinge of misgiving in her solar plexus. Roger hadn't said anything to her about a surprise, but then Roger hadn't said anything about anything of late.

Sophie tutted, "It wouldn't be a surprise if I knew what it was, now would it!"

She made to go to the door, bored now with the conversation with her mother.

"You don't think" she said turning slowly, "that it really will be a pony this time, do you?" Much as Vanessa wanted to say 'yes' she knew that Roger was never going to buy Sophie a pony.

"I don't know," she said instead, "you'll just have to wait and see, like you said, if you knew now, then it wouldn't be a surprise now would it?" Vanessa took the opportunity to hug her daughter. "Anyway, it's a good few weeks till your birthday so we may find out something more before then that'll give us a clue. And you'll be starting your new school in September," she added. Sophie grinned at the thought and Vanessa smiled, but in her heart she felt a vague sense of unease.

Sophie skipped out of the bedroom. "Get changed and wash your hands," Vanessa called after her, "there's a Circle tonight and you'll be going to Mrs Munro's later."

What was Roger up to now? Vanessa pondered. She wished he'd stop filling Sophie's head with nonsense, promising her a pony was bad enough, but building her up again with a mystery surprise wasn't a great idea. Getting Sophie to concentrate on her schoolwork was hard enough, without any distractions from Roger.

The sleep had refreshed her and although the hurt she felt at her father's rejection was acute, she couldn't help but feel there was something more to his refusal than met the eye.

But she was still left with the same problem, how to get herself to a place away from Roger, where she could live at peace with herself and Sophie, as well as her new baby when it arrived.

Chapter 16

Roger was pleased at his daughter's reaction to the 'birthday surprise.'

Using his NLP knowledge to reach her sub-conscious while she slept had worked well. Soon, his plan would be put into play and they'd be together forever, just daddy and his little girl.

But for now, he had to keep building up the bank balance and find time to pay another visit to Darko at his club in London. That was important.

After the Circle that evening, he phoned him.

"Darko my man," he smoothed, aware of his need to keep him onside. "When's the next 'happening'?"

Darko gripped the phone but kept his voice neutral. "Roger, hey, great to hear from you. The next 'happening' eh, well let me just check." He dropped the phone onto the bar top and poured himself a drink."

Roger waited.

"It looks like it's next Saturday. Can I book you, or sweet Kim, anything 'special'?" he drawled out the words heavy with innuendo.

"Well, next Saturday's just perfect," Roger replied, blocking out his appointment book for that weekend, "You know what I like Darko," he chided him, "same as last time would be good, even younger would be better."

Darko tensed. "And Kim, what can I line up for her?"

"Well that's the thing Darko, Kim won't be making it this time, it'll just be me."

Roger could almost feel his disappointment through the phone line.

"By the way, we need to talk a little business while I'm at the club, so keep sober till I get there."

"Sounds interesting?"

"You bet."

Roger hung up the phone and checked his watch. Time for a visit to his favourite Massage Parlour, he had been getting more and more frustrated since Kim had made her exit, but the Madam who ran the 'Relaxation Zone' knew his needs and met them exquisitely, for a price.

He continued to avoid Vanessa as much as possible, but found that even the silent breakfasts were becoming irksome. He had to find a way of even avoiding that soon, especially as she seemed so listless and depressed of late.

The day before his departure to London, he put some money down on the counter in the kitchen and absently told her he would be in London again that weekend.

"Another conference?" Vanessa asked, trying to keep down another bout of morning sickness.

"None of your business," he snapped.

"And this time, when I come back, I'll expect to find you in your own bed and not my daughter's." She could feel his hot breath on her face as he delivered the veiled threat.

Vanessa remained silent as he turned a left the room.

Just in time, she reached the sink and retched. The nausea was draining her physically and she longed for the three month stage of her pregnancy to pass so she could eat properly again.

Sipping a glass of water, she wondered if Hazel might have some magic herbal potion in her pharmacy to ease things and decided she would pay her a visit. She hadn't seen her or Noble since she had found out she was pregnant and she felt the need, to not just get something for her morning sickness, but for some of Hazel's wisdom too for the sickness that was growing in her soul.

She heard the slamming of the front door again as Roger left.

"Can't he just close the door quietly," she muttered, feeling a headache forming over her eyes. The longer her unhappy life went on the more emotionally detached she was becoming. Absently, she stroked her womb. "One day," she told her unborn child, "we'll be free, but right now, you're safe inside me."

By mid-morning she was feeling better and set off to Hazel's cottage.

As usual, the nearer she got to Willow Walk the easier she felt. Hazel knew she was pregnant before she had known and Vanessa wanted to know more about how she knew. 'Had she had some more contact with her mother?'

She parked her bike and called out. "Hazel, it's Vanessa, can I come in?"

She saw movement behind the curtains and the door opened but it was the tall figure of Donald Martin who stood on the doorstep.

"Vanessa," he exclaimed, "how good to see you again. Come in, please. Aunt Hazel is making the tea, as usual. She'll be so pleased to see you."

Donald ushered Vanessa into the sitting room just as Hazel appeared with her tray of tea-things.

"Vanessa, my dear," she smiled kindly, "Donald told me about meeting you in town and about your good news. Congratulations." Vanessa smiled weakly.

Hazel turned to Donald. "Now what were you saying about this new girlfriend of yours?"

Donald blushed. "Well, she's not exactly my girlfriend, not yet anyway, but I think she might be, if I play my cards right."

He was clearly smitten, Vanessa could see.

"She's a very lucky girl if she has you for a boyfriend," Hazel responded roundly. "And does she have a name?"

Donald's eyes misted over. "Mmmmmhhhh, her name is Kim," he murmured, "Miss Kim Mason."

Vanessa couldn't believe her ears.

It couldn't be the same Kim Mason who kept Roger out to all hours, supposedly helping her with her clients, could it?

"That name sounds fffamiliar," Vanessa stuttered, "how did you meet?"

"Oh, she came to work at the local radio station a few weeks ago, where I'm the sound man. You know the one, Hampton fm."

Vanessa breathed a sigh of relief. It couldn't be the same Kim Mason, she told herself, just someone with the same name.

Donald finished his tea. "Well, I'll be off Auntie, I'm sure you and Vanessa have lots to talk about and anyway," he winked at her with one of his big brown eyes, "I have a lunch date with a certain young lady..."

After he left, Hazel refilled Vanessa's cup. "Now, she said, I guess you want some more answers?"

Vanessa braced herself. "How did you know I was pregnant before I did?" she asked bluntly. "And have you been in touch with my mother again?"

"Is that all?"

"No," Vanessa blurted out, "Oh, Hazel, I'm so unhappy at home and I can't seem to find any way out of it. Please help me."

"It's alright," Hazel assured her, "everything's going to be alright."

Vanessa dabbed her eyes.

"Now, tell me about what's been happening to you."

With a deep sigh, Vanessa told her the whole miserable saga, about how Roger had taken to completely ignoring her and how the visit to her father had left her more confused and hurt than ever and as for Sophie, well she seemed to have reverted back to being daddy's little girl and treating Vanessa like her servant.

Hazel's eyes darkened with concern. She could see that Vanessa was getting more and more stressed and, now, with a baby on the way...

"My dear, your mother was the one who told me you were pregnant, but she hasn't contacted me since. Perhaps it is time that I tried to make contact with her. Would you want me to do that?"

Vanessa slowly nodded. "Ask her what I need to do?"

Hazel led her over to a small table with a chair either side and sat her down.

"Hold my hands," she said softly, "let's see if she's there."

Hazel closed her eyes and called Jennifer's name.

"Are you there, Jennifer?" she asked. There was silence. Hazel repeated the request. Then a smile spread across her face. "Vanessa's here," she said, "she's very upset and needs our help. What is your advice?"

Hazel silently nodded, as if she was hearing words. Finally she said, "Thank you Jennifer, I'll tell her."

She released Vanessa's hands and opened her eyes.

"The message is this," Hazel said. "Money will come to meet your needs. Follow the elephant and all will be well."

Vanessa blinked. "What does that mean?"

Hazel shrugged her shoulders. "We don't always understand messages from the other side," she said, "but as the future unfolds, they usually become clear."

"Trust your guardian angel, Vanessa," Hazel reminded her, "she won't let you down."

"Yes, I will," Vanessa replied, feeling calmer now and reaching into her pocket for the glass replica.

"Now, time to get home before Sophie gets in from school." Hazel stood up and helped Vanessa to her feet. "But, before you go," Hazel disappeared into the kitchen. She came back and pressed a little brown bottle into Vanessa's hands. "For the morning sickness," she told her, "three drops in a little water last thing at night before you go to bed."

Vanessa stared at the bottle then at Hazel, "But, how did you know..."

Hazel smiled. "Oh, I just do."

Chapter 17

The day before he was going up to London again, Roger paid a visit to Kim's flat. He didn't particularly want to see her, just to know she was still around before he spoke to Darko.

He parked his car and looked around for Kim's, but it was nowhere to be seen. 'Good,' he thought, now checking out the windows. To his surprise, there was light coming through a gap in the blind. So, she was still living there, he mused, this could prove more interesting than he'd expected.

He knocked loudly on the door. Kim froze and so did Liz. They stared at the door then each other. Liz put her finger to her lips, "Sssshhhhh," she whispered, and pointing to the adjoining kitchen, indicated to Kim to go into the other room.

As she passed the window, Kim quickly peeped through the blind. She turned to Liz her face pale with fear. "Roger's car is outside," she mouthed. Liz nodded and pointed again to the kitchen. The knocking started again, this time, more demanding.

"Just a minute," Liz called, picking up the paint brush and pot of paint she'd been using to help Kim paint over Roger's obscenities.

She opened the door and waited for Roger to speak.

Rapidly getting over the shock of seeing this strange woman, Roger cleared his throat. "I'm looking for Kim," he said, "Kim Mason. I'm a friend."

"Well, you're out of luck," Liz countered, "she doesn't live here anymore."

"And who are you?" Roger asked sarcastically.

"It's none of your business who I am," retorted Liz, beginning to enjoy the verbal joust, "and come to think of it, who the Hell are you?" Roger felt his fists clench. Liz placed her hand on her hip, "I just know that I've paid good money for this pad and it's now mine, so unless there's anything else…?"

Roger eased his head around the door. "Are you sure she doesn't live here anymore?"

"Positive," replied Liz, becoming impatient with Roger's pushiness, "now if you don't mind, I've got work to do."

Forcibly, she closed the door on him.

Roger returned to his car, smiling to himself.

Kim was there alright, he now knew, his glance into the living room showed two mugs and biscuits on the coffee table. He didn't care who the 'sexually frustrated' woman was who answered the door. Kim was still around and that's all he needed to know.

His plan was coming together. Next day he'd get the crucial information he needed from Darko and Kim was the trade-off.

As he travelled down the motorway, he considered his approach to Darko.

The man was nobody's fool and he wouldn't tell Roger what he wanted to know without some kickback for himself. The road was free-running for a Saturday and he made good time, getting into his hotel in London by early afternoon.

Once he'd unpacked and showered, he changed into comfortable trousers and polo shirt, he was going to have to keep his cool if things didn't go his way. He dialled Darko's number.

"Darko," he said knowingly, "it's Roger."

"I've been expecting your call," was the reply and I'm sober. "Soooooo...?"

"So, time for a meet, in about an hour?"

"An hour's fine. See you then."

The line cleared. Darko looked at the mute receiver before slowly returning it to its cradle. "What was Roger up to?"

Darko was soon to find out.

Sitting facing one another in leather tub chairs in Darko's office, Roger put forward his proposition, "So you see, Darko my man, Thailand is the place to be for guys like me and well, it would be useful to have a contact there, just to get things going."

Darko stroked his black beard. "How long do you intend going for?" he asked.

Roger shrugged his shoulders, "How long's a piece of string," he smiled, "I suppose as long as the money lasts till I can get in on the drugs action and if the hot girls are anything like your selection, well, let's say the plan is... forever!"

The thought of never seeing Roger again appealed to Darko, especially as he seemed to be leaving Kim behind.

"Forever's a long time Rog." Roger nodded. "And, now for the burning question," Darko continued, making direct eye contact with the man opposite. "What's in it for me?"

Roger shifted in his chair. This was the make or break question.

"Give me the name, address and phone number of the supplier in Thailand of these beautiful, extremely young Thai girls you bring over here and... I'll give you the address, phone number and mobile number for Kim."

Darko's stomach tightened as he took in a sharp intake of breath and Roger knew he'd hit his Achilles heel.

Access to Kim's private address and phone number was something he had lusted after for a long, long time. His only contact with her in the past was through Roger and he could only have her if Roger brought her to the club.

But now...!

He steepled his fingers together in front of his chin.

"And, how do I know the information you give me about Kim is correct?"

"Darko, Darko," Roger implored, "would I lie to you?"

Darko reached over to Roger, offering his hand. He couldn't afford to miss maybe his last opportunity to get direct access to Kim. "You have yourself a deal," he said, gripping Roger's hand tighter than was necessary, but if you double-cross me... well, you don't want to know what I'll do to you."

"Let's have a drink," Roger nodded amiably towards the bar room, "seal the deal," Darko took his hand, "and if there's any cocaine action going down, keep me in mind," he added winking.

Roger was elated. He had underestimated Darko's lust for Kim and had been prepared to back up his proposition with hard cash, but none of this had been necessary. The two men exchanged their information, Roger carefully folding the paper into his wallet and Darko stuffing his into his shirt pocket. He'd check the details later that day and if they didn't measure up…

"I'll be back this evening," he told Darko, "this cat wants his cream and he wants it fresh."

He tapped the side of his nose and left, the smirk on his face growing with every step. The most important part of his plan was in place, the rest would be easy.

Back in his hotel room, he stripped naked, it was time to start his ritual. He poured a large shot of whisky and lit his candles before lying down on the bed. He reached over to the bedside table and lifted the bottle of Frankincense oil, carefully uncorking it. He breathed in the heavy scent before tipping some of the oil onto his chest. He rubbed it in, all the time anticipating the night ahead. "This would be the best ever," he told himself, "just me and two Thai girls to see to my every need."

He pushed himself up on his elbows and took the two Viagra pills into his mouth, washing them down with the whisky. He could feel himself harden almost instantly. "Yes," he breathed, "tonight would be the best ever."

Chapter 18

Vanessa's morning sickness vanished overnight. She sniffed the bottle Hazel had given her but still couldn't identify the herbal mix, she only knew it worked and worked instantly. She could smell bacon cooking now without feeling sick and her Lady Grey tea was once more on the menu.

Her doctor had arranged an appointment the following week at the ante-natal clinic in Reading and they were going to scan her womb to see how the baby was developing.

She hadn't had any scans when she was pregnant with Sophie, mainly because Roger hadn't agreed to it and with the wedding to plan there hadn't really been the time, so she was a bit nervous about the whole procedure. She held her arms around herself, she would know soon if her baby was healthy and well. On 1 September, Vanessa set off for Reading. Making her way to the railway station she just caught the early train. On her arrival, the busyness of the big city compared to West Hampton almost had her scurrying back to the station so, rather than battling her way to the hospital on the bus, she decided to take a taxi.

The journey to Reading was quite an adventure for Vanessa, as she never really went anywhere on her own that was outside West Hampton and she felt quite pleased with herself, if a little nervous.

The hospital was huge, but the driver dropped her at the entrance of the ante-natal clinic and wished her luck.

What a nice man, Vanessa mused as she paid the taxi fare and patted the little angel in her pocket. "Thanks," she said, "I'm sure everything will be fine."

The waiting room was full of expectant mums and Vanessa found a seat and joined the queue. Looking round her she saw that most of the women were young, just like her, only some were nearer giving birth than others.

"Is this your first time?" the woman next to her asked.

Vanessa returned her smile, "No," she said, "I already have a little girl. She'll be thirteen on her next birthday."

"Oh! quite a gap then."

Vanessa nodded, "How about you?"

"Fourth," the woman grimaced, patting her bump, "and the last."

"Vanessa Lomax," called the nurse.

"That's me," replied Vanessa standing up.

"Good luck," said her companion giving a 'thumbs up'.

Vanessa felt oddly comforted by the two strangers who had wished her well, and realised just how much of her days she spent alone. Apart from Hazel she didn't have anyone to really talk to and now even Roger said little or nothing, it was no surprise that she had begun to feel isolated. She rubbed the little angel, 'just for luck' before following the nurse into a darkened room.

"Hop up on the couch Mrs Lomax," instructed the nurse, "and we'll just take a look at what's going on for you." Vanessa did as she was told. The nurse gently eased her clothing aside and spread some very cold jelly-like gloop onto her abdomen.

"Oh, that's cold!" Vanessa exclaimed, but she was smiling as she said it.

"Just helps me move the scanner better. Here," she swung a TV monitor round so Vanessa could see the screen. "Now, keep your eyes on the screen," said the nurse with professional pride, "and let's see what we've got."

Vanessa watched as shapes began to form on the screen, but none of them looked like a baby. "There," said the nurse pointing to a round area, "that's the head and look, there are the legs." Vanessa was mesmerised. She could see it. For the first time, she could see her unborn child, growing inside her.

"And, it's a boy," pronounced the nurse. "I bet your husband will be pleased."

Vanessa could hardly speak. "You mean... you can tell... a boy?"

The nurse grinned, "Fully formed."

She handed Vanessa some paper towels to wipe off the excess jelly. "Now," she said in her matter-of-fact nurses' way, "get yourself sorted and I'll get your printout for you."

"Printout?"

Vanessa sat on the edge of the couch, adjusting her skirt and tucking in her blouse. "It's a boy," she breathed, "I'm going to have a baby boy."

A feeling of love swept over her, strong enough to bring tears to her eyes.

"And you'll be a lovely little boy," she told her yet-to-be-born son.

The nurse handed Vanessa a card with her name and the name of the hospital on the front and when she opened it, there it was, a picture of her son.

The nurse ushered her to the door, "See you in the delivery room," she said, "when the time comes." Another 'thumbs up.'

Vanessa gazed at the printout of her baby all the way home on the train.

Regardless of the horrible conception, here was proof that she was to be a mother again and, she realised, it was something she wanted now more than anything else in the world.

She longed to show the world the picture but couldn't. There was so much uncertainty around her, she often struggled to see a way through it, but today made things easier to bear. Today, she had met her son.

She pushed the key in the lock and opened the door. The postman had been and a pile of junk mail lay on the floor. She picked it up absently and made her way through to the kitchen, heading towards the bin to dump the bundle of coloured adverts for double glazing, pizzas and garden sheds. As she did so, a long, cream envelope caught her eye. She flicked it over and saw it was addressed to her.

She carefully opened the seal. It was a letter from her father.

Dear Vanessa

I'm sorry I couldn't help you out, but that didn't mean I didn't want to.

News of a new baby is great and when it's born, please come back and visit.

Enclosed is a small cheque to help with odds and ends.

Dad

Vanessa unfolded the cheque. It was for £2,000. She gasped at the amount.

The money would make all the difference to her. She could now buy things for her son without asking Roger for more money. She clutched the cheque in both hands. "Thank you daddy," she whispered, "and when the baby is born he'll be called John, after you."

She put the cheque into her handbag. She'd bank it as soon as possible. What a day this had been, seeing her unborn son and all this money turning up, out of the blue... She stopped in her tracks, her mind going back to the message from her mother, given to her through Hazel.

Money will come to meet your needs. That's what Hazel had said! Vanessa took the cheque out of her handbag and looked at it again. "'Money will come to meet your needs,'" she repeated aloud, "and here it is."

She plucked the angel from her pocket and held it up to the light.

"Thanks mum," she said, stroking the smooth glass, "and I'm not going to be scared anymore, now I know you're still watching over me and look," she smiled, holding up the printout from the hospital, "say hello to your grandson."

Filled with almost more happiness than she could bear, Vanessa took her cup of Lady Grey tea into the garden. It was a beautiful afternoon and Sophie wouldn't be home for a couple of hours yet, so she unfolded one of the garden chairs and sat facing the sun, her hands holding onto the printout. It was almost as though she was afraid it would disappear. The sun warmed her relaxed body and she felt herself drift off to sleep.

The feel of the printout being snatched from her fingers woke her up.

Roger was standing over her, a deep furrow of anger between his eyes as he tried to make sense of the black and white shapes.

"What's this?" he asked, bluntly, waving the printout above her head.

Vanessa leapt up. "Nothing," she blurted, "it's just something a friend gave me to look at."

Roger turned the card over. "But it says here, 'Mrs Vanessa Lomax.' That's you isn't it?" He held the picture closer, "But, WHAT is this?"

Vanessa felt her energy drain from her body as fear gripped her.

Clutching the angel in her pocket, she took a deep breath and stepped back under the branches of the apple tree.

"It's a baby," she said, defiantly, "my baby."

It was as if time had stood still.

She watched as Roger deliberately tore the printout into small pieces and scattered them on the grass.

He stepped towards her, pushing her against the tree.

"It may be YOUR BABY," he seethed, "but it's NOT going to be born."

He grasped her by the shoulders and spat the words in her face.

"I'm going on a trip soon and when I return, YOUR BABY will better be no more. ABORT IT."

Suddenly, there was a flash of white as a ball of fur and claws hurtled itself from the branches of the tree right onto Roger's face.

Vanessa lurched back as the cat clawed and tore at Roger's face and neck, drawing more and more blood with every attack.

Roger fell to the ground, screaming and writhing in agony.

Finally, the cat stopped and disappeared into the shrubbery.

Vanessa was afraid to move as Roger pulled himself upright, blood streaming from his face.

"You did this," he screamed, "somehow, you did this." He pulled out a handkerchief and tried to staunch the blood. "And you'll pay dearly," he added the menace rumbling in his voice, as he lurched towards his car.

Vanessa stood in the aftermath, staring at the torn-up pieces of her baby's picture. She looked around her. "Noble," she called softly. The cat emerged from the bushes, his fur stained red with Roger's blood. She picked him up and carried him into the kitchen. She opened a tub of single cream, poured it into a saucer and placed it before the cat. "Thank you," she said, "I think you just saved my son's life."

Chapter 19

Thanks to Liz's help, Kim's flat was once more habitable. They'd painted the walls and repaired and re-arranged the furniture and, at Liz's insistence, Kim had a new deadlock fitted to the front door as well as a peep-hole and safety chain. 'Just in case', her friend had cautioned.

It was time for Kim to move back home. She felt she had imposed enough on Liz's hospitality and, although it was never suggested, Kim felt it was time to try getting back to normal. It had been four weeks since Roger's visit and there had been no sign of him back at the flat, nor had he phoned or emailed her.

"Are you sure?" Liz asked on hearing Kim's decision.

"As sure as I can be," replied Kim, "and I can't thank you enough, not just for taking me in but for fixing me up with a job at the radio station and," she smiled, "introducing me to Don Martin."

Liz raised an eyebrow. "That's going somewhere then is it?" she asked, noting her friend's downcast eyes.

Kim shrugged, "Well, you know..."

"I think everybody at the station knows," Liz laughed. "Don's like a smitten kitten whenever you're around."

Kim couldn't help the smile of pleasure spreading across her face.

"You think?"

"I think."

That weekend, Kim moved back home.

She unpacked her clothes and filled the fridge with fresh food and while she waited for the kettle to boil she wandered from room to room, savouring the space and freedom she now had back. Her thoughts turned to Don Martin.

Very soon she would invite him up for a meal and then, if things went as she hoped, their friendship may progress to a more 'intimate' level.

Kim frowned. Donald knew nothing of her past and that's the way she wanted it to stay, but there was Roger. Once he found out she was back home and there was another man on the scene, who knew what he would do to ruin things for her.

She pushed the thought from her head. She was meeting Donald that evening and couldn't wait. He was the kindest, most thoughtful and honest person she had ever met and she wasn't going to let anything spoil their friendship, not even Roger.

Donald Martin was holding Noble while Hazel cleaned his paws of blood.

"Do you think he's been in a fight?" he asked, "or maybe had some sort of accident?"

Hazel shook her head. "Who knows, you know Noble, he goes where he wants and does what he wants." She checked over his body and looked into his eyes. "He doesn't seem harmed," she concluded, ruffling his fur, just a bit, well, bloody. Noble purred. "And he doesn't seem bothered," added Hazel, "in fact, he seems positively cheerful... for a cat that is."

Donald shooed him from his lap. "Down you go, old boy," he smiled, "no more sympathy for you."

"Going already?" asked Hazel, as Donald stood up.

"Got to get ready for my date tonight," he grinned, winking at his Aunt. "Kim's moved back to her flat and we're going out to celebrate."

"Moved back?"

"Yes, she was staying with a friend of hers from the radio station while it had... a 'make-over' I think she called it."

Hazel looked bemused. "Young girls nowadays," she said, shaking her head, "always changing things. In my day, you stuck with what you'd got and were grateful for it. And that included your Uncle Charlie, God rest his soul."

Donald gave her tiny frame a hug. "I'll bring her around to meet you soon," he said, "you'll like her, she's really lovely and..." Hazel held up her hand to stop him.

"Go on with you," she smiled, "you don't want to be late for her." She led Donald to the door. "And we'll meet... when the time's right," she assured him sagely.

Donald and Kim had a wonderful evening. They had dinner at the Green

Room, chosen by Donald and then went to a cocktail bar chosen by Kim, for a nightcap. Donald never took his eyes of Kim all evening. She wore a shimmering silver dress which caught the light every time she moved and long silver earrings which danced around her face. She'd had her blonde hair cut in a long 'bob' which she'd topped off with a red velvet rose.

Donald had never seen anyone so beautiful in all his life.

On an impulse, he moved closer to her and took hold of her hand.

"Kim," he said, his voice hoarse with tension. She turned her full attention on him and waited.

He squeezed her hand. "Kim," he tried again, "would you like..." the words dried.

Kim smiled and urged him on. "Yes," she repeated, "would I like... what?" Donald took a deep breath and took hold of her other hand as well.

"Would you like me to be... your boyfriend?" he blurted out, "I mean, your... REAL boyfriend?"

Kim almost burst with happiness.

She leaned forward and kissed him lightly on the lips. "I would like nothing better," she replied softly, "than to have you, Donald Martin, as my REAL boyfriend."

Donald almost spilled the drinks as he pulled her to her feet and to the cheers of the other customers he kissed her passionately and fully.

Suddenly aware of where he was, Donald returned Kim to her seat.

"Sorry," he grinned to the rest of the room, "but she's just agreed to be my girlfriend."

"Then you'd better 'get a room'," the barman winked and to a round of applause and knowing laughter, Kim and Donald went home... to Kim's flat.

After two years of almost brutal sex with Roger and Darko, being with Donald was a revelation to her. She had experienced plenty of loveless sex but never the joy of making love with someone you loved and who loved you.

She now knew for certain Don loved her, as much as she had grown to love this gentle giant of a man.

They lay together in one another's arms and marvelled at the way they seemed to know what the other was feeling and as the sun rose on the couple, Kim rolled over and swung her legs out onto the floor.

"You're hungry," she laughed, "I can tell."

"Hungry for you," Don grinned, pulling her back into the bed.

"Bacon and eggs?" she asked coyly, "or a quick cup of coffee and then off to work."

Don sat upright. "I forgot!" he exclaimed, "I'm on the Sunday Show." He checked his watch and pretending penitence he said, "Bacon and eggs, please and you're right, I'm starving."

The ease of being together continued through breakfast and when Donald had kissed her goodbye, she decided to go back to bed. Donald may have been hungry, but she was happily exhausted.

The ringtone of her mobile phone roused her from sleep. "Donald," she said, "go back to work!"

"Who's Donald?" said the man's voice.

"I'm sorry," said Kim, "turning over and leaning on her elbows, "who's this?"

"Don't you recognise me?"

Kim searched her mind. Very few people knew her mobile number and none of them fitted the voice.

"Sorry, I don't," she said, becoming concerned.

"Kim, darling," he said, "it's Darko."

Kim almost dropped the phone.

"Darko," she repeated, her voice rising in panic. "But, how did you get this number?"

"It doesn't matter how I got your number," he insisted, "aren't you glad to hear from me?"

Kim tried to quieten the thoughts racing through her head. He had her mobile number and she would change that first thing on Monday morning.

"I don't know how you got my number Darko, but don't phone me again."

She could almost see him shrug in amusement. "Well, if you don't answer your phone," he said steadily, "I'll just have to come up to little old West Hampton and pay you a visit."

Kim's grip on the mobile tightened. He seemed to know her address as well.

"Who told..." but even as the question formed on her lips, she knew the answer. Roger Lomax.

She could feel her shoulders tighten as she fought to get back her self-control.

It was plain to her now, Roger couldn't get to her directly, so he was using Darko to keep control over her life.

"No," she said quickly, "don't do that, I'll answer the phone when you ring."

"Good," Darko said smoothly, "now that's better."

"What do you want?" Kim asked resignation heavy in her voice. A few hours ago, everything in her world had been glorious, she'd found love with a wonderful man and now..."

"Kim, sweetie," came the reply, "don't sound so sad, you know how much I lust after you and now with Roger out of the way... well, there's nothing to stop us enjoying one another more often."

"What?"

"I said, there's nothing to stop us..."

"No, not that, did you say Roger was... out of the way?"

"Well, not yet he isn't, but soon he'll be off to..." Darko stopped himself. "But enough of him, how about coming up to London next weekend, you know, pick up where we left off."

Kim felt a wave of disgust wash over her.

"Darko," she began, thinking she might appeal to his 'better nature,' "I'm not into that anymore, so please, just leave me alone."

Before he had a chance to say anymore, Kim switched off the phone and tossed it onto the bedside table.

She lay back on the bed and covered her face with her hands.

Somehow, Roger had managed to bring the past into the present and in doing so, ruin any chance she had of having a future with Don.

She dressed slowly and spent the rest of Sunday in a maze of possible scenarios, what if, she thought, Darko were to come up to the flat and Don was here, what if he insisted on her making the trip to London whenever he felt like sex, what if he told Don about her past.

Each possibility fed her fear and by the end of the day, she felt the only way for her to prevent Don from being hurt by her past was to break off their fledgling relationship.

Chapter 20

The 'bloody' drive to Roger's consulting rooms took all his control to complete. He dabbed at the blood that threatened to trickle into his eyes.

"BITCH," he repeated to himself, over and over, venting his anger on Vanessa.

That cursed cat had appeared from nowhere and he wasn't about to believe that she knew nothing about it.

"Her and her bloody animals," he seethed, "she's probably been feeding it for months."

By the time he arrived at his therapy rooms, he realised that his legs were trembling and his hand shaking as he tried to unlock the door.

"BITCH," he said again, jabbing the key at the lock. Total control was a way of life for him, but after the attack, he was shocked to find that he'd lost it.

"To a BLOODY CAT!" he continued to fume as, with trembling fingers, he finally got into his rooms and poured himself a large Scotch.

He looked at himself in the mirror. "Christ," he muttered, desperate to find a way of explaining the mess of his face to his clients. He took out the First Aid Box and gingerly spread on an antiseptic cream, which stung more than the scratches. He poured himself a second drink and returned to his desk.

Time to take control back. He switched on his computer and Googled riding lessons in London. There was a huge choice, but he settled on the cheapest. He dialled the number. "Redwood Riding Stables," said the plumy voice.

"Good afternoon," Roger cleared his throat, "I see from your website that you offer a 'Learn to Ride in a Day' course."

"We do," came the reply, her voice brightening at the prospect of a sale. "Is it for an adult or a child?"

"Child," said Roger, twelve years old.

"And when would you like to book this?"

Roger looked at his desk calendar. "How about Saturday 2nd November?" he asked.

He listened while pages of paper were flicked over.

"2nd November, yes, that would be fine. And the name is?"

"Lomax," said Roger, it's for my daughter... birthday surprise."

"And her name is?"

"Sophie."

"Great," said the voice, "that's it booked. Do you want to pay by card over the phone or will we invoice you?"

"I'll pay cash on the day, if that's alright," Roger replied, offering his preferred option.

"And could you send me a brochure... to put with her card you know."

"It'll be sent out as soon as you give me your address."

Roger gave her the address of the consulting rooms and hung up.

The second part of his plan was completed. He had intended to wait until nearer Sophie's birthday on the tenth but Vanessa's disquieting news about the pregnancy and the attack by that blasted cat, had made him decide to bring the date of his plan forward. All he wanted now was to take his daughter away with him and live the life he craved. His bank balance had been building nicely and had topped the £8,000 mark.

Hypnotherapy was a very nice little earner, he smiled to himself, and the 'extras' he convinced some of his ladies that they needed, had been a lucrative bonus.

He heard movement on the other side of the door and looked at his watch.

He wasn't expecting any clients. Cautiously, he opened the door and there stood Enid Rawlings. Her hand flew to her mouth when she saw his face. "I saw your car and thought I ought to check and see if everything was alright," she quivered. "You're not normally here on Saturday evening and I was just passing..."

Roger smirked to himself, poor old gullible Enid.

But what he said was, "Enid, how kind of you to be concerned. Yes, yes,

I know," he continued, pointing to his face, "had a bit of a tussle with a holly bush I was trying to cut back. Gardening eh, not the gentle pursuit they say."

"Are you really alright?" she asked, moving towards him deep concern showing in her eyes.

"I'm fine," Roger assured her, "now, if you don't mind." He ushered her towards the door. "I'll see you at the Circle on Monday, as usual."

Enid turned abruptly as she reached the door. "And," she added almost coyly, "will you still be able to take, you know, individual appointments?"

Roger almost felt like slapping her, snivelling slut.

"Of course," he assured her, forcing his mouth into an uncomfortable smile, as he almost pushed her out the door, locking it behind her.

He went back to his computer.

Now that the horse riding part of his plan was in place, it was now time to book the flight. He went on the British Airways website and from then on, it was a piece of cake. The booking was made and he printed off the itinerary.

"Perfect timings," he murmured, "just perfect."

***

He would spend the night at his clinic, he had no wish to go back to the house, in fact, he had no wish to go back there ever again. He treated himself to the last of the whisky. The 2 November couldn't come soon enough.

On the Monday after Noble's heroic attack on Roger, Vanessa felt she should go to Laburnum Cottage and check he was alright. She would have loved to have shown Hazel the picture of her son, but Roger had seen to it, that this was now impossible.

She had heard nothing from him for the rest of that weekend and he hadn't even returned to sleep in Sophie's room. Tonight, however, was the Circle and they'd both have to be there. She hugged herself protectively, she didn't care what Roger said or did, there was no way her pregnancy was to be terminated, either legally or if Roger had his way, illegally.

She put the thoughts out of her head as she wheeled her bike out of the garage. The cycle ride to Hazel's always relaxed her and today was no exception.

"Hazel," she called through the open door. The figure of her friend came bustling towards her.

"Vanessa," she cooed, "and to what do we owe the pleasure of this visit?"

"You mean you don't know?" Vanessa said, in mock surprise.

Hazel gave her a knowing smile.

"It's about Noble, actually," Vanessa continued, sitting on her usual spot on Hazel's sofa.

"Noble?" Hazel echoed, "ah so, do I take it you know something about his red paws?"

"He attacked Roger," Vanessa stated bluntly.

Hazel's eyes widened. "Attacked?"

Vanessa explained about the scan and the printout and Roger's anger when she had told him about the baby..."

"And that's when Noble attacked, is it?"

Vanessa nodded.

"I believe he saved my son's life," she said softly. "He knew the danger I was in and, well... I didn't even know he was there, but he must have been watching everything. Quite literally, he was up in the branches of the apple tree."

"So," asked Hazel, sitting down beside her, "what are you going to do, about the baby I mean?"

Vanessa looked shocked, "Why keep him, of course, there's no way I'm doing anything to harm a hair on his head."

Hazel squeezed her hand. "Good," she said, "but remember, Roger doesn't like to be crossed and Noble might not be there the next time."

Vanessa took a deep breath. "I have you and my mother and Noble and most of all, I have me," she smiled bravely, "and Sophie and the new baby," she added. "How can I fail!"

Hazel wasn't so sure, from what she knew of Roger Lomax, he wasn't the type to give up easily and she sensed there was much more hurt to come for Vanessa before he'd finished.

"I almost forgot," Vanessa said, bringing a cream envelope out of her bag.

"Here," she handed it to Hazel, "read that."

Hazel read the short note. "And look," Vanessa waved the cheque in the air, "all the money I need to buy things for the baby, but didn't you know that would happen. Remember, the prediction about money coming to meet my needs... and here it is?"

Hazel smiled. Jennifer had found a way.

"I think we should celebrate with a nice cup of Lady Grey tea," she said with her usual graciousness.

Vanessa tucked the cheque and envelope back into her bag. "Agreed," she said, "and I'll open my own bank account with Mr Parker this week to keep it safe till it's needed."

"How's Donald," Vanessa asked, as Hazel made the tea.

"Well, he's in love," she replied, "so I think he's feeling pretty good."

"Kim Mason, isn't it? His girlfriend's name I mean."

Hazel turned her enquiring eyes on her. "It is," replied Hazel, "any reason for asking?"

Vanessa felt herself colour with embarrassment. "I'm sure it's a coincidence, but one of Roger's colleagues was called Kim Mason and I wondered if you'd met her."

"Not yet," said Hazel, "but I'm sure I will."

She handed Vanessa her tea.

"Tell me about the Kim Mason you know," she enquired, "then when I do meet her, I'll be able to judge if she's the same person."

Vanessa sipped her tea thoughtfully. "Well, she's very beautiful, young and beautiful, with long blonde hair…; and I think she's a massage therapist. At least that's what I've heard, you know, from the other women at the Circle. One or two of them have gone to her for treatments."

"And, how did you meet her?"

"Oh, she dropped Roger off a couple of times, after he'd been giving talks to her clients. So, I suppose I've only seen her briefly, but I've spoken to her on the phone a couple of times." Vanessa grimaced. "She'd phone to tell me Roger would be late home, you know, held up at one of these meetings."

Hazel could see the doubts in Vanessa's eyes.

"Nothing more than that?"

Vanessa shrugged. "Don't know," she said, "at least I hope not."

"Well," she refilled their teacups, "if and when I do meet her, I'll let you know my thoughts."

They finished their tea.

"Meditation Circle tonight," Vanessa said quietly, "Roger will be there, but if it's like every other time, I'll be in and gone before he shows face."

"How's Sophie," Hazel suddenly asked.

"Sophie?" Vanessa repeated her daughter's name, "fine, I think, just fine. She's like all young girls, wrapped up in her own world of horses and clothes."

"Keep an eye on her Vanessa," Hazel cautioned, "she's young and very vulnerable."

Before she could ask anything further Hazel opened the door. "Looks like rain," she said, sniffing the air, "better get Noble in from the garden. And Vanessa," she added, "he looked very pleased with himself when he came home with his red paws."

Nobel ran in and Hazel gently closed the door, but a feeling of great unease was circling around her. Something was wrong, but what?

Chapter 21

Kim went to work with a heavy heart. She longed to see Don again, but feared their meeting in equal measures, but he wasn't there. She'd forgotten he had the Monday off as he'd worked a Sunday shift and she hoped the window of time would allow her to think things through and avoid making any hasty decisions about their future.

Liz waved at her through the glass and mimed drinking a cup of coffee.

Kim nodded. Her friend was due to finish her broadcast at nine o'clock.

She made her way to the small canteen and poured out two coffees, placing them on a table in the far corner of the room.

A few minutes later, Liz bounced in, her eyes scanning the room.

He face lit up when she saw Kim. "What're you doing in the corner?" she grinned, "been a naughty girl, have we?"

The look of despair on Kim's face brought the banter to a halt.

Liz sat down, coffee forgotten as her concern grew.

"What on earth's the matter?" she asked gently, "you look as though you've seen a ghost."

"I kind of have."

Liz leaned towards her and took her hand. "He's not been back bothering you again, has he? Roger, I mean."

Kim shook her head. "No," she whispered, "but he might as well have."

Liz adopted her big sister voice. "Tell me what's happened."

"You know all about Roger," Kim began, "but you don't know about Darko."

"Darko!" exclaimed Liz, "what kind of a name is that?"

"Polish, I think, or it's his nickname, that's all I know him by."

"OK... but what's he to you?"

"I used to go up to London with Roger to Darko's Private Sex Club." Vanessa's voice was so low, Liz strained to hear her.

"Sex club?" Liz echoed, a hint of shock in her voice.

"Please, Liz, don't judge me. You know Roger had me under some kind of mind control, but I'm not now and I just want to forget everything about the past, but..." her chin began to quiver.

Liz waited till Kim regained control, lifting her eyes to meet those of her friend.

"Roger's given Darko my mobile phone number and probably my home phone number, but worst of all, my address."

"And he's been in touch," finished Liz.

"Does Don know?" but almost as she said it, she added, "no, of course he doesn't."

"Oh, Liz, we had such a wonderful night together on Saturday. For the first time in my life I've found love, real love and..." the chin quivering started again, but this time it was followed by tears.

"Come on," Liz said, "you're in no fit state to work. You're coming home with me, so we can get this sorted out."

Unable to put up any argument, Kim did as she was told.

Liz was kindness itself. She settled her in her big armchair with a box of tissues and left her alone while she made them their coffees.

When she came through with the steaming mugs, Kim had got her self-control back, but the stack of used tissues told their own story.

"Here," Liz said, "drink this."

Silently, they drank the coffee and it was Liz who broached the subject again.

"This Darko," she said, "did you and he...?" Kim nodded.

"So, he's after more of the same thing?" she nodded again.

"But, why did Roger give him your address?"

Kim drew in a deep breath. "He wouldn't say, but he did say that Roger was going away somewhere, so maybe it was a 'parting gift'."

Liz frowned. "How about reporting him to the police, you know, anonymously? Surely, what he's doing is illegal... isn't it?"

Instantly realising the implications, Liz shut up. "Sorry."

"No, I'm sorry," Kim said, standing up and reaching for her coat, "dragging you into this mess. This is something I'll have to sort out for myself. After all, it's my past and my problem."

She hugged her friend. "Thanks for listening," she said appreciatively, "I'll be back at work tomorrow and, Liz, don't say anything to Don, will you."

Liz made a zipping motion across her lips.

She had just opened the door of her flat when Kim heard the ringing of her phone. She threw down her coat and keys and stared at it as if it were alive. After seven rings her answering machine cut in.

"Kim," said the male voice, "it's Don... if you're there, please pick up, I'm worried about you?"

Kim grasped the phone. "Hi Don," she said, "yes I'm here, I was sleeping."

"Sleeping! Are you ill?"

"Just a bit of a cold," she lied, "Liz insisted on sending me home."

"But you're alright?" She reassured him she was.

"Anyway, why the phone call?" she asked.

"Well," he said, "the reason I needed to speak to you is... I'm at Aunt Hazel's and she's invited us both for tea, you know, so the two of you can meet and ..." he tailed off into the silence. "Are you there?"

Kim snapped back to reality. "Yes, yes, I'm here… that'd be fine. I mean, I'd like that too, just not today."

"Of course not," Don laughed, "this is about setting a date while I'm here."

"Right."

"So?"

Kim tried to think, but couldn't.

"How about Wednesday... after work?" Don suggested.

Kim's heart was thumping. She was beginning to run the 'what-if' scenarios again.

"Great," she agreed, just wanting to end the phone call.

"Are you sure you're alright?" Don asked again.

"Just tired," she replied.

She heard Don repeat the date to his Aunt.

"Kim," he came back on the phone, "Aunt Hazel says that's fine and she's really looking forward to meeting you."

"Me too," she said trying to sound enthusiastic.

"See you tomorrow then, at work."

"Yeah, tomorrow. Bye Don."

Kim felt drained, physically and emotionally. What was she to do, she asked herself, but she already knew the answer. Break things off.

That night, Kim slept the sleep of the exhausted and when the morning came she switched on her 'automatic pilot' and made her way into work.

Luckily, Liz read the situation and kept her busy and away from Donald.

"Can I pinch Kim this evening," she asked Don as the clock moved towards home time, "we hardly have any girl-time now and I think she needs a treat."

Don readily agreed. "I know she's got a bit of a cold or something, so a little TLC wouldn't go amiss. You won't keep her up too late though, will you?"

"Oh, don't worry," said Liz comfortingly, "she'll be tucked up in bed by ten."

Assured, Don said, "Get her well for tomorrow. We're going to visit my only Aunt for tea and she's so looking forward to it."

Things had progressed that far, thought Liz. This relationship was serious.

With a cheery goodbye to Don, she went to collect Kim and tell her about the plan to avoid Donald till, at least, tomorrow.

"Thanks, Liz," she said. "I'm going to get in touch with Darko tonight and see if I can get this sorted."

"Good luck," she said supportively, "and if there's anything else I can do, just ask."

Kim pressed her arm. "Just put up a prayer for me, I think I'm going to need a miracle."

After forcing herself to eat a chicken sandwich, Kim poured herself a large glass of white wine and dug out her address book from her handbag.

In the back of the book was a business card with Darko's private phone number on it. She had found it on the floor after one of Roger's visits and decided to keep it. Right now, she was glad she did as it gave her the edge. What Darko wouldn't be expecting was a phone call from her.

A quizzical voice answered on the third ring. "Darko," it said, "who's this?"

"Kim."

Darko flinched. How had she got his private number?

"Kim!" he exclaimed, "what a surprise... hey, how did you get this number?"

Kim fisted the air. "Oh, probably the same way that you got mine," she purred.

Double-crossing bastard, thought Darko, no women had this private number, not even his wife and now... "Well," he replied, "guess that's us even, sweetie. Anyway, why the call? You looking for some action?"

"No Darko," she said, "I just need to talk to you."

"I'm listening."

"Can I be honest with you?" Kim asked, with just the right amount of neediness in her voice.

"Just as long as you don't expect me to be honest back," he laughed.

Kim crossed her fingers and took a deep breath. "It's like this, Darko," she began, "things have changed for me and Roger and I don't think coming to the club is a good idea anymore."

"So you want me to come and visit you there, is that it?"

"No Darko," she said quickly, "I've got the chance to start a new life and... well, I can only do that if you let me."

"Mmmmhhhh, and what's lover boy's name?" he asked, "Donald wasn't it you thought was phoning you but it turned out to be little old me."

"Oh, Darko," Kim began to beg, "please let it go. He doesn't know anything about the past and..."

"And you don't want me ruining your pretty picture."

"You can have any woman you want Darko, you don't need me as well."

"It's not a question of need sweetie, it's a question of desire and, Christ, do I desire you."

The line went quiet. "Let me think about it," he said finally, Darko don't need nobody, but nothing's free Kim, not even your pretty future."

The line went dead.

Kim slowly replaced the receiver. She knew Darko played to his own rules. The more he was pushed, the harder he would hold on to her. She refilled her wine glass. At least he had listened.

Chapter 22

Kim slept better that night. The call to Darko had been her last hope before having to break things off with Donald. Anyway, that was how it felt and she had done something, at least.

She told Liz about the phone call to Darko. "So, the hope is, I can appeal to his better nature, if he has one that is."

Liz looked past Kim's shoulder and waved. "Don's coming down the corridor," she said quietly, "and there're no prizes for guessing who he's looking for."

Kim swung round, her face creasing into a wide smile as Don came loping towards her.

"Are you feeling better?" he asked breathlessly.

Kim glanced at Liz's disappearing back. "Thanks to Liz," she said, "I'm lots better."

"So, are we alright for tea with the Auntie?"

"Looking forward to it," laughed Kim. "See you in the car park around four o'clock. We'll take my car, if that's alright."

"As long as you bring me into work with you tomorrow," Don replied with a mischievous glint in his eye.

"Maybe," Kim said equalling his innuendo, before leaving him in the corridor grinning.

The day flew by and Kim felt her muscles relax as the strain of Darko's earlier phone call and hers, begging him to leave her alone, diminished. By the time she got to the end of the day, she was really looking forward to the promised high tea, her appetite having returned to something like normal.

"Hop in," she called to the waiting Don, flipping the key to unlock the doors of her car from across the car park.

She climbed in beside him and keyed the ignition. "How do I look," she asked, "will I pass muster?"

He kissed her on the cheek. "You look wonderful, as usual and Aunt Hazel will love you as much as I do."

"You think?"

"I know."

Kim was captivated by Willow Walk and Laburnum Cottage. "What a beautiful spot," she said, taking in every detail of the little house and garden. "And there's a cat!" she exclaimed, kneeling down and stretching out her hand.

"Here Kitty," she called softly.

"His name's Noble," whispered Donald, "isn't he a stunner?"

Kim nodded, noticing the cat's eyes as he moved towards her.

"And those eyes," she said, surprised, "they're different colours."

Noble sat down in front of her, allowing Kim to stroke his head and tickle his chin.

"He likes you," murmured Donald. "You're very privileged, you know, he doesn't let everyone get this close."

Hazel watched the scene from behind the muslin curtains and nodded, smiling. Noble was never wrong about people.

"We're here," Donald called, ushering Kim into the front room. Kim saw that the table was laid with a veritable feast, there were tiny triangle shaped sandwiches, scones flanked by jam and cream and a beautifully risen Victoria Sponge. She felt her mouth begin to water.

"Come in dear," said the neat and tidy woman, looking perfectly in tune with her surroundings. "I hope you're both hungry."

Without answering, Don looked at Kim. "Aunt Hazel," he said formally, "this is Miss Kim Mason. Kim," he continued, "this is my wonderful Aunt, Hazel Hazelwood."

The serious introduction broke any ice that could have been forming and both women burst out laughing. Don joined in. "What!" he exclaimed.

"Men," said Hazel, opening her arms, "give Don's old Auntie a hug, my dear."

Willingly, Kim obliged. The afternoon was going to be wonderful.

Hazel warmed to Kim's sunny nature as they ate their fill and Kim felt she had known Hazel forever, not just a few hours.

The cottage seemed to cast a spell over Kim, it was almost as if the walls were listening in and enjoying the day as much as she was. As she sipped her third cup of tea and Don told Hazel about his work at the radio station, Kim looked around the room. No matter where her eyes rested, there was something else she hadn't noticed at first glance. There were sparkling crystals that caught the sunlight, carved figures and alabaster angels, wall hangings depicting far-off lands and candles of many sizes but always coloured white.

"...So, time to do the washing up young Donald," said Hazel, "while Kim and I get to know one another better."

At the sound of her name, Kim's attention came back to the table.

"Slave driver," grinned Donald, "leave the hard work to us men."

Hazel led a smiling Kim over to the sofa.

"That was delicious Mrs Hazelwood, you're a wonderful baker."

"Oh, years of practice my dear," said Hazel, "and call me Hazel, please."

"So, tell me, Kim," she began, patting the cushion next to her for Kim to sit on, "how long have you worked at the radio station?"

"Not long really," she replied, settling herself into the velvet softness, "a friend of mine, Liz, is a presenter there and she managed to find an opening for me on her production team, so there I am and, hopefully, there I'll stay."

"Speaking of friends," continued Hazel, "I believe you know a friend of mine."

"Really," Kim said, stunned that they should have anyone in common. "Who?"

"Her name's Vanessa," Hazel watched Kim's eyes as she said the full name, "Vanessa Lomax."

Kim felt the blood drain from her face. Desperately trying to control her voice she managed to reply... "Vanessa, yes. I know her... but how do you...?" Kim's voice froze. This was just too horrible to bear.

"Oh, she visits here often," Hazel went on as if she hadn't noticed Kim's discomfort. "She's pregnant you know. Doctors say it's going to be a boy too." Kim couldn't believe her ears. Vanessa pregnant!

"Didn't you know?" Hazel asked, "didn't she tell you?"

Hazel's eyes held Kim's transfixed. "No..." she mumbled hoarsely, "I didn't know."

"Are you alright, my dear," Hazel asked, "you look as if you've seen a ghost."

Kim felt herself crumble inside. Was she never to be free from her past and the ghosts it brought with it?

"Not really," she muttered, "I think I need a little air actually."

"Donald," Hazel called through to the kitchen.

"Kim's feeling a bit queasy, I think, perhaps it's time to take her home."

Don came rushing through. "Are you feeling unwell again, darling?" he soothed. Turning to Hazel he told her about Kim's cold earlier in the week. "Perhaps it's back," he decided, helping Kim to her feet.

"C'mon sweetheart, it's back to bed for you. Give me your car keys and we'll soon have you home."

Donald looped her arm through his.

"I'm so sorry," murmured Kim. "And, thanks for the lovely tea."

"My pleasure," replied Hazel, taking her hand and pressing a small black velvet bag into it. "It's just a little something to keep you safe," she said "wherever you go."

Donald settled her into the car. "OK?" he asked. Kim nodded.

"I'll be fine," she said, "must be a virus."

Once she was home and Donald had left, she opened the little drawstring around the velvet bag. Inside was a silver chain, on the end of which hung the tiny silver head of an elephant. Instinctively, she put it round her neck and looked at herself in the mirror wearing it. Almost immediately, the fear and shock seemed to drift from her system and she somehow knew, from that moment, everything was going to be alright.

She lay down on her bed and pulled the fur throw around her. How had Vanessa become pregnant, she wondered, Roger never had sex with her, or so he said and she wasn't the type to play away. Well, she'd had sex with someone, that was for sure. Perhaps Roger had decided to go back to being a family man, after their breakup, perhaps he wanted a son to carry on his name.

But even as she said it, she knew Roger would never want a son, he liked the attention of women too much to share it with another male, even Vanessa's son. Whatever the reason, Kim was just glad to be out of his clutches and reasoned that Vanessa couldn't tell Hazel anything really about her past... unless Roger confessed everything to her.

The new thought hit her hard and she clutched the silver elephant head.

The deception she was continuing to inflict on Donald was getting too much for her and now, it seemed that fate was conspiring against her to also reveal her past to Hazel Hazelwood.

Chapter 23

As the school holidays drew to a close, Sophie became more and more excited. In September, she would start the next stage of her education at the comprehensive school in Reading and that meant a bus journey there and back every day and... BOYS!

She and Jane had spent hours discussing their tactics, how they would wear their new uniforms and which of the rest of their friends would be in their new classes, but most of all they thought endlessly about boys.

Her awakening sexuality had been noticed by Vanessa, her daughter's periods had started and her shape was changing. She knew the primary school had touched on the subject of sex but Vanessa felt that now was probably the time to make sure she knew a bit more about the pitfalls of unprotected sex. And not only that, she wanted to tell her about the baby.

After tea had been eaten and the dishes washed and dried, Vanessa found Sophie lying on her tummy in the living room, flicking through the latest celebrity magazine.

"Anything interesting," Vanessa asked, taking up a position on the floor beside her.

Without looking up Sophie shrugged, "I don't think there's anything that would interest you."

"What, nobody expecting a baby this week?" Sophie looked up, a question mark almost visible in her eyes.

"No."

"What would you say to a new baby brother?" Vanessa asked, unable to think of a roundabout way of broaching the subject.

Again without raising her eyes from the magazine Sophie replied, "I'd probably say 'Hi baby brother!'" She smiled to herself at her cleverness.

"Well, that's good," Vanessa said, taking a deep breath, "because mummy is expecting a baby early next year and it's a boy."

Every muscle in Sophie's body seemed to freeze. She looked at her mother in horror. "But I don't want a baby brother," she said, seriousness written all over her young face.

Vanessa's lips tightened and she raised her shoulders to her ears. "Well," she said, "you're going to get one."

"But, I'm going to the big school soon and I don't want to bring my friends home to a crying baby and nappies... ugh."

"It won't be like that, Sophie, babies are what happens when two people love one another and decide to create a new life, just like daddy and I did so you could be born... and speaking about being..." but before Vanessa could start her monologue on birth control, Sophie interrupted.

"Does daddy know?"

Vanessa nodded. "He does."

With accuracy beyond her years, Sophie hit her mother's Achilles heel.

"Is that why he's hardly ever home anymore?"

Vanessa flinched. "No Sophie, he's just busy at the clinic."

The child in Sophie began to surface and with it, teenage tears.

"Come here," said Vanessa, putting her arms around her daughter.

"I know it's a bit of a shock, but you'll soon get used to it and anyway, just think how grown-up you'll become with a little brother to love."

Then the real reason for Sophie's tears became evident.

"Will daddy still love me, when the new baby comes?"

Vanessa felt a flash of hurt but hugged her daughter closer. "Of course he will, he'll always love you and so will I." Sophie seemed pacified.

"Now, dry those eyes and let's see what these celebs are up to in your magazine and tomorrow, we'll go into Reading and buy your new school uniform. And Jane can come as well if you like."

Sophie nodded. "I'd like."

She was still very much a child, Vanessa knew, despite her bravado and just like children everywhere, all she really needed was to know she was loved.

Roger insisted on taking Sophie to the bus-stop for her first day at the comprehensive. She was developing nicely, he observed, and in her new school uniform looked positively delicious. He felt a surge of jealously as he saw the gathering of boys waiting for the bus.

"Now, Sophie, don't you be wasting your time on boys," he cautioned, guiding her to the bunch of girls hanging back in the queue.

"There's Jane." Sophie squealed, pointing to her friend. "I'll be alright now daddy, Jane and me are going to stick together, so you can go now."

Roger felt his teeth clench. They always did when he felt his control over his daughter slipping.

He dug into his pocket and pulled out a large envelope. "Here," he said, "this is your birthday surprise. I'll see you later. Love you."

Sophie took the envelope. "But, what is it?"

"Open it and see," Roger said, "once you're on the bus."

He hadn't meant to give her the brochure about the horse riding so soon, but the pressure to bring her attention back to him was too strong.

"See you later." He blew her a kiss and was gone.

Once she and Jane were settled on the bus, Sophie waved the envelope at her.

"What is it?" Jane asked.

Sophie shrugged. "Daddy gave it to me, said it was my birthday surprise."

Sophie opened the envelope and extracted the brochure.

Both the girls' eyes lit up.

"Wow," said Jane, "horse-riding lessons... and in London."

Sophie was pleased at her friend's reaction.

"When are you going?"

"Don't know yet, but daddy will probably tell me later."

She stuffed the brochure back into its envelope and then into her backpack.

"And that's not the only news I have," she added smugly.

Jane's eyes widened further. "Tell me."

"Mum's pregnant," she stated feeling very grown-up, "and it's a boy."

Jane's mouth fell open. "You lucky thing," she said, "I wish my mum was having a baby," she said, "I hate being the only one."

Sophie grinned, she was having a wonderful day and when one of the boys at the back of the bus asked her name, she felt her life couldn't get better than this.

Sophie and Jane spent the first day at school finding their way around. It was all so different from primary school and Sophie loved it. By the time the bell rang at the end of the school day, she couldn't wait to get home and tell her parents how wonderful it all was and give daddy a hug for her surprise.

But Vanessa was alone in the house when she came in from school.

She had made her daughter a special tea with all her favourites and could see Sophie blossoming before her eyes.

"Good day?" she asked.

"The best," her daughter squealed. "School is the best thing ever."

The news of the pregnancy had seemed to be have been accepted by her daughter already and Vanessa was glad. She wanted her to feel the freedom of being young and carefree with her whole life in front of her to explore.

"And, look what I've got," Sophie said, taking the brochure from her bag and waving it in the air. "Daddy gave me this at the bus stop this morning."

Redwood Riding Stables, Vanessa read, in London.

"It's my birthday surprise," she said, "I'm going to have real riding lessons at a school in LONDON." Sophie was breathing hard with excitement, "how cool is that?"

"Very cool," confirmed Vanessa, "and when is daddy taking you there?"

"Don't know yet," Sophie tossed the answer back, "but it must be soon."

Vanessa felt a shimmer of disquiet as her daughter skipped from the room and upstairs to change. Roger had given no indication of what he had planned, but it had certainly hit the spot with Sophie. There was nothing she could do about it at the moment, but she took a note of the phone number of the riding school, just in case Sophie lost the brochure, she told herself, or if she needed to just check the place out, which was the real reason. After his violent reaction to her pregnancy, she felt Roger could no longer be trusted. As Hazel had reminded her, Sophie was still a young and vulnerable child.

Chapter 24

Roger made the announcement to both of them at breakfast on the Thursday.

He was taking Sophie to the riding school the following Saturday, a week before her birthday. Sophie clapped her hands with glee and hugged her father, jumping up and down as she did so.

Vanessa looked on, questions without answers forming in her mind.

"So," Roger was saying, "we'll have to leave early on Saturday morning to get to the stables for nine o'clock. The lessons start at ten." Sophie nodded in agreement. "And I want you to pack a little bag so you can freshen up after the lessons and before…"he pulled his daughter's head closer and whispered in her ear. Vanessa strained to hear but couldn't.

"Really?" Sophie's eyes got even wider.

"Really," Roger confirmed. "Now, off you go, I need to speak to your mother."

Without a glance at Vanessa, Sophie almost ran from the room.

"Don't forget your bus pass," she called to her daughter's disappearing frame.

She poured herself some tea and sat very still, facing Roger. Whatever he was going to say, she was determined not to panic or let him overwhelm her.

She waited.

Roger's words, when they came, were cold as ice.

"It pleases me to take my daughter on this trip," he said. "It displeases me that you intend to still be here, in your pregnant condition, when I get back." He pushed a piece of paper towards her on which he'd written a mobile number.

"This is the number of a doctor who will do what is needed." He stood up, staring menacingly at her. "Make sure you use it."

Anger rising inside her, Vanessa also stood up and just like Roger had done to her with the printout of the scan, she slowly tore the piece of paper into shreds and dropped them on the table.

For a moment she thought he was going to hit her, but she remained unmoved. Despite the fact that her legs were trembling and her heart was thudding in her chest, she held his stare.

Roger smirked, his lips forming a snarl around his teeth.

"Feeling brave, are we?" he said his voice low and harsh. Vanessa gulped, wishing she felt as brave as the front she was managing to put on.

The chair grated against the floor tiles as he pushed it back, tipped over and fell with a crash.

"You have till Sunday night," he added, "then we'll do it my way."

Vanessa felt she was going to faint, but kept breathing as steadily as she could, as he left the room.

She almost collapsed into the chair, her fear washing over her in nauseating waves.

She had to get away from here, she thought frantically, but the same blank wall met her every option. And, then there was Sophie, she couldn't bear to leave her behind, not her little girl.

Vanessa went to the sink and splashed her face with cool water. There had to be a way... she just had to find it.

Vanessa hardly slept during the Friday night and at around six o'clock she heard movement coming from Sophie's room. Roger's deep voice giving what sounded like instructions and Sophie's voice, over-excited, doing what he asked. She got up and pulling on her dressing gown went past the bedroom and downstairs to the kitchen. At least she would be able to kiss her daughter goodbye at the door and wave her off in the car.

Sophie came down the stairs first, lugging her little wheeled case behind her.

"Mum!" she exclaimed "did we wake you, sorry."

Vanessa hugged her and kissed her cheek. "I was awake," she said, "and anyway, I wanted to wave you goodbye."

"It'll be such fun," Sophie glowed with anticipation, "imagine real riding lessons and in London. Jane was sooooooo jealous."

Roger joined them, his case much bigger. Vanessa's eyebrows pulled together. Why such a big case, she wondered. What was in it? As if reading her mind, Roger leaned close to her. "Can't ride without riding gear, can she?"

Vanessa's face relaxed, "No, of course not," she muttered, "I didn't know you'd bought her any... that's all."

As he wheeled the suitcase past her, he pushed another piece of paper in her hand. "Don't spoil this one now, will you?" His breath was so close to her face she could feel its heat.

"Sunday night," he growled, "that's the deadline."

Vanessa crushed the paper in one hand and waved to Sophie with the other.

The car pulled away and left her alone, a deep sense of loss gripping her heart.

She went back into the kitchen and there, sitting outside on the window sill, was Noble. She opened the window and he climbed in, his tail held aloft and his beautiful eyes watching her.

"Oh! Noble," she whispered, "I'm so scared."

The cat softly mewed and rubbed his head against her arm.

She picked up his warm body and carried it in her arms through to the front room, absently stroking his fur all the time.

She sat down on her armchair and tried to calm down.

"What am I going to do, Noble?" she asked her white comforter, knowing she would have to find the answer herself, but finding some ease in speaking her fear aloud.

In the silence of the room her thoughts began to form a plan. Not much of a plan, but a bolthole. She would go to the bank and withdraw some of the money her father had given her for the baby and find a furnished room to rent nearby. There were always rooms to rent advertised in the post office. She and her baby would be safe there and she'd be nearby for Sophie when Roger brought her back from London.

She told her plan to Noble, who meowed in what seemed agreement.

A small smile began to play around her lips, as she gently ruffled the fur on the top of his head. She couldn't let Roger win, not now she knew his intentions to harm the baby were real and having a plan, no matter how pathetic, gave her at least a temporary respite from her fears.

She took Noble back to kitchen and poured him a saucer of milk before going upstairs to get dressed. The bank was only open on Saturday morning, so she had to get a move on.

When she got back downstairs, Noble had gone. She closed the window and headed out to the garage for her bike.

Mr Parker was on duty as usual when she hurried into the bank and up to his counter.

"Mrs Lomax," he said politely, "we don't normally see you here on a Saturday, what can I do for you?"

Vanessa opened her handbag and produced her bank card.

"The account I opened recently..."she rummaged for a pen. "I'd like to draw some of the money out, if I may."

Mr Parker clicked the keys on his computer. "The cheque cleared a few days ago, so yes, how much do you want?"

Vanessa blinked. She had no idea how much room rent was, but settled on £500.

The teller took her bank card and counted out the money in large denominations, putting them in a clear plastic bag.

"There," he smiled. "Anything else?"

Vanessa put the money safely in her bag. "No thanks, Mr Parker," she said, "and I'll see you Tuesday as normal to pay last week's fees into Roger's business account."

Mr Parker looked perplexed. "Mrs Lomax," he said confusion settling in his grey eyes and deciding to ignore client confidentiality, "your husband closed that account yesterday."

Vanessa stared at the man.

"Closed the account," she said, "are you sure?"

Mr Parker nodded. "Withdrew everything and closed it." A deafening silence descended over the counter. "Didn't he mention it to you?"

Vanessa shook her head.

The teller could see she was upset. "Can I get you a glass of water?" he asked kindly. He liked Vanessa as much as he disliked her husband, but it was really none of his business he told himself, as she walked slowly out of the door.

Vanessa hadn't expected this news and all thoughts of renting a room vanished from her mind. Why, she wondered, why would he close the account? But no answer was forthcoming and she headed back home.

She reviewed her decision to leave. She would stay and face him, she decided, whatever happened. After all, he couldn't force her to have an abortion. She would go to the police. She would speak to her father again, perhaps now he would realise the seriousness of her situation. Her head swam with choices, none of which she could put into action till she confronted Roger again.

She sank into her chair. Sunday night, when he returned, that's when she would deal with it.

She forced herself to keep busy for the rest of the weekend and by late afternoon on Sunday had exhausted her adrenalin. She felt empty and drained but, at least, she didn't feel scared anymore.

The clock moved slowly but inexorably towards evening, then night.

By ten o'clock her fears were beginning to surface again.

Wide awake, she paced the floor, her ears straining for the noise of Roger's car. Then she remembered him whispering something in Sophie's ear that morning, but couldn't think what it might be. Sophie would be desperate to get home tonight, she knew, as Monday was a school day and she wouldn't want to miss that. 'No,' Vanessa thought, 'I just have to be patient. Perhaps the M4 was busy.'

By midnight, she knew they wouldn't be coming home. Roger had deliberately deceived her to show her who was boss, she thought grimly, probably in some plush London hotel for the night. Sophie would love that.

Wearily, she switched off the lights, locked the door and headed for bed.

Whatever Roger was up to, would have to wait till tomorrow. She was exhausted.

After a fitful night's sleep Vanessa woke up to silence. She got up and looked out of the window to see if Roger's car was there. It wasn't.

Pulling on yesterday's trousers and jumper she hurried downstairs. Perhaps the phone had rung during the night and she hadn't heard it, but the answer machine was unblinking and the caller-display showed no incoming calls.

Her mind veered between panic and anger and by mid-day, a deep concern was forming in her soul. It was a school day. Sophie wouldn't miss a school day. Something must have happened. The thought hit her. What if there had been an accident and her daughter was lying injured somewhere.

Keep calm, keep calm, she told herself as she switched on the morning news. If anything had happened, surely, it would be on the news channel, but there was nothing.

Then she remembered she'd written down the number of the riding school. Quickly, she found it and dialled the London number.

"Redwood Riding Stables," came the cultured voice.

"Yes, good morning," began Vanessa. I'm just checking to see if my husband and daughter, Sophie Lomax, attended the riding lessons on Saturday?"

"Just a moment."

Vanessa heard mutterings in the background. "I've just spoken to the instructor," she said, "and Sophie Lomax did have her lessons and very good she was too."

"And, when did the course finish?" asked Vanessa, aware that the receptionist was wondering why she didn't know."

"Four-thirty on Saturday," she replied, "it was a one-day course."

"Thanks," said Vanessa, relieved that Sophie hadn't had an accident at the stables, but more worried than ever about their non-appearance.

There was a Circle every Monday, surely Roger would have to be back by then. She paced the floor. Think, think, she told herself.

The appointment book, of course, she'd go to Roger's consulting room and see what he had booked in.

The wheels on her bicycle whizzed along as she sped into town. She dumped her bike in the street and rushed the key into the lock. The door swung open. Nothing had changed since she'd been there the previous week and the appointments book lay closed on her desk. Turning it round she pushed the pages over to the last time she had made an entry, Wednesday, 30 October, Enid Rawlings. She turned the page to Thursday, no bookings, then Friday, no bookings. She kept turning over the pages, hoping she would see some appointments booked in, but there was nothing right through to the end of the year.

Vanessa's blood ran cold. He wasn't coming back, she realised with horror, that's why he'd closed the account and withdrew all the money. But her horror intensified when she knew that wherever he'd gone, he had Sophie with him.

Chapter 25

Roger was waiting for Sophie at the end of the riding lessons.

She ran towards him, her face ruddy with the cold wind that had sprung up and the thrill of being able to control the fine pony she had been riding.

"Daddy, daddy," she called out excitedly, "it's been brilliant, thank you, thank you." She threw her arms around his neck. "You're the best daddy in the world."

Just the kind of reaction Roger had wanted. "But, that's not all you're getting for your birthday," he whispered conspiratorially.

"Really!" Sophie unclasped her father, anticipation written all over her face.

"Really," repeated Roger, "now let's get you to the hotel and cleaned up..."

"HOTEL," Sophie squealed, "are we really going to a HOTEL in LONDON."

"Yes, yes, we are, so c'mon, back to the car and let's get going."

Roger switched on the car radio and tuned into a London music station.

The music was dreadful to his ears, but Sophie tapped her feet and joined in with some of the banal lyrics, barely taking in the scenery that was flashing past.

The scream of a jet plane drowned out the music. "Look daddy," Sophie exclaimed, "it's so low. Why is it flying so low?"

"It's coming into land, darling." He pointed to a tower and some long, low buildings. "That's Heathrow Airport over there."

Sophie had heard of Heathrow Airport but had no idea where it was.

Another plane roared over them as Roger concentrated on finding the right exit from the motorway.

Signs for Heathrow were everywhere now and traffic was queuing in long lanes. "Where are we going daddy?" Sophie asked.

"I told you," Roger replied, "we're going to the hotel. It's near the airport, that's all. We'll be there soon." He turned up the volume on the radio, stopping any further questions from Sophie.

The hotel was huge and very modern. Grey concrete lined with identical windows over a covered entrance. A revolving door caught the light as it was spun by people bustling in and out, while others came through an automatic door, wheeling suitcases and carrying bags and computer cases.

Sophie's eyes widened as Roger pulled into a vast car park and removed his large case from the boot.

"What's in there?" Sophie asked in childlike innocence.

"Nothing for you to worry about, sweetheart, c'mon bring your bag and we'll get checked in."

The outside of the hotel may have been utilitarian, but inside the opulence was apparent. Sophie gazed at the pillars, chandeliers and deep sofas dotted in the large reception area. Roger seated her in one of the chairs and went to the reception desk.

"Booking for Lomax," he said. "Twin room."

The clerk checked his computer. "Ah, yes, Mr R Lomax and Miss S Lomax?"

"My daughter."

The clerk looked over Roger's shoulder at Sophie and nodded.

"I'll pay now," said Roger, opening his wallet and producing a bundle of sterling, still with its wrapper on it. "Efficient bank, eh," he indicated, before breaking open the wrapper and paying for the room with the cash.

"We have an early flight tomorrow, so I'd like an early dinner," he said, pocketing his change.

"Dinner begins serving at six o'clock," the clerk told him, "or there's room service if you wish."

"Six will be fine."

He picked up his luggage and indicated to Sophie to follow him.

The lift whisked them to the seventh floor and Room 710. Sophie looked around the spotless room and crossed to the window. The view was amazing. She could see the layout of the airport and the planes taxiing onto and off the runways. She'd never seen anything like it in her life.

Roger switched the lights on in the bathroom. "Here," he said, "have a look at this."

The room sparkled with chrome and mirrors. A power shower was housed in a glass enclosure in the corner and a basket full of coloured bottles and sachets stood beside the gleaming sink. She ran her hands over the thick white towels. "Wow," she breathed.

Rogers squeezed her shoulders, "Now get freshened up. At about half past six you're going to have a birthday dinner in the dining room downstairs, just like a real Princess. And, here," Roger added, "wear this." He opened his case and produced a pink glittering top.

Sophie held it up. "It's soooooo cool," she squeaked. "Thanks, daddy," she blew him a kiss. "This is the best birthday surprise ever."

Feeling very grown up, Sophie took her father's arm as they walked into the hotel restaurant.

"Good evening Sir, good evening Madam." The Maître-de bowed his head.

"Table for two?" Roger nodded.

"This way please."

They were lead to a table in the middle of the room and seated. Roger beckoned the Maître-de closer. "It's my little girl's birthday," he whispered, "can we have the singing waiters later and a small cake perhaps?"

The Maître-de looked at Sophie and smiled. "Certainly sir."

Roger shook his hand, palming him a £50 note.

"Now," he said, "what would Princess Sophie like for dinner?"

Raising her head above the large gold-tasselled menu, she blinked at her father.

"Can I have what I had with mum in the Green Room?"

Roger felt himself stiffen. "Green Room?"

"Mmmmhhh, mum took me for lunch there on her birthday... you were in London I think."

"Well mum's not here now, is she," Roger said forcing a smile, "so you can have whatever you like."

"Beef burger and chips then," Sophie said proudly, "that's my favourite."

Roger rolled his eyes. So much for Vanessa being a wonderful mother!

Pushing all thoughts of her from his head Roger ordered Sophie's beef burger and a steak for himself. The waiter took the order. "And how would Sir like his steak?"

"Rare," Roger said, "but make sure the burger is fully cooked."

"Any wine?" he continued.

Roger glanced at the wine list. "The Rioja," he said, "and Coca Cola for my daughter."

Sophie tucked into her meal and Roger pushed his around the plate. His mind was whirling. This was the critical part of his plan which he couldn't allow to fail. Getting Sophie to agree to go with him to Thailand wasn't going to be as easy as he'd first thought. That blasted school had enthralled her and she wouldn't want to miss out on any of the fun it seemed to offer.

When she'd finished her meal and Roger had drunk half the bottle of wine, he felt the time was right to broach the subject.

He was about to begin sounding her out when the door of the kitchen restaurant flew open and four waiters emerged holding sparklers and heading their way. Sophie jumped in surprise. "They're coming over here!" she grinned, clapping her hands.

"Happy birthday to you," they sang, getting nearer, "happy birthday to you," one of them placed a cake, dotted with candles, on the table in front of her, "happy birthday, dear Sophie, happy birthday to you."

Sophie giggled and blew out the candles and the waiters cheered.

Roger raised his wineglass. "Happy birthday darling," he said, "wasn't that just great?"

Sophie flopped back on her chair as the waiters withdrew with winks and smiles. Thirteen, she thought, next week she'd be a real teenager and her heart soared. Wait till she told them about this on Monday at school.

"Have you had enough excitement for one day, sweetheart," Roger asked, "or would you like to hear about the biggest surprise of all?"

Sophie's eyes turned towards him. "There's more," she said incredulously, "more than this?"

Roger nodded and pulled his chair in closer to her. Control was everything at this point.

"You liked the horse-riding today, didn't you?"

Sophie agreed.

"Well, how would you like to ride on an elephant?"

The words hung in the air between them. A positive response at this point would be crucial.

"Elephant ride, daddy," she said, perplexed. "But they don't have elephants in England."

"You're right," he said, "there aren't any elephants in England, but there are in Thailand."

"Thailand," Sophie repeated, getting more confused, "where's Thailand?"

Roger pointed to the darkening sky outside the restaurant window.

"It's not far," he said, "but we need to get on an airplane to go there."

He quickly finished his glass of wine and waited.

Sophie tried to understand what her father was talking about, but couldn't.

"Will it take long to get there?" she asked, "I have to go to school on Monday remember."

She was taking the bait. Roger's breathing eased.

"Of course you do. That's why I've arranged for us to get up very early, fly to Thailand for your elephant ride and be back before you know it."

The child's desire to ride a real elephant and her trust of her father won.

"OK," she said simply, before asking, "does mum know I'm going on an elephant ride?"

Roger lifted her chin up and kissed her on the cheek. "Of course she does," he said, "it was her idea."

Chapter 26

Vanessa stared at the blank pages of the appointment book, unable to move as the realisation that Roger may have actually abducted Sophie flooded her mind.

What kind of a man had she married? It was true he hadn't been particularly loving towards her but his love for Sophie had always been there for all to see. He wouldn't harm her he *couldn't* harm her, she felt sure. No, this was his way of getting back at her, hurting her because of the baby.

But where were they? She fretted. Where were they?

A very gentle plucking sensation coming from her womb brought her attention back to reality. The baby was moving. She sat perfectly still. Yes, there it was again, rippling under her fingertips. The memory of the scan came back and reminded her of the euphoria she had felt when she'd seen the tiny human form. She moved her hands protectively over the tiny bump. Nothing was going to make her abort her son and she silently vowed she would move heaven and earth to find out where Sophie was and bring her home.

A new resolve took over as she stood up and turned her attention to Roger's inner sanctum. Maybe, she thought, just maybe...

She turned the handle of the oak door and it clicked open. Vanessa breathed a sigh of relief, it had been left unlocked. For the first time, she entered the forbidden territory that was Roger's consulting room. She didn't know what to expect, but found that the room was well, ordinary.

She looked around. There was a treatment table, bookcases of books and magazines, an imposing desk and swivel chair and a computer and printer standing mute against the wall, on a work station.

She wondered why Roger had been so secretive about the room, then realised, almost at once, it was another of his ways of controlling her, stopping her asking any questions, or being part of his life. No, she had to know her place and that was at Roger's beck and call.

The desk had been cleared of any documents, leaving only a desk tidy with a few biros in it, a calendar showing the 30 October, probably the last day he was here Vanessa thought grimly and a revolving index of names and phone numbers. Vanessa sat behind the desk and checked the drawers, empty. Roger had disappeared, literally without a trace.

She picked up the phone index and flipped the cards over. The bank, his office cleaner, a stationery company, a local garage, Kim Mason...! Vanessa froze mid-flip. She stared at the name as if she was expecting it to disappear at any minute. Removing the card from its holder, her old fear resurfaced. Had Roger been involved with Kim Mason? Was she more than just a colleague?

She picked up Roger's phone and dialled the mobile number. A female voice came on. "Kim here," it said, "sorry I can't take your call, leave a message." The mobile bleeped.

Vanessa's mind tried to focus. "It's Vanessa," she heard herself say, "Vanessa Lomax. I'm in Roger's consulting room and I need you to phone me back." She dropped the receiver back on its cradle.

Ten minutes passed, then thirty, but there was no call back.

Vanessa began to fear the worst. Roger hadn't only stolen her daughter from her, she felt herself panic he'd also taken along his mistress.

Just then, there was a noise at the front door.

"Vanessa," a voice called, "are you there?"

A figure appeared at the door of Roger's office. Kim Mason stood before her, as beautiful as she remembered her.

"You left your bike lying on the pavement," she said worriedly, "and the front door was open and..."

Her voice trailed to a halt as she saw the grief and distress on Vanessa's face.

"I got your message," Kim said quietly, pulling across the computer chair to sit on. "You sounded awful," she added, "and now that I'm here, I can see something's very wrong."

She stopped speaking and waited for Vanessa to speak.

"I thought you'd gone with him," she eventually said, her eyes red-rimmed and scared. She pointed to the card on the desk. "Your number," she murmured, "he had your number on his list."

Kim's mouth tightened, ignoring the implication. "Gone where?" she asked.

The women's eyes met. "I thought you might know?" Vanessa said.

Kim shook her head. "If he's gone Vanessa, I'm sorry, but I don't know where."

Tears began to trickle down her face as the words sank in.

"Vanessa," Kim rose, came round to the other side of desk and put her arm around the distressed figure. "Sssssshhhhh," she said, "he'll be back," she tried to assure her, "I'm sure he'll be back, you know Roger," she added, trying to lighten the situation, "he never did tell his right hand what his left hand was doing."

Vanessa shook her head. "You don't understand," she whispered. "I don't care if I never see him again." She looked up at Kim's beautiful face. "He's taken Sophie with him and I don't know..." The tears flooded her eyes as the horror hit her again. Kim held on to her, fear now growing like a cancer in her own stomach.

Memories of Roger and his Thai girls at Darko's sex club rushed into her head. "Vanessa," she said urgently, "please listen. Did Roger say anything to make you think he was going abroad?"

"Abroad," Vanessa managed to shake her head. "He was taking Sophie to London at the weekend for riding lessons, but I've checked with them and they said Sophie and Roger had been there, but that was just London," Vanessa said, "not abroad."

Kim's mind was now racing. "Did Roger take any luggage when they left for London?"

Vanessa's eyes narrowed, trying to focus on the question. "Yes," she said, "a big case on wheels. I asked him what he needed such a big case for but he said it was riding gear for Sophie."

Her troubled eyes searched Kim's face for explanation.

"Vanessa," Kim said, holding her shoulders. "I think Roger may have taken Sophie out of the country. I think you need to phone the police. NOW!"

Vanessa stared blankly at Kim. "And tell them what?" she asked, "that a father has taken his daughter on a trip to somewhere... I tried phoning them but they couldn't help." Kim's lips tightened.

"Have you no idea where they might be?" she asked again, knowing the answer already." Vanessa's head drooped as she folded in despair.

"None," she whispered. Kim went to replace the chair back beside the computer. Her eyes narrowed as hope formed in her mind.

"Vanessa," she asked. "Roger's computer... is it password protected?"

Vanessa raised her head. "What?"

"Password protected."

Vanessa shrugged. "I don't know what that means."

Kim switched on the machine and it bleeped into life.

She clicked on Roger's emails and crossed her fingers.

The screen changed. She was in.

She scanned the list of messages. "Confirmation of flights," one read. She clicked it open hardly daring to breathe.

The email was from British Airways confirming two one-way flights from Heathrow to Bangkok on 3 November, yesterday. There was also a hotel confirmation for the Bangkok Hilton for two nights 3 and 4 November. Kim printed both the emails off and silently thanked technology for pointing the way.

Roger being Roger, hadn't deleted his emails before leaving, but why would he, in his eyes he was infallible and Vanessa, well, she didn't know anything about computers. He'd made sure of that.

Kim placed the printouts in front of Vanessa.

"It looks like he's taken Sophie to Thailand," Kim said quietly, pointing to the flight details. Vanessa grabbed the page and looked bleakly at the printout.

"It doesn't say when they'll be back," she said desperately, "where does it say when they'll be back?" She pushed the email across to Kim.

Kim grimaced. "Vanessa," she said as gently as she could. "There are no return flights booked."

Vanessa was in a bad way. Kim thought of phoning for an ambulance she was so concerned, especially with the pregnancy to consider.

"Is there anyone I can contact Vanessa," she asked, "who could stay with you till you can cope again?"

Vanessa shook her head. She had no friends.

Suddenly, she raised her head and in a low voice said one word. "Hazel."

Of course, Kim realised, why hadn't she thought of Hazel.

"C'mon Vanessa," she slipped her arm around her shoulders, "let's get you to the car."

Kim eased the stricken woman into the front seat and fastened her seat belt.

She went back to Roger's office and closed and locked the front door. With a bit of a struggle, she loaded the bike into the back of her car and took her place beside Vanessa.

Leaning forward to see her face, she tried to gauge Vanessa's state of mind and as she did so, the little silver head of the elephant Hazel had given her, tipped forward on its chain. Vanessa's puffy eyes locked onto it. "It's the elephant," she said, wonder in her voice, as she drew Kim's attention to the charm.

Kim looked down at it. "Yes, it is Vanessa," she agreed, concerned now that her mind was breaking under the strain. Vanessa looked up at her.

"Don't you see," she said, the glimmer of a smile beginning to form around her mouth, "it's the sign."

"The sign?" Kim repeated.

Vanessa nodded, seeming to find new energy from somewhere. "Everything will be alright now," she said, "just as long as I follow the elephant." Kim became more worried. Vanessa seemed to be losing it totally. She started the car and pulled out into the traffic. The quicker she got her to Hazel's cottage the better.

Chapter 27

Roger was euphoric as the jet rose into the air. He'd done it.

He'd done everything by the book in advance of this day. Moving his money to a Hong Kong Bank, arranging long-stay visas, checking how he stood legally, safe in the knowledge that once they were in Thailand, the British Police couldn't touch them. He would find a way of earning money the same way Darko did, sex and drugs and as for Vanessa, he smirked to himself, she could go to Hell along with the brat she was carrying.

Sophie was gazing out of the plane window at the bluest sky she'd ever seen.

"It's so pretty up here daddy," she said, "and the clouds, look at the clouds."

Roger leaned across her, his hand stroking her soft arm. "It's beautiful isn't it," he agreed, "but wait till you see Thailand."

The beautiful girl in her British Airways uniform told them breakfast would be served shortly and was there anything they needed, smiling at Sophie as she spoke.

Roger declined with a wave of his hand. The stewardess moved on.

"How long before we get there?" Sophie asked. Roger flinched.

"Soon, sweetheart, soon." he assured her.

He handed her one of the handful of magazines he's bought at the airport. "Here," he said, "read this, it'll make the time go quicker."

Flight time thirteen hours, Roger thought, Sophie was going to realise sooner or later that there would be no going back to school, to England or to her mother, any time soon. In fact, once they were safely in Bangkok, he'd have to tell her they were never going back.

For a brief moment, he had a twinge of conscience, but he had planned this for so long, he wasn't going to let anything stop him now. On Sophie's thirteenth birthday, in a week's time, he would show her how he felt about her. She would be ready by then, he would see to that.

By the time they had had breakfast and lunch and the cabin crew had closed all the blinds to allow the passengers to sleep, Sophie was becoming more and more agitated.

"Daddy," she nudged a sleeping Roger. "I want to go to the toilet."

Roger grunted and stood up to let her pass, pointing to the sign at the front of the aircraft. Sophie came to the toilet door and found two of the stewardesses sitting on small seats in the little kitchen on the other side of the aisle.

The pretty one who had served her breakfast smiled at her.

"Are you OK?" she asked.

Sophie took her opportunity. "We seem to have been on the plane for an awfully long time," she said, "how much further to Thailand?"

The stewardesses exchanged glances and beckoned her to sit down beside them.

"Didn't your daddy tell you?" one of them asked.

"He said we'd fly to Thailand, go on an elephant ride and be back home in time for me to go to school."

"Honey," said the other one, "I think you may have got things mixed up. We won't get to Thailand till late tonight."

Sophie felt a twinge of concern, "But what about school?"

The stewardess smiled kindly. "I think you need to ask daddy about that," she said, offering her a glass of orange juice.

"No thanks, I'll go to the toilet now."

Something was wrong. Sophie felt uneasy as she slipped past Roger and back into her seat. He pretended to go back to sleep but had seen Sophie speaking with the stewardesses and was worried.

"We won't be back in time for school, will we," she stated with the candour of the child that she was.

So that was it, Roger thought, Sophie had uncovered the lie.

Roger reached out to take her hand but she pulled it away.

"I'm sorry Sophie," he said, his voice contrite and pleading, "but how else were you going to get your birthday elephant ride?"

Sophie folded her arms tightly across her chest.

"Don't want a stupid elephant ride," she hissed, "want to go home."

Roger felt his control over her slipping. "OK," he said, "OK as soon as we possibly can, we'll get flights back to England and home."

Her eyes stared at his, willing him to placate her.

He held up his hands in surrender. "I'm sorry," he repeated.

The rest of the long journey was silent and uncomfortable as Roger got more and more tired and Sophie more stubborn.

When they finally starting making the descent to Bangkok Airport, she could see the city was ablaze with lights. Coloured neon was everywhere and the airport itself was crowded with people of all nationalities, moving around the world. To Sophie, it looked like something out of a movie and despite herself she was awestruck by it all.

Roger clutched her hand as they made their way to Baggage Reclaim.

"The hotel is sending a car to pick us up," he told her, relieved to see she had become less petulant.

"What hotel?" she asked. This was something else he hadn't told her about.

"Where we're staying, silly," he replied, trying to hurry her through the crowd.

"But you said, we'd be going straight back to England," she stopped in her tracks. "Didn't you?"

He grabbed her hand again. "We can't go right away," he said, "there's not another flight at this time of night." His patience with her was being tried to its limit as they were processed through Customs and Passport and Visa Control.

They were carried through the airport along with the crowd, without much attention being paid to the man and his daughter and it was with great relief that Roger spotted the Hilton Hotel car and driver, holding up a sign with his name on it.

"Over there," he urged Sophie, "hurry now, there's our car."

With no option but to go with her father, Sophie slumped down into the back seat of the car. It made its way slowly through the crowded streets of Bangkok and, despite herself, Sophie again was caught up in the newness of it all. "Look!" she exclaimed, as a huge elephant lumbered past.

"Told you," her father said, "elephants."

The hotel was like something Sophie had never seen before in her life, even at the movies. Everywhere she looked, there were marble pillars, velvet drapes, gold trimmed tables bearing bowls of fruit and huge flower displays.

Small, brown men in uniform walked smartly through the massive reception, pulling trolleys piled high with assorted luggage and permanently smiling, regardless of the load.

Roger watched Sophie as she absorbed the opulence all around her.

"You like?" he asked.

Sophie nodded and Roger relaxed again. Everything was going to be alright, he told himself, just as he'd planned it.

After a good night's sleep and tomorrow's elephant ride, they'd be on their way to their final destination. The villa he'd rented at Pattaya Beach, along with two Thai maids, thanks to the contact he'd been given by Darko in exchange for Kim's address, would be waiting for him.

Yes, Missy Areva Wong Sawat had come through with flying colours, for a price of course and once he'd paid her and picked up the key, he would be free and clear to begin his new life, whether Sophie liked it or not.

Chapter 28

Hazel was surprised to see Kim's car pull up outside the cottage and Kim herself hurry towards her door. The look on Kim's face told her something was seriously wrong. "What is it?" she asked, "what's wrong?"

Her first thought had been something had happened to Donald.

"It's Vanessa," Kim said, her rapid breathing making her voice sound higher than normal. "She's in the car, can I bring her in?"

Hazel nodded, concern for her friend and her plight growing by the minute.

Kim half-carried Vanessa into the small sitting room and relaxed her onto the sofa. Hazel was at her side immediately.

"Vanessa, dear, it's Hazel... what on earth's wrong?"

Vanessa tried to speak but couldn't. Kim spoke for her.

She went over the last few hours, trying not to inflame the situation further by adding her own fears to the happenings. Hazel's mood darkened visibly.

"And, he's taken the child with him... to Thailand you think?" Kim nodded. "God help us," Hazel whispered.

"Stay with her a minute," she ordered Kim and went into her kitchen. She brought out a small glass of water to which she'd added a herbal sedative.

"Here, Vanessa," she urged, "drink this, it'll make you feel better."

Vanessa swallowed the mixture and almost immediately fell asleep.

Hazel covered her up and took Kim into the kitchen.

"Do the police know?"

"Vanessa tried phoning them, but because Roger and Sophie had left the

135

country there was nothing they could do and I don't think our police have any power in Thailand anyway," she added.

"What about courts," Hazel asked.

"Well, as far as I know, that could take months and an awful lot of money."

"Poor girl," she said, "what's to be done?" she asked Kim with worried eyes.

"Just before we got here," Kim remembered, "she said a rather strange thing... something about following elephants...?" Kim fingered the elephant head on the chain round her neck that Hazel had given her. "This seemed to have meant something to her."

Hazel's blue eyes pierced Kim's. "So, it IS you," she said dramatically.

"ME!" Kim exclaimed, "what about me?"

"Sit down Kim." Kim pulled out a chair from around the kitchen table and sat down.

"Do you believe in angels?" she asked, "I mean real guardian angels. The ones who look after you when no else does?"

"I don't know," Kim heard herself stutter. "Why?"

Hazel told her about being a Medium and the message she'd received from Vanessa's dead mother. "The prediction was that 'all would be well if she followed the elephant.'" Hazel nodded at the silver talisman. "And you're wearing her guide back to her daughter."

Kim didn't know what to say. The world had suddenly become surreal. Here she was sitting in this cottage and being told that she was some sort of guardian angel for Vanessa, here on earth!

"Nothing is an accident Kim," Hazel told her meaningfully, "no meeting is ever by chance. You never know when you'll be called upon to be an angel helper, but that's what you are Kim, Vanessa's angel helper."

"But, I don't know what to do?" she pleaded, "to help anyone..."

She began to panic as she remembered how sordid her involvement with Roger had been, albeit while she wasn't in her right mind. And now all these people, Hazel, Vanessa and worst of all Donald were caught up in her web of deceit. She felt like running away, escaping to anywhere, as the guilt weighed heavier on her shoulders.

Hazel's voice cut through her thoughts. "Where in Thailand would Roger go, Kim? We need to know, if we're to have any chance of getting Sophie back."

Kim opened her arms in despair, "I don't know I wish I did."

"Ask yourself questions till you get an answer. Somewhere inside you, you know the way forward."

Hazel went through to check on Vanessa leaving Kim alone in the kitchen.

"How am I supposed to know where he is?" she muttered to herself, wishing she could just disappear and go back to the radio station and Donald.

She sat in the kitchen, for what felt like hours, when she heard Hazel speaking to Vanessa. 'She must be awake,' she thought, 'maybe she's remembered something.'

Kim went through to the front room just in time to see Donald bounding up the path. A further wave of panic hit her as he rushed through the door.

"Kim," he said, hurrying towards her. He took hold of her shoulders, "What are you doing here? I've been worried sick about you."

"Liz said you'd got a phone call and just left... I tried your flat..." As he calmed down, relieved to know Kim was alright, he realised that Vanessa was also in the room.

"What's going on?" he asked, looking from one pair of worried eyes to another.

It was Hazel who spoke first. "Vanessa's husband has taken their daughter out of the country without her agreement. I think they call it abduction. And it looks like he's gone to Thailand without any intention of coming back."

"What!" Donald said incredulously. "Vanessa, is this true?"

Vanessa fumbled with the edge of her cardigan. "Things haven't been right for a long time," she began, "but since my pregnancy, Roger has been horrible to me." She looked up at Donald, her eyes pleading with him for support. "He said I had to have the baby aborted or I'd be sorry."

Donald shook his head in disbelief. "And this is his way of paying you back?"

"I think so," Vanessa whispered.

Donald flopped down in an armchair, his head in his hands as he tried to make sense of what was happening. He had come in worried about Kim and found instead that Vanessa was the one who was in deep distress.

"The thing is Donald," Hazel pulled up a chair beside him, "how are we going to get Sophie back?"

Donald raked his fingers through his hair suddenly wondering how Kim had got involved in all this.

He turned to face her. "The phone call," he asked, "who was it from?"

Kim indicated Vanessa with a nod of her head. His brows furrowed. "You know one another?" Kim nodded again. "But how?" Donald asked.

Kim knew there was no way out. Donald would have to know the truth, but not now. "It's a long story," she said, "and once this whole business is sorted, I'll explain everything. But now," she added, "Vanessa needs our help."

All eyes turned to Vanessa.

"What can we do?" Donald asked, focussing his mind on the current problem. He didn't have a clue what Kim was talking about, but she was right, it could wait. The important thing was to help Vanessa.

Vanessa had no doubt about what she had to do, her love for her daughter wouldn't let her do anything else.

"I need to go to Thailand, find her and bring her back," she said simply.

There was silence in the room till Donald spoke. "I don't think it's that easy, Vanessa, Thailand is pretty far away and for a woman alone, it might even be dangerous."

She turned to Kim. "But I won't be alone," she said, "Kim will be with me to guide me and keep me safe."

Vanessa's naivety pierced Kim's heart like a knife.

"Vanessa," Donald said, "Kim can't go with you..." his eyes looking to hers for confirmation... "can you Kim?"

But the confirmation didn't come.

Donald jumped up. "You can't be serious," he said, realising what the silence meant. He looked at Vanessa. "She doesn't have any money for a start," he began... "and I won't allow it," he ended emphatically.

"I have enough money for both of us," Vanessa said evenly.

Donald's head oscillated between the two women as he tried to find a way forward.

"OK, OK," he said. "For a start, how do any of you know they've gone to Thailand in the first place? I take it Roger didn't tell you his plan, Vanessa."

Kim interrupted his questioning. "We found a flight confirmation from British Airways on his computer and a booking at the Bangkok Hilton."

She looked at Vanessa. "That's how we know."

Donald was getting more and more frustrated. "What computer?"

"The one in Roger's consulting rooms."

Kim moved to where Vanessa sat and joined her.

At the mention of the computer, Donald became more grounded. This was something he knew about. "No password protection on it?" he asked Kim urgently.

"None."

"How far did you go into its history?"

Kim shrugged, "Just the emails," she said, "that gave us the information we needed."

"Can you take me to where his office is?" he asked Kim, pulling her to her feet before she could answer. He met no resistance.

"Good," he nodded, "let's go. If he went to Thailand, he must have made contact with someone there and he would have used his computer. If he's clever he'll have hidden these files and emails, but I'm cleverer, trust me, and I'll find them." He smiled at Kim for the first time since he'd arrived.

"Vanessa," he said, his voice calm now, "please stay here with Aunt Hazel till we get back." She nodded. "With a bit of luck, I'll have some answers."

Chapter 29

Breakfast at the Hilton was delicious. Sophie wandered around the buffet tables, choosing from the exotic fruits, breads and strange dishes spread out before her. Roger watched his daughter carefully. She seemed more settled and today was the elephant ride. He was taking her to an Elephant Sanctuary for the ride, then a visit to the fabulous Golden Temple with its enormous statues of the Lord Buddah and finally the floating market where she could choose a gift for her birthday. Roger smiled. It was going to be a good day.

"Ready for your elephant ride?" he asked her as she sat down at the table, her plate laden with her choices.

Sophie had been quieter since her outburst at the airport and Roger hoped this was a good sign.

"I'm ready," she said, "but I still don't know how I'm going to get back to school soon." She drew her eyebrows together as she tackled a slice of orange melon. "Won't everyone be wondering where I am?"

Roger put on a beaming smile. "But everyone knows where you are," he lied, "mummy told the school you'd be going on a trip with daddy for your birthday so stop worrying about school and just enjoy today... alright?"

He was beginning to get a little annoyed with his daughter's constant harping on about school. The quicker he told her she wouldn't be going back to England the better, but not now, not yet. When they got to Pattaya Beach would be soon enough.

After breakfast, Roger packed everything up and checked them out of the hotel. At the front of the hotel the hire car he'd booked was waiting for them.

It was going to be a long trip to Pattaya Beach at the end of the day, but Roger had planned it that way, so that Sophie would sleep for most of the journey and not ask any more irritating questions.

The convertible Peugeot was silver with leather seats and purred like a cat when Roger turned the ignition key. He glanced across at Sophie.

"You like?" he asked.

She smiled back, running her hands over the upholstery. "I like."

And despite her misgivings, she had the most wonderful day. The ride on the elephant was amazing and she waved to Roger from her imperial height on the back of the packaderm as the grey body plodded past him.

Roger smiled to himself. She'd soon forget all about England.

They had lunch, bought from one of the many food sellers that seemed to crowd every available space beside the road. Every taste and sight was a new sensation and Sophie soaked it all up.

"Look," she cried in amazement as golden statues rose up all around her at the Golden Temple, each one encrusted with precious jewels. She watched in awe at the Thai people praying and bowing and placing offerings of fruit and flowers before their gods. And the colours, Sophie was dazzled and Roger's smile got wider.

At Roger's insistence, he bought her a Thai costume at the floating market. The wrap around skirt was green silk with gold embroidery and there was a little matching top to go with it. It was the most beautiful thing Sophie had ever owned. Far prettier than the jeans and t-shirts she usually wore at home.

"Let's eat," said Roger, as they got back to the car. "We've a long drive ahead of us."

The misgivings were back. Sophie dug her heels in, the thrills of the day beginning to be replaced by the returning little knot of disquiet in her tummy.

Her face took on a frown. "Where are we going NOW?" she asked, her voice sounding strident to Roger's ears.

He sighed a deep sigh. He was getting impatient now, the busyness of the day and the heat, soaking his shirt with sweat. "Stop asking so many questions," he admonished her sharply, "you're worse than your bloody mother."

As soon as the words had left his lips, he knew it was the wrong thing to say.

Sophie's eyes widened in real fear now, "Daddy," she said, her voice now almost a whisper, "you swore."

Roger slid into the driver's seat and slammed the door.

"Get in."

The tone of his voice brooked no reply. Sophie got in.

She could almost feel the impatience emanating from her father, but dare not ask any more questions. She had never seen him like this and it scared her.

Roger drove off in silence, leaving Bangkok behind them. They stopped at a small town and ate a silent meal. Occasionally, Roger stole a glance at his daughter, wondering how to repair the bridge that had been broken between them, but glad he didn't have to explain anything more, 90 kilometres to go to Pattaya Beach. Better this way, he decided, as darkness blanketed the countryside.

He stopped and put the hood up, relieving himself at the side of the road.

He opened Sophie's door. "Want to pee?" he asked. Sophie looked around at the dark outline of trees and bushes and shook her head. Roger shrugged and slammed the door.

He was exhausted when they reached their destination, but the place was buzzing. He stopped the car and took the address Darko had given him out of his wallet. Missy Areva Wong Sawat, LuLu Sex Shop, 1217 Walking Street, Pattaya Beach. Sophie woke up. "Where are we?"

"We need to go for a little walk," he told her. "I have to meet someone here who has keys for me."

He let her out of the car and locked it, hoping it would still be there when they got back.

Walking Street was just that, a street where people walked. There were no cars, but running the full length of the walkway were every kind of sexual activity and sex clubs he had ever seen or dreamt of. Everywhere he looked sex was being touted and women and girls were falling over themselves to 'bag' a tourist. He pulled Sophie back into the car. "It'll wait till morning," he said gruffly, accelerating away from the area.

He pulled into a seedy looking motel. This would have to do till morning.

The owner took Roger's money with barely a glance at the young girl half-hidden behind him. He indicated Roger to follow him.

The room was dark and smelled of old sweat and urine. Roger flicked on an overhead light and cockroaches scurried back to their darkness.

Sophie thought she was going to be sick.

Even he felt revulsion at the room. This wasn't how he'd envisaged

Sophie's introduction to Pattaya Beach.

"It's only for a night," he said, taking her towards the toilet which was hidden by a curtain. "Don't touch anything and don't sit down," he said, "just pee."

He pulled the curtain shut. Out of desperation, Sophie peed. How could her father bring her to this awful place, she wondered desperately, what had happened to her daddy. All thoughts of the exciting day were now gone. All she wanted was to go home, to her mum, to her school and to West Hampton.

This was turning out to be the worst birthday ever. Tears began to flow unchecked down her face.

She pulled back the curtain. Roger was shaking out the sheets on the metal bed. "Daddy," she cried, "please, please, take me home."

He opened his arms and she ran into them. "Ssssshhhhh," he whispered, "it's alright. Daddy will fix everything tomorrow. You'll see." He held her close all that night, his emotions fluctuating between love for his daughter and lust for her body.

As soon as day broke, they left that awful place and drove back towards Pattaya Beach and Walking Street. The daylight showed a very different face from the night one. Cars and carts were moving freely down the road and the activities of the previous night were boarded shut. He drove the car slowly down the road, "LuLu Sex Shop," he kept repeating to himself. And then he saw it. "Wait here," he told Sophie, "this is where I will get the keys to your next surprise." Sophie had had more than enough of surprises and sat stony faced while Roger knocked loudly on the black-painted door.

The wrinkled face of an old Thai woman peered round the chink in the opened door. Roger bowed. "Missy Areva?" he asked. The door shut. Roger waited.

A few minutes later, the beautiful face and body of a young Thai woman came out and onto the pavement. "I've been expecting you," she said indicating he should follow her inside. Roger looked over at Sophie sitting in the car. The woman followed his gaze and shrugged her shoulders. "Wait," she said. Another five minutes passed and she returned with a bunch of keys in her hand wrapped in a piece of paper. She gave them to Roger and held out her hand.

He nodded and brought out an envelope from his inside jacket pocket. "It's all there," he said.

Missy Areva smiled. "If it isn't," she said, "I'll know where to find you."

Roger almost skipped back to the car. It was all over. His plan had succeeded. The paper the keys were wrapped in gave the address of the beach-side villa Missy Areva was renting to him. Silently, he thanked Darko. Maybe he would traffic some drugs for him, but right now, he just wanted to get to the house and show it to Sophie. She would love it.

The blue sea was surging in waves onto the white sand and the sun shone hotly onto the idyllic scene. Roger pulled the car off the road and down a dusty track towards the sea. He checked the address and grinned from ear to ear. This was it and it was beautiful.

"Your final surprise," he bowed to Sophie as he opened the car door for her.

The villa was built on stilts and a wooden veranda ran all the way round it. White muslin curtains drifted out of open doors and windows in the breeze and palm trees brushed the air with coolness and shade.

Sophie gulped. "I don't understand," she said.

Roger hugged her. "You will, sweetheart," he said, "you will."

Just then, two little Thai girls ran down the stairs towards them, dressed in the same type of costume Roger had bought for Sophie.

They bowed deeply and waited for Roger to speak.

"What are your names?" he asked wondering if they spoke English.

They did. "I am Nona said one of the girls and this is my sister Thana."

Roger turned to Sophie and pushed her forward. "And this is Sophie," he said. "Say hello Sophie." Sophie extended her hand to shake theirs, but they put their hands together as in prayer and bowed.

She looked at Roger. "It's their custom," he said, "they do things differently here."

Roger felt himself harden at the sight of the two girls. Later tonight, he told himself, when Sophie was asleep, he would have them. But now, he was hungry for food and ordered the girls into the kitchen to prepare a meal for them.

He took Sophie and himself on a tour of the villa. "What room would you like?"

Sophie's lips tightened. "How long are we staying here?" she said. But Roger was giving her no answers. He opened a door into a large airy room, in the middle of which was a circular bed, draped with mosquito netting. White furniture was dotted around the walls, a dressing table, a wardrobe, a set of drawers and two woven rush chairs. Beside the bed were two night stands, one either side, holding small lamps with coloured glass shades.

"How about this one," he said, "isn't it beautiful?"

Before she could answer, the smells of food cooking drifted to Roger's nose. "Aaahhh," he said, "looks like lunch is ready." He put an arm around Sophie. "Hungry?" he asked, ushering her back to the main living room.

The table was laid with salads, rice dishes and little fish parcels. It smelled wonderful and Sophie realised she was ravenous. She ate almost like an animal, using her fingers and hardly stopping between mouthfuls. Roger watched. It would soon be time. Five days till her birthday and her deflowering. He couldn't wait.

Chapter 30

The drive to Roger's consulting rooms was taken in comparative silence, none of them wishing to broach the subject of Kim's relationship to Vanessa and subsequently, Roger, her husband. Don pushed all thoughts about Kim from his head.

"Are you going to phone Liz?" he asked. "She's worried about you."

"Yes," Kim replied absently. "I'll phone her when I get the chance."

Kim felt bleak. She wanted to tell Don everything, to make him understand, but she knew her past was going to be hard for any man to accept, let alone the honourable man by her side. She forced herself to think about Vanessa's plight. How could Roger have been so cruel as to take her daughter from her and was it really to make her pay for not having the baby aborted, she felt a shiver of fear run through her system. Getting to Thailand and finding Sophie was going to be hard enough, but getting Roger to let her go... Kim sighed aloud.

"Are we nearly there?" Don asked, bringing her back to the moment.

Kim glanced around her and pointed to a street running to the left of the traffic roundabout. "Take a left there," she said, "the consulting rooms are on the right half way down the street."

Don found a place to park and they hurried towards the building. It was a very fine building with Georgian windows and pillars either side of an imposing door. "Is this it?" Don asked. Kim nodded and took out the key, letting them into the silence of the premises.

"In here," she said, opening a frosted glass door which lead into a reception area. Don followed, taking in the neatness of the room.

"Where's the computer?" he asked.

Kim pointed to the large mahogany door at the far end of the reception.

"In there."

Don moved past her determinedly. "Let's get a move on then," he said looking around him with indifference, "the quicker we find out where the sod has gone the better for Vanessa."

Kim followed him to the door but hesitated to go any further. She watched from where she stood, as Don powered the machine up and deftly started rapidly clicking the keys.

"I'll just go outside a minute and phone Liz," she called. Don didn't seem to hear her. Outside she lit a cigarette and inhaled deeply as she dialled Liz's mobile. Liz picked up after the first ring.

"Kim," she said, trying to keep the anxiety out of her voice, "what's happening?"

Kim leant against the metal railings and looked up at the clouds in despair.

"I can't talk too much just now Liz, but things are pretty bad. Roger has abducted his daughter and taken her to Thailand."

"WHAT!"

"I know, I know," Kim said, "it sounds incredible, but that phone message that made me drop everything and run, was from his wife, Vanessa. She'd found my phone number in Roger's consulting rooms and thought I might know where he'd gone."

"And did you?" interrupted Liz.

"No, of course not," Kim replied her guilt making her overreact, "you know I've been moving heaven and earth to avoid him."

"Sorry."

"And there's worse news," Kim continued, "Don knows there's something wrong about me knowing Vanessa and Roger, but I've managed to put off telling him anything more till after we find Sophie."

There was a long pause while both women realised what this was going to mean for Kim's relationship.

"Anyway," Kim managed to continue, "it looks like I'll be going to Thailand with Vanessa to try and get her daughter back..."

"YOU!"

"Yes, me," replied Kim, quietly. "Please don't ask me anything more just now. If this is to happen, I'll need to take some time off, a week or so. Could you clear it at work?"

"Leave it with me Kim," replied Liz, "and I won't ask any more questions. But, Kim, do take care of yourself we both know what Roger is capable of and I shudder to think how he'll going to react if he's cornered."

"He'll react like the rat he is," said Kim through gritted teeth.

She heard footsteps behind her. "I have to go now Liz, see you later."

Don came down the front steps waving some paperwork in triumph.

"Got it," he grimaced. "I was right. Roger had been surfing the net for information on Thailand, especially a place called Pattaya Beach and hiding his history. Unfortunately, for him, he didn't cover his tracks enough."

Kim looked at the printouts on Roger's business letter heads.

"But these are copies of letters," she said.

"Exactly!" He grabbed her arm, "let's get back to Aunt Hazel's and Vanessa, hopefully, this will lead us right to Roger's door."

Don folded the papers and put them in his inside pocket. "Can't I read them," Kim asked.

Donald shook his head. "Not till we're all together," he said.

The drive back to Hazel's was as silent as the journey out. Donald's eyes were fixed on the road, but his mind was becoming fixated with Roger Lomax. His trawl through Roger's computer had revealed the depth to which the man had descended. There were visits to child pornography sites and websites extolling the dubious virtues of Pattaya Beach, especially targeted at middle-aged white men with money, who were looking for no-strings sex with young Thai women. There were also emails from someone called Darko in London, who seemed to be procuring Thai girls for Roger. Donald felt a deep anger and revulsion building inside him. Normally an easy going, peaceful man, Roger's depravity was bringing out a side of himself he hadn't, till then, realised even existed. By the time they got back to Hazel's, he had made up his mind. He too was going to Thailand. He was sure Vanessa knew nothing about Roger's depraved lifestyle and, hopefully, neither did Kim and there was no way he was going to let the women go alone to find this sexual monster.

Vanessa jumped to her feet when the pair came in the door.

"Well?" she asked fearfully, "did you find anything?"

Don eased her back down onto the settee. "It's alright Vanessa," he said, "I think we know where he's gone in Thailand." He looked around at the others.

"Let's sit down at the table and talk this through," he said, taking control of the situation. "Aunt Hazel," he asked, "can you make us some of your wonderful tea. I think we're going to need it."

Hazel hurried through to the kitchen while the others gathered around the table in the front room. Don was considering how much to tell the women without panicking them about the possible danger that Sophie could be in at Roger's hands. Hazel handed out the cups of hot tea and joined them.

"Well," she asked Donald, "what can you tell us?"

Don cleared his throat. "Before I say anything else, I've decided that I'll be going with you to Thailand." The response was positive as Vanessa sighed with relief and Kim visibly relaxed. Hazel nodded sagely in acknowledgement of her nephew's decision.

"Now," he continued, "when I dug around in Roger's computer, amongst other things, I found three letters to someone called Missy Areva Wong Sawat, in a place called Pattaya Beach in Thailand. The women exchanged glances of ignorance.

"Who is she?" asked Vanessa.

Donald frowned. "I think she's the contact in Thailand he's been in touch with and who has arranged a place for him to stay out there."

"How did he know who to contact?" Vanessa asked, "he's never been to Thailand before."

"According to his emails, he contacted someone called Darko, in London. I assume it was him who gave him Missy Areva's name and address."

Kim felt herself go numb. 'God, no,' she thought, 'now Donald knows about Darko.'

Her lips tightened as Don went on. "I suggest we book flights to Thailand as soon as we can and find this woman. She's the only link we have as to where Roger may have gone with Sophie." He looked round the faces at the table. "Vanessa," he asked, "do you want to do this?" Vanessa nodded.

"I'll draw out the money from the bank tomorrow and we can meet at the travel agency in town. I know Mr Rennie and he's very nice. I'm sure he'll do all he can to get us on an early flight." The fight was back in Vanessa's eyes, now that she could see a way forward.

"Kim?" he turned towards her. "What about you?"

Kim looked at Vanessa and saw her neediness. "Count me in," she said.

Donald nodded. "Right then," he said, "we'll meet tomorrow at ten o'clock at the travel agency and Vanessa," he added, squeezing her hand, "everything will be alright."

"I know," she said in a whisper, "all I have to do is follow the elephant," she looked at Kim, "and that's what I'm doing."

Donald didn't understand the statement but he also put it down to the stress she had been under. His concern was Roger Lomax. He now knew he was a paedophile and that he had taken his twelve year old daughter to a far off country, to do with whatever his warped urges desired. Don prayed to God they would be in time.

Chapter 31

Sophie lay staring at the mosquito netting all around the bed. The sun had been up for a couple of hours and already the heat was beginning to build.

She could hear Nona and Thana speaking and giggling in the kitchen as they prepared breakfast. They sounded so normal, but nothing in Thailand was normal to Sophie. She missed everything about home. She missed her school and her friends, especially Jane, who must be wondering where she was. She missed her mum and thought of all the horrid things she had said to her when she didn't get her own way. Sophie felt very lost in this strange land and couldn't understand why daddy had brought her here. The surprises he had planned for her birthday were no longer happy thoughts. Everything was confusing.

She pushed the netting aside and slipped out of bed, padding her way to the bathroom adjoining her room. There was a pile of her clothes sitting on a chair alongside the Thai dress her father had bought at the floating market. Where had they come from, she wondered, she hadn't packed any clothes for herself except for her little overnight bag when they'd left for the Riding Stables.

Her thoughts flashed back to the horse and how happy she'd been when she'd been able to ride him, but now...

Gloomily, she washed and dressed in a t-shirt and pair of shorts, pushing her feet into a pair of flip flops which had also magically appeared and went to find her father.

Roger was sitting on the veranda in a high-backed wicker chair, his feet resting on a stool and a cup of coffee in his hand. He indicated the table to her. "Help yourself to breakfast," he said, "the fruit salad and eggs are particularly delicious."

Sophie did as she was told, more driven by hunger than because she wanted to. He daddy seemed so normal too. She looked around her. Everything seemed to be normal in this strange place to everyone but her.

After eating, she joined him on the veranda. "How about a swim?" he asked, beaming at nothing in particular.

Sophie looked out at the water, sparkling in the sunlight. "I don't like the sea," she said emphatically.

Roger pursed his lips. "OK," he said evenly, "what would you like to do?"

Sophie took her chance. "Go home," she said.

This pussy-footing wasn't going to work any longer, Roger thought, it was time to tell her, she was here to stay.

"Let's go for a walk," he suggested passing her a wide brimmed sunhat. "You'll need this."

Sophie put on the hat and followed her father down onto the beach.

He sat down near the edge of the water and motioned her to join him.

"Thing is, Sophie," he began, "we're not going back to England. We're going to live here."

The bluntness of his words hit her like a physical thing.

"What do you mean?" she asked, her chin beginning to quiver.

"Just what I said. We're not going back to England, ever and the sooner you get used to the idea, sweetheart, the better it will be for everyone."

Sophie drew her knees up to her chin and hid her face in her hands.

"But, I don't want to stay here," she said desperately through her fingers, "I want to go back home."

Roger sighed, "Sorry Sophie," he said, "no going back." Defiance brought on by fear filled Sophie's heart and she jumped up.

"But what about mum," she shouted, tears beginning to flow freely, "and the new baby," she suddenly remembered, "the new baby needs me."

A darkness came over Roger at the mention of both Vanessa and the baby and he pulled Sophie roughly back down onto the sand.

"You'll do as I tell you," he growled at her, "nobody needs you, not your mother and not the baby, so get used to it. You're staying here with ME."

Waves of shock and fear reverberated through her young body. What was her daddy saying and why was he being like this? He'd always given her everything she'd ever asked for, but now... he was behaving as if she was a stranger, not his little girl at all.

"And stop staring," he said bluntly as her eyes of disbelief bore into him.

Just managing to control her tears, Sophie stood up and started to back away from him. "I feel sick," she said looking towards the villa.

Roger kept his eyes fixed on the sea. "You'd better go and vomit then," he grunted.

Sophie ran for all she was worth back to the house. She almost knocked Nona down as she barrelled blindly through the living room and into her room, throwing herself down onto the bed and sobbing tears of fear and confusion.

Startled, Nona listened at her door till the sounds lessened, before knocking gently on her door. "Sophie," she called, "are you alright?"

After a while, the door opened and Nona could see Sophie's swollen eyes and face red with weeping.

The young Thai girl took her hand. "It'll be alright," she counselled, "the first time is always the worst, but after that, you learn to take it and it becomes easier." Sophie didn't understand what Nona was talking about but gave her a weak smile. She liked Nona and the food she cooked and now she felt too that she had maybe found a friend.

"Please," she said to Sophie, "wash face and look pretty and Mr Roger will be happy with you again."

"You don't understand, Nona," she said, "I don't want to live here with daddy, I want to go home to England."

Nona frowned in disbelief. "Not happy here?"

Sophie shook her head. "Nona sorry," she said softly.

Just then the sound of Roger coming up the steps to the veranda ended the conversation. "Must go," Nona whispered. Silently she slipped away from Sophie's door as it was firmly closed.

By the time she could smell lunch being prepared, Sophie had calmed down.

There had to be a way to get away from here. Surely, her mother must be worried about her by now, if only she could get word to her where she was, she'd come and get her. Roger had the only mobile phone, but Nona must know where there was a phone she could use. She resolved to confide in her as soon as she could, ask her to help her.

She splashed her face with water and put on a clean t-shirt. She had to pretend she was willing to stay, till she could get to a phone.

Making her way through to lunch, she heard Nona giggling as her father's deep voice urged her to go faster. Peeping around the side of the door she saw her father sitting on a low wooden chair, his bare legs stretched out either side of Nona who sat astride him with her back to Sophie. What were they doing!

Frozen to the spot, Sophie stared at the scene in front of her as Roger pulled Nona, in stronger and stronger thrusts, towards him. Nona's giggling filled her ears and only stopped when Roger roughly pushed her away. Sophie watched as Nona fastened her skirt back around her waist and bowed out of the room. Roger sat with his head back and eyes closed, breathing heavily, the long white shirt he had taken to wearing pushed between his legs.

Sophie felt herself tremble. Whatever it was that had happened, she knew it was wrong, but that Nona had been happy. All thoughts of asking her for help faded. Sophie felt totally and utterly alone.

All emotion spent, even fear, Sophie went through to lunch. Roger waved her in as if nothing had happened. "Here," he said, "try this chicken it's delicious." He waved a chicken leg at her, before biting into it and tearing chunks of meat from the bone. Sophie picked at some fruit and rice, her appetite having deserted her. "Still feel sick?" Roger asked, shrugging his shoulders when she didn't answer.

Sophie looked at the man in front of her and a coldness entered her being. This wasn't her daddy, this was a monster and she was trapped.

Chapter 32

The trio met at ten o'clock at the travel agency. Mr Rennie was kindness itself, just as Vanessa had promised and they spent the next hour arranging their flights to Bangkok and a cheap hotel for the night when they got there.

"We'll also need a hire car," Don said, "enough for four people and luggage."

Mr Rennie looked at them, he'd had enough understanding of Bangkok to know it had a seedier side. "But there's just the three of you," he said, "unless..."

"Someone will be joining us in Bangkok, Mr Rennie," Donald advised.

He wrote out their flight tickets. "These are your tickets," he said, "and you will have to pick up visitors' visas at the airport. The currency is Thai Bhatt," he added, "do you want any Thai currency?" Vanessa looked at Donald.

"Some US Dollars would be better," he replied, "say £500 worth."

Mr Rennie disappeared through to the back of the shop. "Why do we need US Dollars?" Kim asked.

Don drew her aside. "From what I can gather from Roger's correspondence," he whispered, "Missy Areva doesn't give anything away for free. I just hope £500 will be enough for her to tell us Roger's address in Pattaya Beach."

Mr Rennie handed the money over to Vanessa and the tickets to Don.

"Anything else?" he smiled.

"No, thanks, Mr Rennie," said Vanessa, "you've been very helpful."

"Anytime," he nodded, but there was something about the transaction that made him uneasy. Their return date was only five days after their departure, a long way to go for a very short stay!

Just as they were leaving the shop, he called after Vanessa, "How's that little girl of yours by the way? Haven't seen her at the school bus stop for a few days."

Vanessa hesitated for a moment. "She's fine, Mr Rennie, just has a bit of a cold, that's all."

"That why she's not going with you then?" Vanessa nodded and moved quickly out of the door and onto the pavement.

"What was that all about?" Kim asked Vanessa.

"Don't know," she said, "maybe just genuine concern."

But it wasn't. David Rennie knew of Roger Lomax and the therapy he used to treat his clients. Enid Rawlings was his sister and she was currently in a mental hospital due, he was sure, to Roger Lomax's treatment. Ever since she had started attending his clinic she'd become more and more depressed and reclusive and had become hysterical when he had closed his practice a couple of weeks ago. Eventually she had broken down completely and the doctor had insisted she be admitted to the hospital for observation and treatment. And now, Roger Lomax's wife and two of her friends were going to Thailand, leaving the daughter behind? Something didn't add up, David Rennie surmised, he'd speak to Enid at their next visit, tell her the news and hope it would get her to open up about what was eating away at her.

Vanessa, Kim and Donald went into the small cafe nearby to consolidate their plans. "When we get to Thailand," Donald said, "we'll pick up the hire car at the airport and after the night in the hotel to recover from the trip, we'll motor down to Pattaya Beach."

The two women nodded.

Now came the difficult bit. "Vanessa," he began, "once we get to Pattaya Beach, you and Kim needn't come with me to Missy Areva's place in Walking Street. I can drop you both off at some cafe or other and pick you up when I've got the information we need." They both looked concerned.

"Why can't we just come with you?"

"Walking Street," he explained slowly, "is the place where western sex tourists go, I believe in their thousands, looking for young Thai women for, well..."

Kim and Vanessa sat waiting. Don cleared his throat before continuing.

"Well, that's where Missy Areva Wong has her sex shop."

Kim blinked and Vanessa's muscles tightened.

"Is that where he's taken Sophie?" Vanessa asked, hoping against hope she was wrong.

Donald nodded. "I'm sorry, Vanessa," he said, trying to think of a way of breaking the news to her that Roger was a paedophile, but Kim interrupted before he could answer.

She took Vanessa's hand. "If that's where he's gone then the quicker we get there the better." She glanced at Donald, a warning in her eyes. "Let's not get worried before we have to," she said, "we'll be on the flight late tonight and by tomorrow we'll be in Thailand. Let's just focus on that first and deal with whatever we have to when we get there."

"Right," Don said briskly, "let's get packing and I'll pick you both up around four o'clock for the drive to Heathrow. Remember your passports," he concluded, "see you both at four."

The three parted company, each with their own thoughts and fears. Kim phoned Liz when she got back to her flat. "Just to update you, we're heading for Thailand tonight," she told Liz. "God knows what Roger is up to with Sophie, it turns out he's taken her to a place called Pattaya Beach, notorious for sex tourists."

Kim heard her friend's sharp intake of breath. "You don't think he's going to do anything horrible..."Liz's voice faltered.

"The short answer to that is, I don't know," Kim replied. "I know he's capable of some pretty sordid stuff but, his daughter?" Kim quickly changed the subject, pushing aside the thought of Roger lusting after his own child. "Don's been great," she said, "he's taken charge of the whole trip and no matter what happens to us in the future, I'm so glad he's coming along."

"What about Vanessa?" Liz asked.

"I think she's got much stronger, especially now we have a way forward. I don't think she realises the extent of Roger's 'activities' and certainly not regarding Sophie. She seems to think he's just paying her back for keeping the baby."

"What a mess," Liz said with feeling.

"Well, the quicker we get started the better," Kim said, "so it looks like we'll be away for at least five days, if that's OK."

"Of course it is. I told you I've got things covered at the station."

"Thanks Liz."

"Kim," said her friend, "take care of yourself and I'll be thinking of you all till you get back, hopefully, with Sophie."

Kim hung up and looked around her flat. How she longed for life to be normal again. She couldn't believe how distorted life had become since meeting Roger Lomax and now, here she was about to go to Thailand to rescue a little girl! She fingered the silver elephant head on the chain around her neck.

"Just follow the elephant," she intoned, "and everything will be alright."

She dragged her case off the top of the wardrobe and started packing, hoping that the guardian angel was paying strict attention to what was happening.

Don picked her up at exactly four o'clock. Vanessa was already in the car.

"Ready," he said, wheeling her case to the car and lifting it into the boot.

"Ready," she said, "how's Vanessa?"

"Seems pretty calm," he said, "let's hope she keeps that way."

The drive to Heathrow was slow due to sheer volume of traffic, but they finally got to the long stay car park where Don left the car and his credit card details.

"C'mon," he said, "let's get our visas and check in."

The airport was crowded with people of all nationalities. "Stick together," he ordered the women, "we don't want anyone going missing." As soon as he said it, he regretted the words. "I mean, getting lost," he corrected himself.

"It's alright," Vanessa said, "we know what you meant."

Everything checked out as they were processed through the airport and finally, at nine-thirty they were on the plane and ready for take-off.

The Gulf Air stewardesses were beautifully dressed and exotically made up. If the reason for the journey hadn't been so serious, it would be have been exciting, but none of the three were saying much, each just wanting to get to Thailand and find Sophie.

Kim and Donald dozed most of the way, but Vanessa remained fully awake. Her brain was racing from one possibility to another. Why had Roger gone to such a place as Pattaya Beach? If what Donald said was right, it would be the last place on earth her daughter should be. And why did he want to punish her like this? She couldn't have had the baby aborted, even though its conception had been forced on her, she had seen its little shape on the scan and couldn't have hurt it for the world. Then she realised, before the baby, Sophie was her world and Roger had taken her away as the worst punishment he could think of. She felt her mouth turn down with a new emotion. Hatred.

It was late afternoon when they landed at Bangkok and the humidity hit them as soon as they stepped from the air-conditioned plane and down the metal stairway to the tarmac.

They followed the snake of passengers into the airport, through Customs and Baggage Reclaim, before finding the Car Hire Desk. The paperwork was all there and Don signed for the people carrier. The agent smiled and nodded towards the exit door. "There is a little bus," he said politely, "it will take you to the car compound." Wearily, they completed the last lap of their journey as Donald drove the car to the hotel. They were all hot and exhausted and arranged to meet for dinner in the restaurant around eight o'clock. To give them time to freshen up and cool off. There were no arguments from anyone.

Dinner was quiet and quick, each wanting to get as much sleep as possible before the drive to Pattaya Beach. "Breakfast around seven o'clock," Don said, "then we can get an early start before it gets too hot."

Kim and Vanessa nodded. Just being in Thailand had raised their spirits that they were getting near their goal of rescuing Sophie. Tomorrow couldn't come soon enough.

Chapter 33

It was two days till her birthday and Sophie couldn't have felt more miserable.

She had come to realise that Thana and Nona were more than just housemaids. Nona, at least, was doing 'things' with her father that didn't seem at all right to her young mind. So too, probably, was Thana, Sophie thought objectively. They were sisters after all, she concluded.

She had taken to avoiding her father as often as possible, but that morning he had sent for her. "Mr Roger wants to see you," advised Nona, "and he say, right now."

Sophie felt herself cringe, but had no option but to do as she was bid.

She stood before him, looking at her feet and trying to magic him to disappear. "I want you to begin to blend in," he said, "and look at me when I'm talking to you."

Sophie raised her head and tried to meet his eyes, but only managed his nose. He called for Nona, who came hurrying in, hands clasped in front of her and bowing as usual. "Yes, Mr Roger," she asked, "what is your wish?"

Roger took a moment to savour her subservience.

"Bring me the package I left with you last night."

Nona backed out of his presence and returned in a couple of minutes with the package, which she placed on the table beside him. She went to leave.

"Stay here," he ordered her, "and open the packaging."

Nona did as she was bid and produced a box with the picture of a smiling Thai girl on the front and strange writing at the top. "Tell my daughter what it is," he instructed.

Nona looked at Roger non-plussed. "It is lady's hair dye," she said, turning the box over in case she'd misread something.

"Now," he said, "look at the colour of Sophie's hair and look at the colour on the box." Nona looked.

"Which is the prettier?" he asked.

Afraid to give the wrong answer, Nona replied, "Whatever one you say Mr Roger, that one is the prettiest."

Sophie wanted to disappear through the floor boards, as she realised what her father had in mind.

"Take her to the bathroom," he said to Nona, "and don't bring her back till her hair is the colour on the box."

"But, I don't want to have black hair," Sophie pleaded, "I like it the colour it is."

"Tsk tsk, Sophie, I've told you, I want you to blend in."

Sophie looked at Nona in desperation. "I don't want to blend in," she cried, "please don't do this."

"Nona will do as I say," Roger said harshly, "won't you Nona."

Nona bowed her head and Sophie knew she was as trapped here as she was.

"Yes Mr Roger," she said meekly, taking Sophie's hand in a firm grasp as she led her away from her father and into the bathroom.

She put her fingers to her lips. "Ssssshhhh," she whispered, "please do as he says or I am the one who will suffer."

Sophie saw her own fear reflected back at her in the eyes of Nona and understood. "There is no way out," she said, "is there?"

"Not for Thai girls," said Nona, "and also not for you."

Sophie sat dejected while Nona mixed the colour and combed it through her blonde hair. "It's not too bad, being a Thai girl," she said with more assurance than she felt, "and if it keeps Mr Roger happy, it will be easier for all of us."

Sophie tried to keep her eyes shut till Nona had finished, but when she finally looked in the mirror her heart sank. In place of her beautiful blonde locks was jet black hair, making her pale skin look even paler. She felt like crying, but knew it would be of no use. Nothing was going to stop her father doing whatever he wanted. Nona towelled and brushed the miserable girl's hair dry and smiled. "It is very pretty," she said, comfortingly, "you can be our new sister."

She took Sophie's hand and brought her back before Roger.

"Well," he said admiringly, "what a difference."

Sophie said nothing.

"But you know, something's still wrong," he added, stroking his chin as if in deep thought. "Of course," he said, "it's your clothes." He looked his daughter up and down. "Your clothes don't go with your hair."

"Nona," he said, "take her away again and dress her properly and when that's done, get rid of those ridiculous shorts and t shirt. I never want to see them again."

"And Nona," he called after them, "show her what to do with her face, pretty her up a bit."

Nona grasped Sophie's hand firmer this time and led her away. She felt heart sorry for the young English girl who was so innocent in the ways of the world, especially the Thai world which she had learned about, some five years ago, at the hands of her own father.

Sophie felt herself diminishing by the minute. Everything about herself that she knew was being stripped away and replaced by a stranger. She didn't know why her father was doing this, but she knew it was bad and very wrong.

Powerless to do anything about it, both girls did as they were told and Sophie was dressed in the green and gold costume bought from the floating market in Bangkok, then Nona painted black lines around her eyes and red on her lips.

"There," she stood back. "Mr Roger will be happy now."

Looking like a china doll and feeling just as fragile, Sophie was brought back before her father for a second time.

"Perfect," he murmured, already aroused at the thought of what tomorrow held. He had planned everything so meticulously, and on Sophie's thirteenth birthday, he would finally claim his prize. His daughter's virginity.

Ever since she had been born, he had watched her grow from a toddler to a young, pubescent girl, her body changing as she developed. He had talked to her night after night as she slept in her room, eating into her subconscious with his carnal suggestions. All the time, preparing her for the moment when she would invite him in. Tomorrow, he would give her something to relax her, keep her subdued till he was ready. He positively glowed at the cowed child in front of him. This was what he lived for, this was what he lusted after, young, fresh, virginal flesh.

In his mind, she was no longer his daughter but his concubine, just like Nona and Thana, ready and willing to meet his every sexual demand and he had many. She would find that out tomorrow.

He dismissed Nona with a wave of his hand and sat Sophie down opposite him, where he could savour her. "Tomorrow is your thirteenth birthday," he said, an edge of anticipation creeping into his voice. "And we're going to celebrate in a very special way."

Sophie had had enough of her father's celebrations and surprises and now knew that whatever it was, she wasn't going to like it.

"I don't want to celebrate anymore," she said, "I want to go home."

Roger felt a surge of anger that she was ruining his fantasy for him.

"Stop talking about home," he shouted, "I've told you, you live here now, with ME."

Sophie felt herself cringe as Roger's anger blazed from his eyes.

"I'm sorry," she said, scared now that he was going to actually hit her.

His smile returned. "That's better," he said, "now let's have some nice dinner," he smoothed, "just the two of us and then an early night for you. Don't want you missing any of your birthday celebrations, do we?" The way he said 'birthday celebrations' filled Sophie with foreboding and thoughts of escaping once again filled her head. Her only chance would be to speak to Nona, get her to help her escape, but her childlike mind couldn't see any further than the walls of this villa. Where could she escape to with no money and nobody she could run to.

Roger watched her eat their meal and sip on some fruit juice. "How would you like a little wine?" he asked, "now that you will soon be a grown up lady."

Without waiting for an answer, he poured some from his glass into Sophie's fruit juice.

"Try it," he urged. "You'll like it."

Fearful of what would happen if she refused, Sophie took a sip of the drink. It tasted bitter and made her face screw up. "The first taste is always like that" Roger laughed, and poured some more into the glass. "Try again."

Over the course of the meal Sophie was forced to drink again and again from her glass. She felt her eyes lose focus and her hands begin to move uncontrollably. She could hear her father laughing, but it was somewhere in the distance. Her eyes closed and she slumped across the table. She felt herself being carried through to her room and dumped onto her bed. "Sleep well, sweetheart," she heard her father say, before blackness enveloped her.

Chapter 34

Vanessa was already seated at the table when Kim and Donald joined her for breakfast. Kim wondered if she had slept at all.

After they had eaten and drank several cups of coffee, Donald prepared them for the day. "First stop is Walking Street," he said, "I've found out that during the day, it's actually quiet, it isn't till night that things start to happen, so we should be able to find Missy Areva's sex shop without too much trouble."

He looked at the women. No one queried how he'd found this out and when he asked if they still wanted to go with him to find the place, Kim and Vanessa both nodded. "We might as well know what we're getting into," said Vanessa nervously.

Don wasn't so sure, but both women seemed determined to face whatever was in store.

"Once we know where he is and, more to the point, where Sophie is, here's what I suggest."

Don outlined a loose plan of attack. The most important thing was to first of all get Sophie and also, vitally, her passport, if they were to get out of Thailand and back to England without any awkward questions being asked by the authorities.

"The thing to remember is that Roger won't be expecting us, so we have the element of surprise, but after that, we'll just have to play it by ear and hope for the best."

They checked out of the hotel and loaded up the car. "Everybody ready?" Don asked. The two women looked at each other.

"Ready as we'll ever be!" said Kim, taking hold of Vanessa's hand. "It'll be alright," she whispered, "as long as we follow the elephant." Kim smiled.

"I remember."

In the morning light, Walking Street was the most shabby sight Vanessa had ever seen. Everywhere she looked, she saw painted cardboard figures of naked women, with sleazy signs for live sex shows in every window. Small Thai men were unloading boxes of alcohol and food supplies for the night ahead and miniature Thai women were either helping, or picking up rubbish from the areas around the shop fronts. The whole street was a hive of industry, with people going about their business as if it were any high street in any town in England. Except that here, the only thing on sale was sex.

"Is it much further?" she asked Don, who was scanning the shop fronts for the LuLu Sex Shop.

"Hope not," he muttered, beginning to panic that he'd somehow got the information from Roger's computer wrong.

"Over there," Kim pointed. Don breathed out in relief and pulled the car to a halt. He turned to the two women in the back seat.

"Sure you don't want to wait here?" he asked. Both women shook their heads and stepped out of the car. Vanessa shuddered. How could Roger have brought their daughter to a place like this?

The door of LuLu's opened at the first knock, almost as if the owner had seen them pull up. A very lovely Thai woman faced them.

"Missy Areva?" Don asked, politely.

"Who's asking?" came the cautious reply.

Don cleared his throat. "We're friends of Roger Lomax," he lied, "and thought we'd pay him a surprise visit."

Even as he was saying the words, Don felt his face redden. He was useless at lying, but couldn't think of anything else to explain their appearance at her door.

Kim could see the look of suspicion on Missy Areva's face. "I'm also a friend of Darko," she said hurriedly, hoping that she would make the connection with the Soho Club and relax.

Her eyes lit up. "Ah," she said, "Darko from London."

Kim nodded and smiled. "He wants more Thai girls?" she asked sensing money.

"No," Kim said, quickly, her fingers crossed behind her back, "but he did say you knew Roger and where he was living."

Missy Areva's eyes narrowed. "He told you that?"

"He did."

There was an uncomfortable silence while everyone wondered what to say next to convince Missy to tell them what they wanted to know, but it was Vanessa who spoke first.

"Would $500 help?"

Missy's eyes fixed on the bundle of green currency Vanessa had produced from her handbag.

"Wait here," she ordered.

The door closed and three pairs of eyes stared at the chipped paintwork, willing it to open again. After a few minutes, Missy Areva came half way out of the door, her hand reaching to Vanessa and the money. Vanessa handed it over and in return received a slip of paper with writing on it, before the door firmly closed again.

She handed it to Donald. "Money talks," he said, "let's go."

The address was 'Shangri La Villa, 116 Beach Road.'

"Should be easy enough to find," said Don, starting the engine, "just head for the ocean."

If Donald had been surprised at the mention of someone called Darko, he kept it to himself, for now. The important thing was to find the villa and get Sophie out. He reminded the women about not only finding Sophie, but also getting her passport from wherever Roger kept it. It was agreed that Don would deal with Roger, while Vanessa grabbed Sophie and Kim searched for her passport. The plan was vague, but it was all they had. There was much that could go wrong, but Don pushed all 'what if' scenarios to the back of his mind and focussed on the task in hand.

Had their mission not been so serious, the drive to Roger's villa would have been breathtaking. The ocean rollers surged onto pure white sand and stands of palm trees waved their welcome to Thailand, but no one in the car was looking at the view, they were looking for Shangri La.

A weathered wooden board, nailed to a post had the words they had been looking for painted on it, in red. A track headed south towards the beach and Don could see tyre treads left by another vehicle etched into the sand.

"This is it," he announced nervously, "keep your eyes peeled for any sign of life, especially Roger."

Don inched the people carrier forward, blipping the accelerator only enough to keep them moving forward. The track widened and opened out as the villa came into view. "Shangri La," Don whispered, "this is it."

He pulled on the hand brake and cut the engine. There were no signs of movement anywhere. "Probably still in bed," he suggested, wishing once more he could take the words back the minute he said them, but Vanessa remained impassive.

They all felt the tension of the unknown as they watched the scene before them, but nothing moved. "C'mon," he said trying to inject confidence into his voice, "we know what we've come for and we're not leaving without her."

Kim fingered the silver elephant. Now she was here and about to face Roger, she could feel the fear beginning to surface unchecked. Vanessa's hand grasped hers. "Please," she whispered to Kim. The rest went unsaid, but Kim knew she had to see this through, if it was the last thing she ever did.

She nodded to Vanessa, she owed this pregnant lady so much for the mistakes of the past and now it was payback time. "Let's get Sophie," she said firmly, "and her passport," she added with a hint of humour as she tried to lighten the task ahead.

Don tugged the bell-pull that hung beside the door, its tinkling sounding inadequate to summon anyone inside. He made a fist and banged it on the wooden lintel. The sound of slow, shuffling footsteps came closer, a bolt was pulled back and the door swung open. A bleary-eyed, middle-aged man, wearing a long white shirt and sandals blinked at the figures before him.

"Who the hell...?" he began, trying to clear his head from last night's drinking.

"Hello Roger." Vanessa's voice was calm and firm. "I've come for Sophie."

Disbelief filled Roger's eyes. "Vanessa," he muttered bewilderedly. If the ghost of Christmas Past had stood before him, he couldn't have felt more stunned. How had she found him here! Stupid, dull Vanessa? His eyes moved to the gangly, bespectacled giraffe of a man beside her. "And who the hell are you?"

"Just a friend," said Donald, deciding to take advantage of their surprise appearance by pushing past Roger into the house, followed by Vanessa.

Roger began to gather his wits about him and felt the anger generate indignant energy inside him. "Fuck off," he yelled, "both of you before I get really angry and break your fucking necks."

Kim had stayed outside till then, but hearing Roger's threats gave her the courage to enter. "Blame me," she said, emphatically, "I brought them here."

For the second time, Roger felt he was seeing a ghost, but not for long.

"Well, well," he sneered, "if it isn't my favourite whore. Miss your spankings, Kim dearest." He moved nearer to her. "Want a bit more punishment from old Roger do you?" Kim could feel her heart racing in her chest as he closed in on her, his breath reeking of stale whiskey and old curry.

Before she could move, she felt his hands encircle her neck and start to squeeze. "This is what happens to naughty little girls like you," he spat, the words foaming from his mouth. Kim felt her knees buckle and her eyes bulge. She grabbed his hands to loosen them from her throat but they were locked hard. She was going to die! She could sense everything around her become silent and darkness began to cloud her vision.

Don, who had been frozen to the spot at Roger's words, suddenly reacted.

He wrapped is arm around Roger's neck to try to pull him away, but it was useless, Roger had the strength of someone out of control. Rapidly, he looked round the room for something to use to knock Roger out. And then he saw it. On a table nearby was the elongated statue of an Egyptian cat carved in white marble. He grabbed it by the neck and brought it down with as much force as he could muster on the back of Roger's head. Almost instantly, the grip on Kim's neck loosened as Roger fell into a sea of darkness.

Kim staggered backwards, gasping for air. Vanessa rushed over to her and eased her down onto a chair, stroking her hand and reassuring her she was alright.

Don stood over the slumped figure of Roger. The back of his head was bleeding, but he was breathing. He dropped the statue as if it was burning and fell to his knees. He could have killed a man, he realised shocked at the level of violence he had felt. He gazed over at Kim, white and shaken and wondered how he had got mixed up in all this mess. It seemed like years ago, that he was living a normal life, even falling in love, but now!...

It was Vanessa who took control of the situation.

"Don," she said, shouting at him to get his attention. "It's alright," she assured him, "it's nearly over. We just need to find Sophie and we'll be out of here and heading home." Don felt his head nod in agreement. "Just stay with Roger," she said, "I'm going to find her."

She squeezed Kim's hand and hurried from the room to start her search.

Kim opened her eyes enough to see Don staring at her. His look said it all. If he ever loved her before, he didn't now. Roger had won in the end.

She struggled to her feet, rubbing her neck. "Passport," she whispered, her voice rasping against her tonsils, "must find it."

Vanessa found herself in a corridor with two doors opening off it. The first one she tried led into a bedroom. In the middle of the room was what looked like a round bed surrounded by mosquito netting. She could see a small figure lying there, her black hair spread over the pillow and her Thai dress crumpled around her knees. She crept closer. Perhaps this girl would know where Sophie was. She pulled aside the netting and shook the girl by the shoulder. A sleepy head turned towards her, "Go away daddy," she said, her eyes squeezed tightly shut, "I don't want any more birthday surprises."

Vanessa took a moment to realise who the child was. "Sophie?" she whispered anxiously, stroking the black hair. "Sophie, it's mummy, I've come to take you home."

Two blue eyes opened wider and tears immediately began to spill out of them. "Mummy?" Sophie asked incredulously. "Oh mummy, you've found me."

Two small arms wrapped themselves round Vanessa's neck. "It's alright now Sophie," Vanessa said, grimly, "mummy's going to take you home and you need never see this place again."

She bundled Sophie out of the bed. "Are there any of your own clothes here?"

Sophie pointed to the bathroom. "In there."

Vanessa went through and grabbed a pair of jeans and a couple of t-shirts from the pile. "C'mon," she urged, "these will do till we get home."

Roger still lay comatose but Donald had begun to react again. He was sitting on a chair, his head in his hands and the sound of muffled sobs coming from his throat.

"Don," Vanessa called, "I've got her. Look."

Donald Martin raised his eyes. "Sophie?" he asked.

Vanessa nodded, "It's alright, she's just had her hair dyed and been dressed to look like a Thai girl." She hugged her daughter, "Nothing that won't wash out."

Sophie gazed at her father, lying in a heap on the floor.

"Is daddy alright?" she asked Vanessa, real concern showing on her young face, despite what had happened. Vanessa held her face with both hands and established eye contact.

"Daddy will be fine," she said, "but he's going to stay in Thailand for a while after we leave. Is that OK with you?"

For what seemed like an eternity, Sophie said nothing, part of her confused and part of her just wanting to go home, then she nodded, "Yes," she said quietly, "I guess so." Vanessa turned to where Don was sitting.

"This nice man is Donald, go with him and wait in the car. Mummy and her friend will be down in a minute." She handed Sophie her clothes and indicated to Donald to take her to the car. Feeling beyond useless, Donald stood up and took Sophie's hand.

Vanessa looked around her, "Where's Kim?"

"Gone to look for the passport," Donald replied woodenly.

"I'm going to find her," she said. "We'll be with you as soon as we've got Sophie's passport.

Chapter 35

Kim had headed out through the opened door onto the balcony. She needed air. Breathing deeply, she stood still letting the awfulness of the situation sink in. She'd nearly died! If Don hadn't stopped him, Roger would have surely killed her. All around her, everything seemed so peaceful. It was hard to believe the sordidness of Roger's world on the other side of the door. And, there was Sophie. What had his plans been for her? She felt herself chill at the possibilities.

"Passport," she shook herself, "must find it."

She moved along the balcony till she came to another open door. The smell of cooking wafted through to her nostrils. Cautiously, she peered into the dimness. The shapes of two small girls came into focus.

"Can I come in?" she asked. As one, the two Thai girls shrank into the corner of the kitchen at the sound of the English voice. "It's alright," Kim said, placing her hands in front of her in Thai greeting, "I won't hurt you."

Nona and Thana looked at one another, eyes wide with fear.

"Mr Roger angry?" Nona finally asked. Kim's mind went back to Darko's club and the two young Thai girls she had seen there with Roger. She felt sick to her stomach. So this was Roger's big plan. To live in Thailand with young girls on demand, to meet his perverted needs, for the rest of his evil life.

Kim felt her heart break at the life these girls were forced to lead and anger welled inside her. "Get out of here," she suddenly yelled, "and never come back. DO YOU HEAR ME?" She pointed to the open door. "JUST GO."

The two sisters scampered past her and onto the balcony. Kim watched as they ran down the stairs that led to the beach. And may God go with you, she added silently to herself, knowing that their future was already

171

written.

Further along the balcony she could see another entrance. Carefully, she peeped in. From the size of the bed and the laptop on the table beside it, she figured this was Roger's room. She looked around. Passports, where would he keep the passports? She began to search. The room wasn't big and there weren't many places to secrete things away. She pulled open drawers, nothing, she rummaged through his clothes hanging in the wardrobe, nothing. Then she spotted it, a wooden box sitting in the bottom of the wardrobe. She lifted it out and opened it. It was full of banknotes. Sterling and US Dollars and underneath them, there they were, the passports. Roger's and Sophie's.

She pocketed them both. If Sophie couldn't get out of Thailand without a passport, then neither could Roger, Kim smiled for the first time since Roger's attack on her. At last, she had got one up on him.

She hurried back out of the room and along the balcony to the living room.

Vanessa was kneeling beside Roger, just looking at him with a mixture of sorrow and hurt. For all he had done, Kim realised bizarrely, Vanessa still seemed to have feelings for him!

She coughed to get her attention. "I've got the passport," she said, holding it up in front of her. She could see tears in Vanessa's eyes.

"It could have been all so different," she whispered, the calm assurance she had shown earlier, seeming now to desert her. "I loved him, you know," she told Kim. As she spoke Roger began to stir. Kim hurried over to Vanessa, grabbing her arm and hoisting her to her feet.

"C'mon," she said urgently, "we need to get out of here, he's coming round."

Vanessa straightened up. "Sophie's in the car with Don," she said, breathing deeply, her eyes still shining, "let's go home."

Kim and Vanessa hurried through the door and ran to the car. Don had the engine running and took off as soon as the doors closed.

"Did you get it?" he asked Kim. She handed him the passport.

"Good," he acknowledged. "Our flight's booked for tomorrow," he said, his practical side now reasserting itself, "I'll try to get Sophie booked on the same one. Keep your fingers crossed."

They drove for a couple of hours before Donald pulled into a small roadside motel.

"This'll do for the night," he said, turning to Vanessa, "book us in and

I'll head to the airport, see what I can get arranged for Sophie."

Vanessa nodded and placed her hand on his arm. "Thanks, Don," she said, "for everything."

Don nodded grimly. "We're not home yet," he said, "but we're nearly there," he added reassuringly. "I'll be back in about a couple of hours."

The drive to the airport gave Don a chance to settle his thoughts. Their objective had been accomplished and barring accidents, they should be back on English soil late afternoon the next day. Going to Thailand had been the right thing to do, he confirmed to himself, but he hadn't expected to have to club a man who was strangling his girlfriend in front of his eyes. His girlfriend, he mused, was she really? What did he actually know about Kim Mason and her past? If Roger was involved, he bet it would be murky and as for Darko, how did she know him? The questions without answers tumbled through his brain till he got to Bangkok Airport.

The airline was more than helpful and managed to book Sophie on the same flight as the rest of them. He almost maxed out his credit card but it was a small price to pay for Sophie and her mother's peace of mind. He found a quiet corner in the busy airport and sat down to rest, his eyes felt gritty and his body was sweating.

Aimlessly, he watched people go by as he waited for his energy to return. Coffee would be good, he thought after a while, forcing himself to join the queue at one of the many cafes dotted around the concourse. He pointed to his choice on the blackboard behind the counter and a smiling woman filled a cardboard cup with the black brew. Back in his seat, he sipped the hot, strong Americano.

It was nearly over, he told himself. Just one more night and day and he'd have everyone safely home, then he would have time to think things through properly regarding his relationship with Kim, but till then, he had to keep hold of his emotions and control the deep unease which had formed in his gut.

He finished his drink and stood up tightening his belt a notch, which stress had unexpectedly loosened and set his mind to 'neutral'. One step at a time, he repeated to himself till he was back in the car and on his way to the motel.

Vanessa had booked a twin room for herself and Sophie and, at Kim's insistence, two single rooms for her and Don.

"Is everything alright with you two?" Vanessa asked.

Kim's mouth set in a straight line. "Oh, you know," she replied, dropping her head and suddenly finding her feet very interesting, "sharing a bed in this climate isn't recommended."

Vanessa let the subject drop and turned her attention to Sophie's hair.

"How about we try to wash some of the dye out," she said, "try to get those lovely golden locks back." Sophie obediently took her mother's hand and nodded. She vowed, silently, she would never be horrible to her mother again.

Kim found her room and flopped onto the bed allowing her thoughts to roam back to her first meeting with Roger. He had seemed so helpful and caring then and she had trusted him immediately. Like Vanessa, she too had thought Roger was the most wonderful human being she'd ever met. She hadn't noticed the signs of his control over her mind developing, the insistence that he chose her clothes, because he knew best what suited her, his direct contradiction of her every opinion, foolish little Kim, his comparing her with other women, especially younger ones and how she didn't quite measure up to being as sexy as them.

His sexual demands had become more and more bizarre, as the months had gone on, forcing Kim to comply with his every wish in case he left her for someone who would. She drew her knees up to her chest and clasped her hands around them. How could she have been so stupid, so naive and now, he had tried to kill her. His hatred of her must have been total but in her too, like Vanessa, there was still a strange need to be around him. She pushed the thought from her head and sat up. She and Vanessa would have to have a conversation about it all when they got back, she decided, try to understand what had happened to them and find a way to heal.

The sound of Don's car pulling up in the small car park outside brought a fresh train of thought into Kim's head. She watched him park the car and go through the front door. Did she really believe that she could have a new life with any man, never mind someone as honest and straight thinking as Don, after what she had done! She shook her head to chase away her bleak future and felt for the little silver elephant round her neck for comfort. Would she ever find happiness again she asked it? There was a knock at her door. She opened it. Don stood there, looking strangely calm given the events of the day.

He ran his fingers through his damp hair. "Flights are booked for all of us," he said, "check-in around one o'clock tomorrow afternoon. Tell Vanessa," he continued, "I'm going for a lie down."

Before Kim could say anything, he turned and left her watching his back disappear down the short corridor. She looked at the elephant again. "I guess the answer's no," she said sadly.

Vanessa had managed to get most of the black dye out of Sophie's hair when Kim knocked at her door. "Look," she said pointing to her brownish blonde daughter. "I think it was a vegetable dye, so most of it's gone, a couple more washes should do it..." Kim's eyes registered misery and Vanessa asked Sophie to go to the small bathroom and replace the Thai dress with her jeans and one of the t-shirts. Once her daughter had left the room she took Kim's hand and led her over to the bed. "Here," she said, "sit down." Kim sat.

"What's wrong," she asked Kim worriedly, "everything's working out alright. Sophie's safe and we'll be home soon."

Tearful eyes turned to Vanessa. "I don't think Don loves me anymore," she whispered, "he just came to my room to tell me the flights were all booked and there wasn't a trace of affection or even friendliness in his voice."

Vanessa had heard Roger's rant at Kim at the same time Don had and could understand his hurt and betrayal at what was said, but she also understood how powerful Roger could be in getting his own way in everything. Hadn't she accepted his moods and anger that kept her cowed in his presence, hadn't she accepted his sexual perversions as normal, even the rape that had resulted in her pregnancy, he had convinced her, was her fault. She had even stood by as he slept in Sophie's room, despite her unease at his reasoning. But now, now it was clear, the man she had married was nothing more than a sexual predator and a perverted one at that.

She wrapped her arm around Kim's shoulders and hugged her closer.

"I know how you feel," she told her, "we've been used by my husband in a way that only we can understand, but it's over now," she said, "he can't hurt us anymore."

"And you can forgive me?" Kim blinked.

"There's nothing to forgive Kim," Vanessa whispered, "what we need to do now, is forgive ourselves." She pointed to the silver elephant. "Remember what Hazel said, follow the elephant and everything will be alright."

Kim felt a smile begin to tug at her lips. She wouldn't need to have that conversation with Vanessa when they got back to England she just needed to trust in herself again, they both did. She looked at the calm face of her fellow sufferer, her blue eyes willing love back into her heart and nodded in acknowledgement. Some good had come out of her encounter with Roger, after all, in Vanessa she had found a soulmate for life.

Sophie bounced back into the room, delighted to be wearing her own clothes again and towelling her hair dry. "Look mummy," she said, "it's nearly all gone." Vanessa high-fived her daughter, the relief of having her safely back again once more threatening to overwhelm her.

"Kim's got good news," she continued, bringing her into the happy circle.

"The good news is," Kim smiled, "we'll all be flying home tomorrow together."

And in that small hotel room in Thailand, three souls were united in true happiness.

Chapter 36

The trip to the airport went like clockwork and the flight home was on time.

"I'll just get something to read on the plane," Don said, pointing to a rack of newspapers before they went to the Departure Gate, "any requests?"

Vanessa and Kim shook their heads, but Sophie asked for a magazine.

"Nearly home," Vanessa smiled to Kim and Sophie as they waited for Don's return.

He handed Sophie the magazine he hoped she would approve of and tucked the newspaper under his arm. "Let's go," he said brightly, but Kim noticed that a fear had crept into his eyes.

"Everything alright?" she asked quietly.

"Later," he said tightly, "let's just get on the flight."

They found their seats, Vanessa and Sophie were together and Kim and Donald were in seats two rows behind. As soon as they were settled, Kim asked again if everything was alright.

Don's whole posture seemed to tighten as he handed Kim the newspaper.

"Read that," he said, pointing to a headline on Page 2.

"Villa Blaze," it read, "Police Suspect Arson."

Kim's eyes widened as she read on. "Yesterday afternoon, the beachside villa Shangri La, on Pattaya Beach owned by a local business woman, was destroyed by fire. Police are investigating a possible arson attack, as a hire car was said to be seen in the area just before the fire started. Anyone who saw anything suspicious are asked to contact the Pattaya police as soon as possible."

No wonder Don had been worried.

"But... we didn't start any fire," Kim whispered... "I don't understand?"

"And if they find a body," Don said grimly, "we could be charged with murder."

"But I've just said," she repeated, her voice rising on hearing the word 'murder', "we didn't start any fire."

A grey head from the seat in front turned and glared at her. "Sssshhhhh," it said.

"Sorry," Kim apologised, trying to calm down.

She re-read the story. The only other people at the villa, had been the two Thai girls cooking food, and she'd chased them off the premises. She told Donald about them. "But they wouldn't have had the nerve to start a fire," she concluded. "They were terrified."

"They maybe didn't start a fire," Don agreed, "but you didn't notice if there was anything on the stove that could have caught fire, accidentally I mean?"

Kim tried to recall the scene. "They were chopping vegetables, I think, and yes, there were pots and a wok on the stove, so maybe... if there was any oil it could have ignited after we left."

Donald visibly relaxed. "Then that's what the Thai police will find, accidental cause."

There was silence between them as each tried to reassure themselves that it was an accident and it was Don who broached the subject of Roger.

"Was Roger still out of it when you left?" he asked Kim.

"No," she said, "when I went back with Sophie's passport, Vanessa was kneeling beside him and he began to come round, so we left rapidly."

"You don't remember if you shut the door, do you?"

Kim felt herself becoming angry. This was like a cross-examination.

She glanced upwards. "I don't think I shut the door," she said, pacing her words to keep calm, "but I can't be sure."

After another heavy silence, Kim asked, "Will you tell Vanessa about this?"

"Don't know."

"But what if he's dead, she'll need to know that surely."

"Look, until we know more, let's just assume that there was an accidental fire and that Roger escaped unhurt."

"But how will we find out?"

"I'll go on the internet when we get home and follow-up the story. Let's not panic before we have to."

The rest of the long journey home was broken by meals and intermittent snatches of sleep, until finally the Captain announced that everyone should return to their seats and fasten their seatbelts for landing.

Sophie felt tears of joy springing in her eyes. She would be home soon and then she could go back to school and be with her friends. What a story she would have to tell them, especially Jane. She would be soooooooo jealous.

She wouldn't tell her about the horrible bits though, she decided, not realising how close she had come to being sexually assaulted by her own father, just the good bits.

Vanessa held her hand as the plane touched down. The stewardess welcomed everyone back to England and Kim and Donald gave Vanessa a half-hearted 'thumbs up' sign. Vanessa frowned, 'What's up with them,' she wondered, hoping Don hadn't upset Kim again. "See you at the Luggage Reclaim," she mouthed, putting her jacket around Sophie's shoulders. The temperature in London was getting wintery and Sophie would feel it more than the adults.

They loaded their bags into Don's car and headed home to West Hampton.

They were all exhausted and little was said as Kim was dropped off at her flat before Don headed to Vanessa's home.

He helped her with her bags to the front door. "We need to talk," he said, "but now just now. When are you going to see Hazel?" he asked. Vanessa tried to think of a date, but her mind was too tired.

"Phone me in a couple of days," she said, "then we'll arrange something." She looked quizzically at the man who had succeeded in reuniting her with her daughter against all odds. She would forever be in his debt.

"Thanks for everything Don," she said gently, "and I'll see you very soon."

With an enormous sigh of relief, Vanessa returned to her home. Sophie ran upstairs to her room, reuniting herself with all her things while her mother filled the kettle. She poured herself a cup with Lady Grey tea and took it to the back door. She looked at the darkening sky the days were noticeably shorter, ready for Christmas. She sipped her tea, hardly daring to believe, after all that she and

Sophie had been through, that they were safely back in England. Thoughts of her mother flooded her mind. "Thanks mum," she whispered, "for everything." Just then a flash of white caught her eye and there, jumping down from the branches of the apple tree, came Noble.

She bent down and picked him up. "Hello Noble," she cooed, "have you been waiting long?"

"Meow," said Noble. And she knew that he had.

As usual, after he had assured himself that Vanessa was alright, he turned tail and left. Back to Hazel, who must be wondering where he'd got to, but perhaps not, she probably knew.

That night, Vanessa slept solidly for ten hours. On waking, she had to give herself a moment to remember where she was. "HOME," she breathed, taking in the welcome sounds of normality. She could hear Sophie singing to herself as the shower made splashing noises on the tiles, probably giving her hair yet another wash to remove the last of the hair dye. They would have a birthday celebration lunch at the weekend, Vanessa decided, just the two of them. Put all the bad things behind them and start their new life together, free at last from Roger.

Vanessa was in the kitchen as usual when Sophie came in, her hair almost as good as new. She'd even pushed on a sparkly headband with a sequinned butterfly on it for added effect. "Very pretty," observed Vanessa admiring the result of her efforts.

"Can I go back to school soon," Sophie asked, longing too for normality.

"How does Monday sound?" Vanessa asked, "I thought we might go the Green Room tomorrow, you know, celebrate your birthday."

Sophie clapped her hands. "Oh, yes please mummy," she giggled, the weight of worry from the past week dropping from her young shoulders by the minute.

"Good," said Vanessa, "now let me just look through the pile of mail I found behind the door last night, and then we'll go food shopping." Sophie went through to the front room and Vanessa heard her switch on the television.

She sat at the kitchen table and sorted out the envelopes and flyers. "Such waste," she tutted, as yet another pile of junk mail was deposited in the kitchen bin, but amongst the junk was a cream envelope. She thought it was from her father, but she didn't recognise the writing. Carefully, she opened it.

"Dear Miss Vanessa", it read, "Your father has asked me to write you this letter. He's not too well and would like to see you as soon as you can manage it." It was signed by Mr Dobson. She looked at the postmark. It had been posted over a week ago.

She knew her father hadn't been well when she last saw him, but he'd assured her everything would be alright. With trembling fingers she dialled her father's phone number. Mrs Dobson answered.

"Mrs Dobson," said Vanessa, trying to sound relaxed, "can I speak to dad, please?" There was a moment's silence.

"Just a moment," came the reply.

"Miss Vanessa?" Vanessa felt her legs beginning to shake.

"Mr Dobson," she said, before asking for the second time, "can I speak to dad?"

Mr Dobson's voice sounded very deep and very grave. "I think you'd better come over as soon as you can Miss Vanessa, it's not good news."

Vanessa felt herself freeze to the spot, "I'll be there within the hour."

She dropped the phone and called for Sophie.

"We need to go to Grandpa's," she told her, as she pulled on her coat and grabbed her handbag. Sophie could see from the expression on her mother's face that something was badly wrong and she reached for her own coat without a word and nodded to her mother. Vanessa quickly phoned a taxi and while they waited explained things to her daughter.

"He's not been well for a while now," she said, as calmly as she could, "and he's asked to see me." Sophie nodded, her eyes serious and her mind again trying to understand the world of grown ups'.

The taxi made good time and soon she was knocking on the front door of her father's house. Mr Dobson opened it. "Hurry please," he said quietly, ushering her in.

Vanessa looked from Mr Dobson to Sophie. "Can Mrs Dobson look after her?" As soon as the words were spoken, Mrs Dobson appeared at her husband's side and guided Sophie through to the kitchen.

"Have you had breakfast my dear?" Vanessa heard her ask before following Mr Dobson through to her father's bedroom.

The blinds had been lowered and the room smelled strongly of antiseptic. Her father lay absolutely still, attached to a drip that was feeding something into his arm from a bag that hung from a metal hook by his bed. Vanessa moved closer. Even in the dim light, her father's wrinkled skin was yellow but his eyes flickered when he heard her voice.

"Daddy," she whispered, "it's Vanessa, come to see you."

Her father made a great effort and turned his face towards her. She took his hand and she could feel how weak his grip was in her own. His eyes opened a bit more so he could see his daughter, as he tried to tell her that he loved her, but no sound came out. Vanessa looked to Mr Dobson. "We need to get him to hospital," she said, her throat almost closing up with tension.

But Mr Dobson shook his head. "There's no more can be done Miss Vanessa," he told her, "it's the cancer you see, it's all through him."

Vanessa looked at the drip, "Morphine?" Mr Dobson nodded.

He pulled up a chair alongside her. "He's been fighting to keep going till you got here. Perhaps now, he'll go to his rest in peace."

Vanessa heard a gurgling sound coming from her father, as he breathed his final breath. "He's gone Miss," her father's trusted friend and servant said, "and may God rest his soul." Vanessa felt a sob rush to her throat.

"Can I have a moment alone with him Mr Dobson, before you call anyone?"

Mr Dobson nodded. "Take as long as you want."

Vanessa sat holding her father's hand, going back over the years and remembering when her mother, his wife, had died so young and how it had left him a broken man and her a needy child.

He had never let her get close to him and, even in the days and weeks before his death, he had been alone, not telling her anything, nor asking her for anything. At least, she had been here at his moment of passing and she thanked God and Mr Dobson for that.

Carefully, she kissed his cheek for the first and last time, before closing the blinds fully. Mr Dobson was waiting outside the room and took her through to the kitchen where Mrs Dobson had fed Sophie with blueberry muffins and milk. She reached out her hand for her daughter. "Time to go home, Sophie, Grandpa has gone to be with Grandma now and we shall be happy for him."

Sophie didn't fully understand, but knew enough not to ask any questions.

"What about the funeral," Vanessa asked Mr Dobson, tears backing up now and ready to overflow. "I don't know..."

"It's alright," Mr Dobson reassured her, "your father's solicitors will deal with everything. I'll look after the house till they've completed their work and then, well, let's just wait and see shall we."

For Sophie's sake, Vanessa kept a tight hold on her emotions till they got back home. She and her daughter spent the evening quietly in each other's company, both aware that they had been subjected to some extraordinary and, at times, frightening experiences, but they were together now and safe.

Tiredness overcame Sophie around nine o'clock. "C'mon young lady," Vanessa said, "time for bed." The hug she gave her mother was the most genuine emotion Vanessa had felt from her daughter in a long time. It seemed like Roger's influence had loosened its grasp on Sophie. Maybe, one day, she would be able to talk to Vanessa about all that had happened to her during that terrible week, but in the meantime, she was just glad to have her daughter back.

She listened till everything went quiet and she knew Sophie had gone to bed. Only then, did she allow herself to cry. The stress of going to Thailand, the worry about Sophie, the horror of Roger's true nature, the death of her father all came together in a deep sobbing and Vanessa vowed, she would never again let any man into her life. The pain was too much to bear.

The ringing of the phone forced her to regain her control. It might be Mr Dobson needing some question answered, she thought, but it wasn't Mr Dobson, it was Kim.

As soon as she heard Vanessa's muffled voice, she knew she'd been crying.

"Is this a bad time?" she asked.

"Just a bit," replied Vanessa and she went on to tell her about the death of her father. It helped to talk about it and although Kim could do nothing to change anything, Vanessa knew she had found a true friend she could confide in.

"Don says he wants to meet at Hazel's sometime soon," she told Kim. "Will you come along too?"

Kim grimaced. "I don't think so," she said, "I'm not exactly the flavour of the month with Don and, anyway, I never go anywhere I'm not invited."

"Well if you don't go, then neither shall I."

Kim smiled to herself. "Hey, sister," she said, "I'm all for solidarity, but I think Hazel needs to see you, whether Don's there or not."

Vanessa told her about Noble, being there to greet her when she got home.

"And, he liked you," she reminded Kim, "and that cat is never wrong. Please say you'll come too."

"Let's talk about it tomorrow," said Kim, "it's too late for making decisions."

Vanessa let her off the hook and hung up.

Tomorrow, she would take Sophie to the Green Room and they'd have a lovely lunch. Vanessa felt herself cheer up despite everything. Not only had she got her daughter back, but she also had a friend she could trust.

The Green Room was busy and Vanessa was glad she'd booked. She'd dressed up again and made sure she applied Hazel's cream to her skin. As she twirled in front of the mirror, she was positively glowing.

Sophie had ditched her usual jeans and wore a red velvet dress for the occasion. After all, she was thirteen now, not a little girl any longer. Mother and daughter linked arms as they made their way to the table. Several pairs of eyes watched Vanessa go by and one pair belonged to Donald Martin.

He was standing at the small bar, ostensibly waiting for a table, but secretly hoping Vanessa would show up like before. Through all the madness, she was the one who held steady and stayed calm when Roger started screaming at Kim, she was the one that had the presence of mind to get him out of the room as the shock of what he had done froze him to the spot. She was some special lady.

He finished his drink and made his way to Vanessa's table. "Mind if I join you?" he asked, looking at Sophie.

"Please do," she said beaming, "you're my hero."

Don looked at Vanessa. "May I?" Vanessa didn't object. How could she, he was her hero too.

Lunch was fun for all of them and Vanessa allowed herself to relax and enjoy it. Don treated Sophie like she was very grown up, which pleased her no end and when she wanted to go to the loo, he held her chair for her while she stood up.

"Thank you again," Vanessa said, while they waited for Sophie to return. She placed her hand on Don's arm, "thank you for everything and especially for today, you've made a little girl very happy."

Vanessa felt Don's hand cover hers. "And what about her mother," he said fixing his gaze directly at her, "have I made her happy too."

Surprised at his words, Vanessa quickly withdrew her hand. "I'll tell Kim we met today and by the way, she'll be with me when I visit Hazel," she said defensively, "whether you're there or not." The mood was suddenly gone and no sooner had Sophie returned and sat down again, Vanessa announced it was time to go. Sophie shook hands with Don and followed her mother from the restaurant. Vanessa felt hot and uncomfortable. What was Don playing at! She vowed to keep as far away from him as she could and she would go and see Hazel with Kim and without Don.

Chapter 37

Kim needed someone to listen and bring the events of the past week into some kind of perspective. She phoned Liz, who immediately invited her over for dinner and a bottle of chilled white.

"I was beginning to think you'd got lost," her friend grinned, happy to see her again. "Come in, come in, dinner's on the way. But first, this! She handed Kim a large glass of cold, cold Chardonnay."

"Now," she began, plumping up the cushions on the sofa, "tell Auntie Liz all about it."

It didn't take long for Liz to realise that things had got pretty bad out in Thailand and that Don had found out about her relationship with Roger to boot.

"Oh, Kim," she soothed, "I'm so sorry, I didn't mean to make light of things..."

Kim held up her hand, "Please," she said, "don't be, you weren't to know."

They sipped their wine while Kim tried to hide the hurt.

"Where's this dinner then?" she asked Liz, forcing a smile and changing the subject. "I'm so hungry my stomach thinks my throat's cut." Kim froze at the words, remembering how close she had come to being strangled by Roger.

Liz sat down beside her. "Kim what is it?"

Kim felt a mixture of tears and anger flow through her. "He tried to kill me," she murmured.

"Tried to kill you," Liz echoed, "who tried to kill you?"

Kim blinked back the mist forming over her eyes. "Roger did."

Once the flood gates opened, Kim told Liz everything. Her friend interrupted only to refill her wine glass as the sorry tale unfolded.

"And is he dead," she asked, "did he perish in the fire?"

Kim shrugged her shoulders. "I don't know," she said, "Don's going to check the newspaper's website."

Liz finished off her wine and put the glass down with a clatter. "Let's hope the bastard is dead," she said, through gritted teeth, "best thing for him."

Kim silently agreed.

"And Don," continued Liz, "what's happening with you and him?"

"Pass."

"You mean it's over?"

Kim sighed. "Not officially over, he hasn't dumped me yet, but Liz, you should have seen his face when Roger turned his venom on me. Shock doesn't cover it." She shook her head sadly at the memory.

"But you said he saved your life!"

"He did, but I guess it must have been more of an instinctive reaction rather than 'rescuing a damsel in distress.'"

"C'mon," said Liz, "let's eat. I think you've had enough drama to last you a life time and, by the way, you're staying here tonight, I insist."

Kim hugged her friend. "You're the best," she whispered.

After Vanessa and Sophie had left, Don remained at the table, his silly emotional outburst making him wish he'd never been born. How could he have been so naive? One minute he was Kim's boyfriend and now, here he was, making a stupid pass at Vanessa and after what she'd been through!

And what was he doing about Kim anyway? Did he love her, really love her, or was he just lusting after her body, much as Roger had done? The memory of the words Roger had used about Kim made his stomach tighten and his eyes sting. Had she really loved all the pain Roger had said she did? The more his troubled thoughts took hold the more sickened he felt. Surely she could have stopped it if she'd really wanted to he told himself, after all, Vanessa lived with the man and Roger hadn't said those things about her.

By the time he'd finished his one-sided argument, he had decided that whatever feelings he'd had for Kim were now dead and his ego wouldn't let him think otherwise.

Pushing back from the table he left the restaurant and headed home. He had to check the internet, find out if Roger had survived the fire or, as he dreaded, find out that Roger had perished in the burning villa. What had he got himself into? He was a Sound guy for a local radio station, he wore glasses, he visited his Auntie for goodness sake, he wasn't a killer or, as Sophie had told him, a hero. "Bloody hero!" he muttered, "bloody idiot more like."

He was so lost in his thoughts that he almost ran into Mr Rennie from the travel agency, who had arranged their hasty trip to Thailand.

"Ah, Mr Martin isn't it?" he said, placing his hand on Donald's shoulder.

Don hesitated, the last thing he wanted was to have a conversation with the travel agent, but Mr Rennie seemed determined to have a conversation with him.

"Got back from Thailand then?" Mr Rennie enquired benignly. Don nodded and tried to sidestep him. Then he felt the grip of Mr Rennie's hand on his shoulder tighten.

"I need to talk with you," David Rennie said firmly, "about Mr Lomax."

Don straightened. "What about Mr Lomax?" he asked.

"Not here," he looked around and pointed to a tearoom on the other side of the street. "Over there."

The two men crossed the road and found a table in the corner. The lunchtime rush was over and apart from a couple of people finishing their meal, the place was empty.

They waited till their tea arrived before anything was said, then David Rennie leaned forward, his voice low and concerned. "There's something I have to tell you about Roger Lomax," he said, "and I think his wife may be in danger."

Donald sat still, his eyes fixed on David Rennie.

"How so?" he asked cautiously, wondering what other horrors were about to unfold.

"My sister, Enid Rawlings, was a... client of Mr Lomax." Don noted the hesitation over the word 'client'. "She's now in hospital recovering from a severe mental breakdown brought on by her contact with... that man."

Don waited for him to continue, as David Rennie composed himself.

"It took a long time for the psychiatrists to get Enid to open up, but when she did..." David Rennie's chin began to quiver and his eyes became cold.

"Go on," Don said quietly.

"Roger Lomax had manipulated my sister's mind and turned her into a... sex slave..." he almost spat the words out. "When she started attending his

'Circle' to help her relax, she quickly became a different woman. She stopped seeing her friends, stopped visiting me and seemed to spend her days in isolation, only going out when she had to. She even stopped attending the Circle, instead having 'one-to-one' consultations at his hypnotherapy practice.

"Then one night, she came to my door in a state of near collapse. She was so distressed, I called an ambulance and she was admitted to the Observation Ward at the hospital. Her state was brought on by finding out that Roger Lomax had shut down his practice and had effectively disappeared. She was so under his influence, she felt she couldn't live without him in her life and, of course, she blamed herself for his disappearance. Without him, her guilt at what she had done and what she had become surfaced and broke her completely and it's only now that she's beginning to understand what happened to her at the hands of that evil man."

David sighed deeply and gulped down his now cold tea.

"So you see, Mr Martin, if he could do that to my sister, what could he have done to poor Mrs Lomax."

Donald knew only too well, the depth of Roger's depravity, but he hadn't understood how far he had cast his sex obsessed net. He thought of Kim and realised, she too, must have been caught in his perverted trap, only she had been strong enough to break free. His shame deepened at what he had thought about her. Blaming her for something she had virtually no control over.

David Rennie continued. "So, what I want to know is... where is he?"

Don focussed once more on the travel agent's words. What could he tell him without incriminating himself? "He's not in the country Mr Rennie, but that's as much as I know right now, but if I find out anything more I'll be sure to let you know."

"It's not me who needs to know," said David, "it's Mrs Lomax and that young daughter of hers and also... the police."

Don felt cold with fear. He had to find out if Roger was dead or alive and only then could he decide who to tell, if anyone.

He left David Rennie gazing blindly at the people passing the tearoom window and hurried home. He switched on his computer and brought up the newspaper's website. He typed in the date of the first report and re-read it.

Then he typed in the next day's news. There it was the update on the fire.

"Villa Fire was Accidental," he read. "Police and fire officers say the source of the blaze was the kitchen area where cooking pots had been left unattended on the stove. The owner of the house, Madam Areva Wong Sawat, confirmed that it was a holiday rental and that only housemaids were living there at the time. It was thought that one of them had forgotten about the pot and she has since been dismissed from her job. No other enquiries would be necessary."

Don stared at the screen, re-reading the article. There was absolutely no mention of a body or of Roger. "He must be alive," he told himself relief flooding through him. But it was short-lived. If he was alive, he reasoned he may return to England some day and begin his evil life again.

Don switched off the computer after printing out the article. Kim needed to know, but more to the point so did Vanessa.

Chapter 38

Vanessa phoned Hazel and briefly told her the good news.

"I thought you were home," Hazel said, "Noble disappeared on the day you left for Thailand and he only returned day before yesterday."

Vanessa smiled. "Beautiful Noble," she said, "can we come and visit?"

"We?" asked Hazel.

"Yes, Kim and I have so much to tell you, so can we come today?"

Hazel wondered at the omission of Donald's name in Vanessa's request, but said nothing.

"Of course come today," she said warmly, "I'll put the kettle on."

"See you soon Hazel," Vanessa said, "we've so much to thank you for."

Kim had just got back from her stay with Liz when the phone rang.

Part of her hoped it was Donald but another part hoped it wasn't.

"Kim? It's Vanessa."

"Good timing," she said, "I've just got back from an overnight stay at Liz's."

"How do feel about going out again," Vanessa asked, keeping her fingers crossed, "I've just been on the phone to Hazel and she's expecting a visit from us today. Sophie's going to her friend Jane's house, you know, to catch up, so it'll just be the two of us."

Kim wasn't sure if Vanessa had deliberately implied Donald wouldn't be there, but she was glad it would be just them.

"Great," she said, "I'll pick you up in about an hour."

Her talk with Liz had clarified things in Kim's mind regarding Don. It had been great at the beginning, but under the stress of the last week, cracks in the relationship had quickly begun to show. Was Don really strong enough for her? She'd seen a pretty dark side of life when she'd been Roger's mistress and she couldn't deny it had changed her. The romantic dream she had started out believing in had been badly tarnished by reality, but for Don this hadn't been the case. She wondered if he could ever get over her past and trust her. Ruefully, she had to concede it was very doubtful.

She freshened up then drove with Vanessa to Hazel's. The cottage looked exactly the same as she remembered and it was hard to believe that so much had happened since she was last there.

Hazel was as welcoming as before to both of them and Noble purred from one pair of legs to another as they sat down on the velvet sofa.

There was so much to tell Hazel, that it was hard to know where to begin, but Vanessa took a deep breath and began from the point where they arrived at the villa. Kim took over once or twice, especially the bits that concerned her, concealing nothing and expecting nothing. "And so," Vanessa ended, "here we are safely back and really grateful for all your guidance and strength."

"And your father?" Hazel asked, knowing the answer already.

Vanessa's blue eyes blurred. "Is he with mum?" she asked. Hazel nodded and took her hand.

"Jennifer has been agitated for a while and I thought it was because of what was happening to you, but it wasn't, she knew John was dying and was using all her spiritual energy to keep him alive till you got home."

Vanessa blinked away a tear. "You can tell her I was with him at the end," she whispered, "and that I love them both very much."

"She knows," said Hazel gently, "and so too does your father."

The moment was interrupted by the arrival of Donald. Whether Hazel had phoned him, or it was just a coincidence, neither Kim nor Vanessa knew, but he hurried into the cottage without knocking as if he was expected.

"Does she know everything?" he asked Vanessa, nodding towards Hazel.

"I know everything Donald," said Hazel, "unless you've got something to add."

Don took the folded printout from his inside coat pocket and read it out.

There was silence while the implications of what he said, sank in.

"So, Roger's still alive?" said Kim.

"Looks like it."

"Do you think he'll come back, for Sophie I mean?" he asked Vanessa.

"If he does, he won't get anywhere near her," she said with blunt determination, "and Sophie now knows he's not to be trusted, so I don't think she'd go anywhere with him again without telling me."

Don nodded. "Let's hope we've heard the last of him then."

Kim cleared her throat. "I don't think it will be too easy for him to get out of Thailand without this…"

She produced a plastic folder holding a British Passport and Visa from her handbag and handed it to Vanessa.

"When I found Sophie's passport, I also found Roger's, so just thought…" she let the words trail off with a shrug and a smile.

Vanessa took the passport and wondered at the presence of mind of her friend. Despite being nearly strangled by Roger, she had the calmness to carry out the simple act which would effectively stop Roger in his tracks.

"There was money there too, but that would have gone up in smoke, so Roger Lomax has been left with nothing." No one moved as the knowledge fed into their brains.

Kim took her chance. "Well," she said, standing up, "time I was off. I've a hot date for tonight," she lied, "I'm sure Don will give you a lift home Vanessa." Kim made for the door, before she lost her nerve. She didn't want to be left alone with Don so he could dump her, so had to make good her escape from the cottage first. "Bye everyone," she waved, as she disappeared out of the door.

"Hot date," Don repeated to himself, "she's found someone else already!"

He'd been coming round to the idea that Kim was a victim more than a willing partner to Roger and how they might give it another go, but now… she had dumped him!

His face reddened and Vanessa secretly cheered. She knew how much Kim had been hurt and was glad she'd had the courage to take back control of her life.

Hazel cringed at Donald's discomfort, but she was sure he'd get over it. Kim was Vanessa's guardian angel on earth and she'd served her purpose, it was time now for her to move on with her own life. Her path and Don's path may cross again in the future, but it would be as friends only.

Vanessa took out the passport from its folder and as she did so, something else dropped onto her lap. Carefully she picked it up. It was the silver elephant. She showed it to Hazel, who smiled in that knowing way she had. "It's for Sophie," she said, "Kim and you have no more need of it but it will keep Sophie safe no matter what the future holds."

Don looked dismal, still disbelieving Kim's exit. He may be tall, but he knew he needed to grow emotionally before he could hope to win the love of someone as brave as Kim.

"How about that lift," he heard Vanessa say.

The embarrassment of their meeting at the Green Room rekindled the heat in his face. He had some major thinking to do about women, especially what he called 'women of the world.'

He shrugged. "It would be my pleasure Mrs Lomax."

Hazel hugged Vanessa goodbye and Noble meowed his farewell.

"Next time I call," she said, "I'll bring Sophie with me, if that's alright?"

"Do you think she'd like a new Grandma in her life?" Hazel asked with a twinkle.

"She'd love it."

Don drove her home and decided against telling her about David Rennie. He felt sure, as time went by, Roger would become a distant memory to both him and his sister and, hopefully, to everyone else.

Before leaving the car, Vanessa turned to Don and kissed him softly on the cheek. "Don't be a stranger," she said, "I don't have many friends and I think I'd like you to be one of them."

For the third time, colour flooded Donald's face. "I'd like that," he said meaning it. "And Kim," he finished, "when you see her, tell her I'd like to be her friend too."

Vanessa patted his hand. "I will."

Chapter 39

By the time Sophie came home, Vanessa had spoken to her father's solicitors. The funeral would be on Friday and his body would be buried in the family grave alongside his wife. There was also the matter of her father's Will and Mr Nelson asked her to come to his office on the Wednesday at two o'clock.

Vanessa felt her whole body become still. Her father was dead and the realisation of its finality settled in her soul. Despite the fact that they saw so little of each other since her marriage to Roger, she knew he was there. Suddenly, she felt very alone. Events had moved too fast and she was having difficulty absorbing the changes. She was a single parent now. Solely responsible for her daughter and the new baby boy she was carrying. A feeling of panic raced into her mind. How would she cope when the baby was born, how would she manage everything on her own? She thrust her hands into the pockets of the old cardigan she had pulled on, reluctant as always to switch on the central heating before evening.

The fingers of her left hand folded over something cold and hard. She brought it out into the light and stared at it in wonder. She'd forgotten all about the little angel that had given her so much strength when she tried to stand up to Roger's temper. "Hello mum," she said, clutching the tiny form to her cheek. Just then, the baby decided to play football in Vanessa's tummy.

"Hey", she said smiling, "we know you're there too." She placed the little angel over the baby's kicking foot. "Sshhhhhhh," she said, "everything's going to be alright."

***

A delighted Sophie went back to school on the Monday. There was a time when Vanessa thought she'd never see her daughter again, never mind

195

see her so happy. By the time Vanessa's visit to the solicitors came round on the Wednesday, things felt almost normal, but fate had another surprise in store for her.

Mr Nelson welcomed her into the plush office he occupied. As the senior partner in the business, he took care of the firm's important clients and Vanessa's father she soon found out, was one of them.

"My condolences," he said to Vanessa, "Mr and Mrs Dobson will be here shortly and then we can begin. Perhaps you'd like some coffee while we wait?"

Vanessa nodded and looked around the panelled walls, each panel holding an oil painting of past partners. The heavy brocade drapes at the windows were held open by gold coloured tie-backs and Mr Nelson's desk had been polished to a deep mahogany shine. It reminded her a little of Roger's consulting room. He too had a great sense of his own importance, she recalled. The coffee arrived only minutes before Mr and Mrs Dobson.

Mr Nelson signalled that he would like to start and Vanessa placed her cup on a side table. She glanced at Mr Dobson. He must be eighty if he's a day, she thought and Mrs Dobson, the last few months looking after her father had taken their toll.

As they were all there, Mr Nelson began. "As Mr Anderson's Executors," he stated, "it's my duty to read John Anderson's Last Will & Testament. This document has been witnessed by two of my staff members and was written when he was of sound mind and body." He looked over his glasses. "Are we all ready?"

Everyone nodded. "Firstly, there are two donations to his charities which he has supported over the years. £50,000 to Cancer Research and £50,000 to The Heart & Stroke Foundation. To Mr George Dobson and to Mrs Isabella Dobson, the sum of £100,000 and the use of the house they occupy adjacent to the main house, rent free and maintained in good order till both or either of them no longer wish to live there."

Tears began to flow down Isabella Dobson's face as she gripped the hand of her husband. "Thank you," said George Dobson, "thank you very much."

"The final part of this Will is for the ears of Mr Anderson's daughter alone, so if you would both leave now." Mr Nelson indicated the door.

They both stood up to leave, but before going, Mr Dobson took Vanessa's hand. "He loved you very much, you know," he whispered, "just got scared of letting anyone into his heart after the Missus died."

Vanessa nodded tearfully. He had confirmed what she had suspected since she was a little girl. "Thank you Mr Dobson," was all she managed to say.

After they left the room, Mr Nelson cleared his throat. "Mr Anderson was very concerned about the agreement he made with Mr Roger Lomax. He regretted forcing the marriage on you, by financially supporting Mr Lomax, but felt at the time it was the best thing to do for you and your unborn child."

Vanessa nodded agreement. She remembered begging her father for help and would have done anything to be Roger's wife. "I wanted to marry Roger Mr Nelson, my father shouldn't have felt bad about it."

"Please," said Mr Nelson, holding up his hand, "there's more."

"Subsequently, it came to light that my daughter was actually very unhappy in the marriage and it is now my express wish that she agrees to bring a divorce action against Mr Roger Lomax at the earliest opportunity. On her signed agreement that she will carry out this instruction, my bequest to her is that the remainder of my estate, including the main house and contents and all monies, stocks and shares amounting to £25.3 million be passed to her and her issue."

Vanessa felt faint. What was Mr Nelson saying? She knew her father had a good standard of living, but never in her wildest dreams did she imagine he had so much money. And now, he had given it all to her!

"Are you alright, Mrs Lomax?" Mr Nelson asked, noting the whiteness of her face.

Vanessa gulped. "I'm alright," she managed to say hoarsely. She wrapped her arm around her now expanding womb. Baby John Anderson would never know a day of want, nor would Sophie or herself. Her father had seen to that. And as for Roger, he'd made sure he wouldn't benefit from his death as he had benefited when he was alive.

Mr Nelson got her to sign the prepared document. "Leave everything to me," he said, "we'll see to it that the divorce goes ahead unimpeded."

Reality returned in a flash. "But I don't know where my husband is," she said, "he disappeared to Thailand a few weeks ago and took Sophie with him."

Mr Nelson's brows frowned. "Abducted your daughter you say?"

Vanessa nodded, "But we got her back, two friends and I went out to Thailand and brought her back."

"I think you need to calm down Mrs Lomax and tell me exactly what has been happening."

Vanessa tried to recount the events again, as accurately as she could.

"Do you expect him to return home?" Mr Nelson asked.

"I don't know if he can," Vanessa said, producing Roger's passport from her bag where she'd put it when Kim had given it to her at Hazel's.

"How did you come to get your hands on this?"

"I found it," she said stuttering out the lie and not wanting to implicate Kim in any of this, "at the house where he'd taken Sophie."

"This could be construed as theft by finding," Mr Nelson intoned, switching on his legal head again.

He could see how confusing it all must have been at the time and how frightened she would have been. From what John Anderson had told him of Roger Lomax, he was quite an overpowering figure.

"I'll report your husband to the police as a missing person," he said, "then it's up to them to decide how to proceed. They'll probably want to see you and your friends, but depending on what they hear from you all, will indicate what action they take."

Vanessa felt a wave of relief sweep over her. She had never felt comfortable with what she had done, but her over-riding aim had been to get her daughter back whatever the consequences. She felt guilty about involving Kim and Don and to an extent Hazel, but she could do little about it now, except take full responsibility for everything and face the consequences.

Mr Nelson removed his spectacles. "Vanessa," he said kindly, "I know you're an honest and good person and I'm sure the police will do what is for the best."

Vanessa stood up. "What now?" she asked.

"Well," Mr Nelson said, also standing up and coming around from behind his desk, "I think you should arrange to move in to your new home as soon as possible."

He pointed to Vanessa's bump. "And when's the new arrival due to grace us with his or her presence?"

Vanessa smiled. "It's a boy," she said, "due to make his debut next February and he's to be called John Anderson after his Grandpa."

"A very fine name," Mr Nelson said, "now let Mr and Mrs Dobson take care of you for a while, till you find your feet and, please, try not to worry about Mr Lomax. Leave him to me."

Vanessa didn't know what he meant, but she was glad to do just that.

John Anderson's funeral was a quiet affair. Like his daughter, he didn't have a huge circle of friends, mostly just business acquaintances and Vanessa was pleased to see how much he was respected. Kim and Don came too, as friends and at the wake afterwards when everyone else had gone, she told them about the Will and what Mr Nelson intended to do. She saw both of them flinch. "It's alright," she said, "Mr Nelson already knows it was all my idea and my responsibility, including the passport," she said directly to Kim, so please, if the police want to speak with you, just be totally honest with them and I'm sure everything will be alright. After all, Roger caused all of this harm, not us. I think Mr Nelson intends hiring the services of a Private Detective to try to track him down, just to get him to sign the divorce papers, nothing else."

"And if they can't find him, what then?" asked Don.

"I think the divorce would go ahead anyway without him. Mr Nelson said after five years a missing person is presumed dead."

So, it wasn't over yet, Don felt. Right now, part of him wished Roger had been burnt in the fire, but the thought didn't last long. He was too much of a humanitarian to wish that on anyone, even people like Roger.

"C'mon," Vanessa said wearily, "let's just take one day at a time till we know what's happening, if anything."

Don and Kim agreed. "Can I give you a lift home Miss Mason?" asked Don.

Kim smiled. "No thanks," she said, "my car's outside."

"Got another hot date then?" Don asked. Kim punched him gently on the shoulder.

"Grow up," she said and she meant it. Don would never be man enough for her, no matter what, she knew that for sure now.

"See you at the radio station," she called over her shoulder.

"Do you mind if I stay a bit longer?" Don asked Vanessa.

Despite feeling sleepy, Vanessa felt she couldn't refuse.

"Sure," she said, "how about some hot chocolate?"

"Sounds good to me," he said, following her into the huge kitchen.

"Quite a spread," he said as he watched her making the drinks, "and all yours."

"Provided Roger divorces me," Vanessa replied.

"Don't you think he will?"

Vanessa waved her arm around the room. "Would you?"

Don knew what she meant, "So better he knows nothing about this till the divorce is signed, sealed and delivered."

"You got it."

Don took his cup of hot chocolate. "Vanessa," he said, "there's something you should know about Roger, or maybe the police should know about him."

"Oh," Vanessa said, "and what's that?"

"Do you remember Mr Rennie from the travel agency?"

"Yes."

"Well, did you know he had a sister, Enid I think her name was?"

"Enid Rawlings, yes, she was one of Roger's most devoted followers. Why do you ask?"

"I don't want this to upset you but..."

Vanessa sat perfectly still while Don related the story of David Rennie's sister. Her hot chocolate became cold as she took on board the depravity of Roger's activities. No wonder he wouldn't let her into his 'inner sanctum.'

She had always believed that his behaviour was in some way due to her and her failure as a wife and mother, now she knew differently. She thought back to all the times he had used the same manipulative behaviour on her, realising for the first time that her husband was the failure, not her.

"I'm sure the police would be happy to arrest him for professional sexual misconduct and David Rennie's sister would be very happy to bring about the charge." Vanessa felt empty.

"Could I ask you to go now, Don?" she asked, "please."

"I'm sorry," he replied, "I didn't mean to upset you."

Vanessa hushed him. "It's alright," she said, "it's not you, I just need to come to terms with Roger's behaviour and how he did it right under my nose and I didn't realise..."

"Hey," Don said, "don't beat yourself up about that lowlife."

"I'm very tired," she said, "please, just go now."

Reluctantly, Don left. "I'll phone you tomorrow," he said, "sleep tight."

She heard the door close quietly. Sleep. If only she could.

She looked around the beautiful room. All hers, yet she felt totally drained.

What was it about her that drew her into abusive situations, she asked herself. Her distant father, only able to tell her he loved her on his deathbed. Marriage to a monster, who had broken and abused everything and everyone he touched.

She thanked God she'd got to Sophie before he'd had the chance to destroy her innocence. No matter what the future held, going to Thailand was one thing she would never regret. And Enid Rawlings, what horror had she endured at the hands of her husband. The caring hypnotherapist with the healing hands, they'd said. It sounded so pathetic now it was almost unbelievable that they had all been so easily taken in by him. She must go and see Enid, tell her she wasn't to blame.

Then there was Kim. How had he managed to bend her to his will? She was young and beautiful, not needy like Vanessa or Enid Rawlings had been.

The questions spun around in a never ending circle in her head till she fell asleep, fully clothed on the sofa.

In the morning when she awoke, she found a warm duvet cover had been placed over her and her shoes had been removed. She blinked at the sun coming through the blinds as Mrs Dobson quietly rolled them up.

"Mr Dobson's making coffee," she said softly, "shall I bring you some in?"

"Yes please Mrs Dobson," Vanessa said, "and I'm sorry, I must have fallen asleep…"

"You had a busy day Mrs Lomax, it's no wonder you dropped off."

Don's revelation about Enid Rawlings returned to her mind. She would tell Mr Nelson about it, let him decide how to proceed, in fact she decided she would let Mr Nelson deal with everything to do with Roger. She had enough to do preparing for the baby and looking after Sophie.

Mr Dobson came through with the coffee. "Do you want me to collect Sophie for you?" he asked. "Your father would have wanted me and Mrs Dobson to help you all we could, especially now with the baby and all."

"It's alright Dobson," she said, "I'll get her myself from Mrs Munro's, but perhaps you could get the best room we have ready for her. We're moving in right away."

"Good," said Mr Dobson, "Mrs Dobson will be delighted to have two young ladies to cook for."

After her coffee, Vanessa showered and dressed. The closets in her old room still held clothes belonging to herself and her mother. She'd forgotten how beautiful they were. Sophie was going to love it here.

The next two weeks passed in a blur of activity. Vanessa and Sophie packed their belongings and personal things and transferred them to their new home, while Mr and Mrs Dobson prepared the old house for rental. Mr Nelson had suggested this option and assured Vanessa he would look after all the details. Till Roger could be traced, the house couldn't be sold and she didn't want it just boarded up.

One afternoon, after she had had her first driving lesson, Vanessa was about to phone for a taxi to pick up Sophie from school when the doorbell rang.

Mr Dobson came through to the lounge. "It's the police madam," he said, moving aside to let two men and a woman police officer enter.

"Could you collect Sophie for me Mr Dobson," she said, "this may take a while."

"I'm DI Walker and this is DC Thompson. WPC Whitelaw is here to observe and take notes."

Vanessa nodded. So this was it, the dream of her new life was over. "Please, sit down," she said, trying to keep the tremor in her voice under control.

"We were contacted by Mr Nelson of Nelson and Grant, a few weeks ago and he had rather a strange story to tell us about your husband and a trip to Thailand. Perhaps you can give us your version of events." It wasn't a request, it was more a command.

Vanessa clasped her hands in front of her and retold the whole sorry saga again. WPC Whitelaw wrote furiously and flipped over pages as Vanessa talked. "So, whatever I've done wrong," she concluded, "I'll accept my punishment, but I'd do it all again to get my daughter back with me and away from her father."

The two detectives exchanged glances.

"I have to tell you Mrs Lomax, we've found your husband."

Vanessa almost collapsed at the news. "Found him... but how?"

Before we came to see you, we talked to Miss Kim Mason and a Mr Donald Martin and what Miss Mason told us was very interesting. I'm afraid your husband was leading a pretty nasty life Mrs Lomax."

DI Walker explained further. "Miss Mason directed us to a man called 'Darko' who ran a private sex club in London. Your husband used to go there to have sex with underage Thai girls. Under questioning by officers from the Met, Darko told us about Roger's plan to live in Thailand and also about Missy Areva Wong Sawat, who supplied girls to Darko and with whom Roger made contact on his arrival in Thailand. As you may have found out, it was she who rented the villa to Mr Lomax, along with two Thai sisters for his 'personal' use.

The Met contacted the Bangkok police and they arrested Missy Areva for child trafficking. But, there's no honour among thieves, as they say and it wasn't long before she told them where Mr Lomax was hiding. Trying to save her own skin, I guess. Unfortunately for him, he couldn't leave the country with his stash as his passport and money had been lost in the fire."

"Where is he now?" Vanessa asked incredulously.

"In prison, in Bangkok!" Vanessa gasped, "he's awaiting trial on suspicion of procuring and using children for sexual purposes and also on trafficking drugs. A kilo of cocaine was found hidden in the boot of his car. The plan was for him to send the stuff to Darko who would sell it at his club and they would split the proceeds. And you know what the Thai police think about drug trafficking!"

She didn't, but she could imagine.

"What happens now," Vanessa asked nervously.

The two detectives exchanged another knowing glance.

"I think we can safely say that Mr Lomax won't be around for a very long time, and if he ever does return to this country, we'll know about it. He's now on our sex offenders' register."

The detectives shook her hand in turn. "Have a good life Mrs Lomax and we're sorry to have troubled you."

As the detectives turned to go, the front door opened and Sophie ran in.

"Mummy, I've had a wonderful time at school today, Mrs Hadley has picked me to be in the school play and... who are these people?" she asked bluntly.

Vanessa hugged her. "These very nice gentlemen were here to tell mummy some news from Mr Nelson, that's all, now get changed out of your school things and we'll have tea."

DI Walker smiled. "Sophie, I take it?" he asked Vanessa.

"She's a very lucky girl," he added, "having a mum like you."

"And I'm a lucky girl, having a wonderful daughter like her."

The detectives left and Vanessa and Sophie went into the kitchen.

"Hungry?" Vanessa asked.

"Yes," said Sophie, "but not for chips," she mused, "I think I'll have chicken salad."

Vanessa suppressed a grin. "Very good choice madam," she said, "and how about a coke to go with it?"

Sophie pondered again. "Not a coke, no," she said, "I think I'll have a Lady Grey tea."

Baby John gave Vanessa a kick as if to say 'what about me'?

She placed Sophie's hand over the rippling movement. "That," she said, "is your little brother wanting a cup of tea too."

Sophie's eyes opened in amazement. "I think I'm going to love having a little brother," she said, "just think how much I can teach him about EVERYTHING."

Their laughter rang through the house and George and Isabella Dobson smiled to one another. Vanessa was back where she belonged. John Anderson would be very pleased, wherever he was and somewhere in heaven, Mrs Dobson was sure, the angels would be having a ball.

Now that everything was over and she wasn't going to be thrown in jail, Vanessa decided she would throw a dinner party. She'd invite everyone who had helped her, especially Kim and Don, not forgetting Hazel and Noble the most beautiful cat in the world. Mother and daughter ate their salads and drank their Lady Grey tea. Vanessa and Sophie and not forgetting baby John, were truly home at last.

THE END